Bloodlines

Brian T. Seifrit

Email: **briantseifrit@gmail.com**
Web site: www.booksbybriant.ca
Cover art by AFRIna

Edition 3

ISBN: 978-1-9992595-6-3 Paperback
ISBN: 978-1-990215-16-2 Hardcover
ISBN: 978-1-9992595-7-0 eBook
Copyright Brian T. Seifrit (C) 1998-2020

This book is in memory of Skidder.

Special Acknowledgements to: *Christine Fenton* who brought the image of Shala to life. To *Stacy Brown* for being so critical. To *Lloyd* (Yellow Hair) and *Amy Lubbers*, for insisting I finish the book.

To my wife for being there.
Thank You.

Bloodlines

Chapter 1

"I figure Eli and I should head back to the first camp," Hank began as he bowed his head, and the others stirred uncomfortably. "I reckon we could all use some food; there ain't no animals going to be showing up here in the next while. I've done some calculations and reckon we could make the trip in ten days. There's enough food in the cache that'll last the rest of you, leastwise that long."

He turned his attention to his wife. It was clearly out of the question to her. "Now, Renee, before you start nitter-nattering, it ain't something I'm fond of doing, but a man has to look out for his kin, especially in situations like this one here."

"I'm not denying that, Hank," Renee began, her blue eyes piercing his soul. Her long black hair jutted across her cheek. "Think about the weather. Unless you are a mountain goat, it is cold enough to kill any red-blooded man," Renee pointed out as she bit her bottom lip.

"It doesn't matter how damn cold it is, woman. I'd much prefer to have some frostbite around my ears than watch us all die from lack of substance. No sir. We'll leave at first light. The boy can man the rifles if needed. Ain't that right, son?" He asked, looking into his son's eyes and smiling.

"Yes, sir. I don't reckon there'll be a need, though. Ain't nothing out here that ain't scared away by a few screaming women," William replied with humour as he brushed his bangs from his face.

"William Vanfell, you watch your tongue, boy, and show your mama more respect than that," Renee said as she shook her finger at him.

"Sorry, Ma. I didn't mean any harm," he said bashfully as he shrugged his shoulders.

"Ah, that's all right, lad. Most women do scare away most things, 'cept maybe a young whippersnapper like you," Eli added as he chuckled. "Ain't that right, Bethy?"

"Don't 'Bethy' me, Eli. I feel the same way as Renee," Beth Ann responded as she stared her man down. She was a firestorm of a woman. With fire-red hair and deep green eyes, she was as cagey as any Irish woman was, except she wasn't Irish. The cave became silent for a moment. Everyone present knew what kind of wrath she could wreak.

"I'd like to add my thoughts, since we are all in this together," Shileen began as she broke the silence. Shileen's youth and good looks would lighten up the darkest room. She wore her dark blond hair long, almost to the small of her back. Her hazel brown eyes matched perfectly with her angelic face. "I think they should go back. They could retrieve food, warmer blankets, medicine, and whatever else would help us through this winter. Spring is a long way off. Both Honey and Sinclair need warmer clothing, and I know each of us would like the same."

"Yes, yes, I need warm clothes," her daughter, Honey, sounded off as she reached for Shileen's hand.

"Me, yes, too," Sinclair followed.

The monotony was finally broken, and they began to laugh. "Well then, it's settled. Tomorrow Eli and I will head back, and as Shileen suggests, we'll gather what's most important. That, most certainly, Miss Honey, will include warmer clothes for both you and Sir Sinclair," Hank chortled as a smile crossed his face.

"Sure, you couldn't use an extra hand, Pa. I'd join you," William responded.

"Not this time, boy. You're gonna have to keep everyone back here safe and content, man the rifles as I implied earlier."

"Yeah. I reckon that's best. All right then, that's the way it'll be," William responded, half-relieved and half-disappointed.

"Don't sweat it, Willy. Wouldn't you rather be in the company of us women?" Shileen joked.

"Yeah. Perhaps if the women weren't my two aunts and my mother, maybe if you were all some hoochie dancers," William replied with a wry smile. They all knew he was joking; he was always joking.

Hank chuckled then took on a more serious demeanour. "Since they are your kin, son, it is all the more reason for you to protect them."

"I know that, Pa, and rest assured, I will. I was only joking. There is nothing I wouldn't take more seriously than protecting my kin," he said with conviction and assurance.

"You best take good care of the woman folk whilst we're gone," Eli began to chortle, "because I'm going to need a cuddle when we get back."

"Eli Vanfell! Watch your tongue around the little ones. Must all you men talk with such vulgarity?"

"Vulgarity? I never swore once," Eli responded.

Hank shook his head as he added wood to the evening fire. "You two best get your cuddling in 'cause ten days ain't going to be no picnic. Ain't that right, Renee? If I have things my way, I'm getting mine in tonight as well." Hank looked over to Renee and winked.

"Come on, Pa. I don't want to hear that. Ain't never going to be able to sleep now," William said as he rolled his eyes in disgust.

"Stuff cotton in your ears then, boy," Eli snickered.

The following morning, on January 20, 1826, Hank and Eli began their trek to the first Vanfell camp. Their goal was to return no later than February 1. One cold evening after the men had been gone, an unfamiliar sound resounded outside the cave. William reached for and loaded a rifle. He edged his way along the cave wall to the entrance and cocked the gun. Peeking out, he saw one of the horses thought to have been killed days earlier. "It's one of the horses," he called. Greeting the horse gently so as not to startle it, he reached out his hand and took it by the halter. "She seems to be in pretty good shape, all things considered. She's got a bit of a limp, likely caused by this cut on her flank," William commented as he pointed it out.

"Will she be okay, son?" his mother, Renee, asked with concern.

"I reckon so. I reckon also, Ma, our chances of getting out of this alive have improved. Pa is going to be pleased that the old mare found her way back," he replied as he walked the old mare out to what remained of the pen. Tying her to one of the trees, he fed her some of the hay he was able to dig out from the snow. Grabbing the big tin washtub they used to water the horses, he filled it up with snow. "I'll have some water for you in a short while, once this here snow melts down. Hang tough, old girl," William said as he turned and walked back to the cave.

To the northeast, Hank and Eli sat in silence as timber wolves in the distance howled. "Seems to me they're a might too close for my liking. What do you suppose the meaning of that might be, Hank? Makes me a bit edgy."

"Ah, probably don't mean a thing," Hank responded as he waved his hand through the air. "We'll toss some more wood on the fire, bring up the flames a bit. That should keep them at bay." At that moment, the trees stood still and silent. Suddenly, Hank heard the growl to his left. Spinning around, he fired his rifle. The loud clap echoed like thunder.

Too late. Eli was attacked and pulled to the ground. Gouged and bleeding, he found enough energy to pull himself to his feet, reaching for his pistol as the ravaging wolves disbursed. "Go on, get out of here!" Eli exclaimed as he fired a few rounds into the pitch-black evening. Flames from the pistol reflected the horror on his face. Hank, too, fired repeatedly into the darkness until the barrel of his .44 glowed with an orange hue.

"Where the heck do you suppose they sprung from? In all my years, I ain't ever seen that happen. Pretty brazen, I reckon. Looks like we have three pelts if we want them. I tell you, Eli, I hated having to do that." Hank looked at the dead wolves he was full of remorse.

"Didn't have much of a choice. I like the way it played out. I'd rather see three dead wolves than another dead Vanfell. Let's count our lucky stars, the few we have left, leastwise." Eli responded.

"Yeah, I suppose you're right. Let's get these flames going again and let me have a look at those wounds on your back. You seem to be bleeding from one or all of them."

"No worries there. They ain't as bad as they look." Eli looked over his shoulder at the wounds. "Superficial, I'd say."

"I can't argue, you're the doctor of the family. I reckon you'd know best," Hank commented as he spat on the ground. "For safety precautions, I reckon we take turns keeping watch. I'll pull the first shift."

"I ain't going to argue that point. What do you figure… four-hour intervals?" Eli questioned.

"Yeah, that'd be about right." Hank added sticks to the fire, then kicked a few fist-sized rocks out of the ground and tossed them into the fire.

"Now what's the meaning of that?" Eli questioned, scratching his chin.

"Get them to the right temperature, and they'll radiate heat into our bedrolls all night. A man has to be careful, though. Get them too hot, and the rock will burn right through, might even catch a bedroll on fire whilst a man sleeps."

"You mean to tell me we're gonna sleep on them? What man in his right mind would want to sleep on fire-roasted rocks? Sounds a might uncomfortable."

Hank rolled his eyes in the back of his head. It was hard to believe they were brothers. Hank loved the outdoors and spent as much time in them as he could. His weathered face and scarred-up, bulky frame proved that. Eli, however, never did. His idea of outdoors was a short jaunt on a dirt trail to a patient's farm, not this kind of outdoors. "I never said we were gonna sleep on them, but you're quite welcome to do so. I prefer to put mine down by my feet, maybe one up near the belly… crotch even, if you like."

"Well then, that makes more sense," Eli responded with doubt as he pulled his bedroll up over his shoulder and tucked his head.

Hank just snickered. Looking over at his younger brother, he began to think of his wife and son, William, and the death of their youngest son. Trent died as the others had from 'flu-like' symptoms and the freezing cold they endured in the first few weeks of their journey. Taking a deep breath to clear his head, he decided that no matter what, he would see them all make it safely to the Double-U.

During his watch, a moose approached its chest had been ripped open, its belly protruding. Wolves or other animals had tried to kill it. It looked at Hank with agony, then walked a few steps before stumbling and falling. Rushing over to it, Hank poked it with the barrel of his gun. Satisfied it was dead, he drew the blade of his hunting knife across the big animal's throat. The meat would feed them for weeks to come. As the moose bled out, he roused Eli from sleep. "Rise and shine, sleepy head. We have us a moose that lies here dead," he rhymed. "Come on, get up," he repeated a few times as he lightly kicked his sleeping brother.

Finally, a groggy Eli responded. "Moose? Wha?… what in God's creation are you going on about now, Hank?" Eli sat up, and his eyes grew big as he fumbled to get out of his bedroll. "You've got to be kidding. You weren't pulling my leg after all. That is one big fella. How did you manage it?" Eli asked with elated excitement. He could almost taste the succulent moose meat as it melted in his mouth.

"Truth is, I was sitting at the fire when he wandered in. His guts were sloshing. I was going to shoot him, 'cept I didn't have time to cock the rifle before he stumbled and fell. I reckon the wolves had a go at him, maybe a mountain lion. Whatever it was, it didn't kill him. Not then, at least. Nope, he chose to die in our laps and, by God, we're going to feast on him. Come on, let's get him skinned and quartered," Hank replied. Eli knelt next to Hank, and the two of them spent the next few hours skinning and quartering the massive beast. There was no way they were going to be able to transport the entire animal back to the cave, not before every carnivore that walked the winter landscape had a nibble. "I figure I'll carry on from here alone to the first camp. Now that we have meat, it would be wise to pack a hundred pounds or so back to the others," Hank suggested as he cut away a big piece.

Eli nodded in agreement. "You got that right. Figure what's left will be rancid when you return from the first camp?"

"Nope, not in these freezing temperatures, but the animals will have had a good go at it. Whatever is left on my return will only be fit for animals. That's all right, though; they deserve to eat as well. Besides, a hundred pounds can go a long way. We get that much back to the others, along with what I'll gather, we should be okay 'til we can train our sights on more game."

"All right. Now let's get some of this meat roasting on the fire. Almost tempted to eat some raw," Eli chuckled. The aroma of the cooking meat made them salivate. How they wished for a potato or a piece of bread. They wasted no time in letting the meat cool, and it burned their tongues as they began to devour the few pieces they cooked. It gave them the energy and strength their bodies craved. Sitting cross-legged, as near to the fire as the flames allowed, they conversed and sipped tea. The evening was cold, but the food in their stomachs elated their spirits.

"When you head back in the morning, follow our trail, and I reckon you'll be okay. Lose the trail, though, and things might be different," Hank spoke up as he tossed another stick into the flames.

"I'll stick as close to it as I can. If it doesn't snow, I think I'll be okay, Hank."

"Yeah, I suppose," Hank said with mild concern, as he finished the last of his tea. "I'm gettin' tired of tea, I'll tell you that much."

"Yep," Eli agreed.

The following morning, each man went his separate way. The late winter air was cold and brutal, and clouds hung over the mountains, threatening it with snow or freezing rain. Hank looked back at Eli to see him slip into the woods. He would not see him again for another six to seven days. As he walked, Hank thought not of all the setbacks; instead, he thought of the life they had lived. He remembered returning from one of his cattle drives on Trent's fifth birthday, beaten up and scarred because of an old cougar that had been taking his cattle nightly. He'd tracked it for three days and nights until he finally ran it down. *That was five years ago,* he thought to himself as he stopped to rest.

Fifteen miles in the opposite direction, Eli struggled with the hundred pounds of meat strapped to his back. A wound to his right shoulder split open, and the blood was freezing on the outside of his jacket, making it stiff and uncomfortable. Throwing the pack of frozen meat over his good shoulder, he continued onward. Noting the area, he realized he was only capable of travelling half the distance that he would otherwise be able to travel under different circumstances.

Hank was having problems of his own. Unexpectedly, he slipped on a frozen log; a broken branch impaled his left buttock and then broke off. Squinting with agony, he slowly stood up. Fully erect, he reached around and felt the wound. There didn't seem to be much blood. Prodding with his finger, he tried to remove it, but to no avail. Finally, deciding he best leave the splinter alone as he couldn't risk losing any blood and, for now, the splinter had plugged the wound. When he returned to the cave, he would have Eli remove it.

He could tell that the lodged broken branch was the circumference of his thumb. It made walking unpleasant and painful. With every step he took, he felt the branch grinding and twisting. It was excruciating. As the last bit of sunlight vanished behind the mountains, he found a well-treed area and set up his camp. Building a fire, he noticed that the branch had worked almost all the way out. He could now feel it with his fingertips; *maybe it would be a good idea to pull it out,* he thought.

Brandishing his hunting knife, he put the blade into the burning embers of his fire. He knew that if he were to remove the broken branch, he'd have no choice but to cauterize the wound. While the knife heated up, he slid his wool pants and long underwear past the wound. Twisting to his side, he could see its red hue protruding. To make sure the knife was hot, he spit on the blade. Then, he grabbed it with one hand and the broken branch with the other. At the count of three, he pulled the jagged splinter out and pressed the hot steel of the blade against his flesh, cauterizing the wound. Calling out in agony, he fainted as his outcry of pain echoed in the silent wood. Waking some time later, he applied snow to the wound. The cooling effect on his seared flesh gave him some relief from the agonizing burn.

That evening, as the two brothers slept, a blizzard blew in. The temperature fell below -30 °, and in the morning, when they awoke, they discovered that their way was now snow-covered. Hank walked for two hours when, he came across a scattering of human remains. The blood appeared thick beneath the snow, frozen like puddles of mud. There were five bodies in all. The sight caused him to vomit. What he could see of the remains told the story, they had been cannibalized. *How could any man eat another...* he thought out loud as he shook his head in disgust. Moving now as quickly as he could in a heated rush to their first camp, the pain in his leg was all but a memory as he traversed the distance. He didn't stop or slow down until the familiar camp came into view. Looking to the sun, he estimated the time to be around 2:00 p.m. He had made good time.

Gathering wood from the broken old wagon and other materials, he built a skid that he would use to haul back the supplies. It would be crude, but he didn't want to spend too much time on it. It took him a little over three hours. With the task done, he began amassing the supplies. The sun was almost gone when he packed the last of the cargo. With evening approaching, he had no choice but to spend the night on the consecrated grounds of his dead kin.

While gathering wood for the evening, his right leg gave out, and he crumbled to the ground. Crawling closer to the fire for light and warmth, he pulled his pants down to look at the wound. It was turning a dark black-green. He realized the wound was showing symptoms of gangrene. *Got to take care of that. If it spreads, I'm as good as dead, and that ain't part of my agenda,* he thought. *When will this run of bad luck end,* Hank contemplated as he looked up to the clear star-studded sky. A tear rolled down his cheek, and he wiped it away with the back of his hand. *As God as my witness, I'll make it back. We'll get out of this. We have to. It's up to me to see to it…* Making himself comfortable, he curled up near the fire. The flickering flames of orange and blue lulled him to sleep as he stared into the dancing flames.

In his dreams, he was back home in Greenfield. The entire Vanfell clan gathered to celebrate a prosperous year. Their harvest had been good. The cattle market was at its peak, Eli's medical practice was going into its tenth year, and his wealth was only now beginning. Then, like a crack from a whip, the scenario changed, and Hank found himself burying one of the last living members of the Vanfell family. A feeling of loneliness, defeat, and sadness swept over him, and he awoke in a cold sweat. Sitting up, he winced in pain as he added wood to the glowing embers of the fire. *I hate dreams like that…* he thought as he stirred the coals.

Chapter 2

At dawn's early light, now stricken with fever, Hank blew gently into the glowing coals of his past night's fire, igniting the flames. He shivered as beads of sweat formed on his forehead. He desperately needed to clean the wound. Again, brandishing his hunting knife, he set the blade deep into the embers and waited for the blue steel to become red-hot. He knew that when he cleaned it, he'd have to cauterize it for a second time.

As for Eli, he travelled a good distance considering the pain he was in. He noticed the symptoms the night before: mental depression, restlessness and a high fever, as well as an overwhelming thirst. All this meant one thing: hydrophobia. That was why the wolves had attacked. Reaching for his journal and a pencil, he wrote: *Beth, the date is January 26 or 27. Wolves attacked us. Hank, as far as I know, is well. I myself have become deathly ill. If I make it back alive, you must do whatever it takes to subdue me. I may have hydrophobia. With love, Eli.* Finishing the letter, he put it where it could easily be reached. Convulsing, he vomited as his head began to spin. His face contracted as he spewed the contents of his stomach. *I'm into it now… undoubtedly*, were Eli's last thoughts as he crumpled over, clenching his stomach in deplorable pain.

With apprehension, Hank took note of the blade he set into the fire. It glowed orange like molten lava. The time had come. He removed his outer clothing and slid his long underwear past the wound. Picking at it, he pulled the crusted scab off, revealing an oozing mess from his own rotting flesh. Flicking the scab into the fire, he doused the wound with warm, melted snow water. The repulsive odour the wound emitted told him it was *gas gangrene*. This usually meant amputation or death. As clean as he could get it now, he reached for his knife, the blade red-hot, and he pressed it against his wound for the second time, and for the second time, he passed out from the excruciating pain. Coming to his senses some hours later, the fire that once gently flickered with flames had diminished to only a few glowing coals. Reaching for some wood to add, he tried to stand, but to no avail. He would not be leaving yet, and so he rested.

After finding the strength to gather more wood, he prepared for his stay. He managed to cut down some poles and cedar boughs and built a shelter. It was not the best, but it would have to do. Settling in, he stretched his bedroll out close to the fire and closed his eyes.

The following morning, overwhelmed with what he thought to be hydrophobia, Eli was disoriented and confused. Having no sense of direction, he was unaware that he was only a short distance from the cave. Hallucinating and frothing from the mouth, he stumbled into the path of help, guided by what he thought to be the spirit of a wolf. Oblivious to the pain from his wounds in his state of delirium, he left the meat he'd packed behind. His mind completely blank, he sauntered on with no purpose whatsoever, or so it seemed.

It was only by luck that south of the cave, William was tracking a snowshoe hare. From the corner of his eye, he glimpsed in the distance someone darting through the underbrush. Odd as it was, with caution and curiosity, he approached in silence, keeping hidden from sight. Discovering tracks, he followed them a short distance. He called out but received no response. Minutes dragged on as he waited. Finally, he turned and coursed his way back to the cave, his imagination running wild.

A turn of events for Hank that morning was all in favour of his leg. He felt no pain, and although his leg was weak, with the help of a stick, he was able to stand. Inhaling deeply, a smile crossed his face. *Perhaps he would survive to see his family once again,* he thought. He looked around one last time at the lonely graves on the little knoll. "I'd best get on my way. The others will be expecting me soon. Rest in peace, Vanfell kin," he said solemnly to himself as he strapped the skid of supplies to his waist.

Turning, he began the trek back to the cave. Before dusk, he came across one of Eli's camps. A small pile of wood, as well as a clump of birch bark, waited for him. Eli had even managed to erect a half-decent lean-to. For Hank, it was quite welcoming, and he sighed in relief as he removed the strap around his waist. He felt ten times lighter with the skid removed. Stretching his back, he looked in the direction of the cave. It was only a matter of days before he would once again be in the arms of his wife.

Igniting a fire, he opened a jar of preservatives. This one in particular was his favourite, crab apple jelly. Renee made it from the apples they picked from the old tree in the backyard of their house in Greenfield. Scooping some of the sweetness up with his fingers, he lavishly licked them off. It reminded him of the life they used to have. As the flames from the fire danced gently in the wind, he slid his pants down to check on his wound. The flesh was not nearly as black as it had been. The stink was almost gone, and the swelling had reduced. He was pleased with the recovery.

Eli spent the entire day chasing after the spirit wolf. Exhausted as evening approached, he curled up beneath a tree and began to convulse. The spirit wolf sat nearby, not venturing far from his side. It stared at him and waited hungrily for Eli to become still. Sensing there was something wrong, it cautiously approached him and lay at his side, keeping vigil. With the approach of dawn, the wolf followed a scent that had been present the night before. Following it, he came upon a cave. Scenting the air, he was satisfied that this was where he would find help, and he darted back the way he came. Approaching Eli, the wolf tried to get his attention. However, the man remained silent. Licking the man's face, he heard a mumble and stepped away. Eli began to convulse and slobber. Painfully dehydrated, he needed liquids.

Looking around to get his bearings, he noticed again the spirit wolf in the distance watching him. Agitated with nervous anxiety, he sat motionless. After what seemed like hours, the wolf ran forward, stopped and ran back, finally approaching close enough for Eli to realize that it was a wolf pup. With all the energy he could muster, he stood up and ran towards the pup, hoping the pack was nearby and would kill him. It would be better than dying slowly and painfully from the symptoms he suffered. Falling down face-first into the frozen ground, he awaited his doom.

The pup approached him and only licked his bloody face. Lying in confusion and exhaustion, Eli could smell the smoke from a fire. Slowly, he stood and averted his eyes. The forest was too dense for him to see any smoke in the sky, but he could most definitely smell it. The wolf was leading him either into an Indian camp or perhaps a trapper's cabin. Wherever it was leading him, maybe he would find help. Staggering, he walked a short distance and clamoured for help. His head began to spin, and his eyes rolled back as he collapsed, feeling only briefly the many cuts he received from the crusty snow as he fell face-first. Then silence.

Honey heard the distant cries for help and promptly informed the others. They searched only for a few minutes until spotting him lying face down. His face was swollen with lacerations, his eyes too puffy to open. Blood trickled down his cheeks like tears. His breathing was laboured, and he looked like death itself. His tongue was grossly swollen, and he was frothing at the mouth. Renee called the others. "He is here, I've found him. It is Eli; come quick." Renee rolled him over onto his back and put her ear close to his mouth, but could not confirm that he was breathing; the cold breeze that blew hindered her attempt. Finally, she felt a twitch. A sigh of relief exhaled deeply from within her. "He'll be okay; he'll be okay." She repeated with hope and prayer.

Beth Ann darted to Renee's side, followed closely by William and Shileen. Beth Ann gasped and began to sob. "Eli, Eli… oh dear God, Eli, can you hear me. I'm here, right here. Squeeze my hand, Eli. Please, please, squeeze my hand." Tears streamed down Beth Ann's face. Her whole world seemed to crumble until she felt her husband's hand squeeze her own ever so gently.

Eli could not speak, but he heard what he thought to be a familiar voice and, for a brief moment, he had a relapse of normalcy. He pointed to the pocket that held the letter. Frantically, Beth Ann reached for and grabbed the note. Tears continued streaming down her cheeks as she read it aloud to the others. "We must hurry. Come on, let's help him back to the cave," Beth Ann said as she swallowed deeply.

Shileen and William stepped forward and helped Eli to his feet. They each put an arm around his shoulders and scurried him to the cave. Beth Ann dabbed Eli's brow with melted snow, giving him some relief from the fever that burned. She could not believe the shape he was in. The wounds on his back seeped pus and blood; the few scabs that formed were discoloured and hard, like calluses on one's hand. While she tried to put disinfectant on the wounds, Eli fought her tooth and nail. He was like a crazed animal, leaving Beth Ann with no recourse other than to let him be.

Concern for Hank was now the topic. "What do you figure, Ma? Figure I should harness up the mare and go have a look for Pa? I reckon I can pick up Eli's trail easily enough and follow it back the way he came. It could be that Pa is in need of some help. With the mare, it shouldn't take long to track him down," William suggested.

"I don't know, William; I've already lost one son," his mother responded with worry. "I know your heart is in the right place, son, but if something were to happen to you, my heart would never heal."

"What if the two of us went?" Shileen spoke out. "It would be safer. We'll be a lot sorrier if Hank never returns." It was the truth, and they all knew it.

"Yes. Perhaps it is best that we find him," Renee responded as she averted her eyes toward her son. *How he has grown…* she thought.

"So then, it's settled," William said with hope.

"Yes. It is settled. You're like your father, William. He would do the exact same thing, even if his nagging mother plainly said no. You make me proud, son."

"Thanks, Ma," he replied, as his face grew flush. "I reckon, Shileen, and I can head out at first light; no use putting it off any longer. It won't take long, I promise." For the remainder of the day, they huddled around the fire and reminisced about a time not long ago, when they were all together, alive and well. *In such a short time, so many of their kin had died.* Sadness crossed their minds, but what they had to hold on to most of all was *hope*.

Packing up his bedroll and supplies, Hank looked to the horizon. He guessed he was probably two days behind schedule. Strapping the skid around his waist, he started off. The weather wasn't as cold as he had first surmised. Stopping for a short while, he removed one of the jackets he wore. Today, he would walk well into the evening and put as much distance between himself and the last camp as he possibly could. It was tough going, but his determination and perseverance outweighed both the terrain and the wound he endured. Unstoppable, like a locomotive, he strode on. No bush or bramble slowed him down.

Somewhere between late noon and early dusk, he lost Eli's trail. Stopping momentarily, he gathered his thoughts. The last few tracks of Eli's that he was able to follow had been going in the right direction. Hank averted his eyes as he looked to the horizon. *I must've wandered off his trail…likely, I'll pick it up soon,* he hoped. He looked around to make sure that he hadn't lost his own bearings. Satisfied that he was travelling in the right direction, he shook his head and continued on, although at a slower pace. The short rest did its damage and wore him out; now he was low on stamina. "Come on, old boy. Don't give up the ghost yet. A couple more miles and then we'll call her a day; that's all, just a couple more miles." Inhaling deeply, he searched for any remaining energy his body could muster. It was of no use; he was simply out of poop.

Sighing in defeat, he removed the strap from around his waist. As the weight he was pulling released, he stumbled forward, his lower back and legs shuddering with exhaustion. "Nope. This'll be as far as I make it today," he muttered. Squinting, he looked back the way he came. *I guess I ain't got a real cause to be upset about the distance I've made. I reckon near five, maybe six miles, not bad for an old folk,* he half-chuckled. *Not bad at all,* he thought. Checking over the cargo once he rested, he was satisfied it all remained intact. The crudely built, thrown-together skid was worth its weight in gold in his humble opinion.

He settled that evening, huddled around the fire he managed to light after the third or fourth attempt. His fingers and face were chilled to the bone. He lifted the collar of his felt jacket up around his ears. The wind came at him from all directions, cold and unrelenting. Birch, cedar, and aspen quivered, swaying this way and that as the wind lashed out, breaking weak branches as it swept by. Shivering, he warmed his hands above the flame. Gusts of ice pellets pelted his face as whirlwinds glided across the frozen snow like an entourage of dancing fairies. As magical as it seemed, it was as unwelcome as ticks in July. It meant one thing. The night was going to be cold. He knew what to expect, and he prepared for it accordingly.

Stoking the fire, he waited for the flames to give him the light he needed, then strategically removed the items from the skid. Draping a large piece of canvas over the top, he made a crawl space big enough to climb into. It was an instant shelter. He anchored the canvas on either side with a few of the heavier tools and such that he had reluctantly packed, then tossed his bedroll inside. "May not have known what I was doing when I did it, but I did something right," he mumbled, referring to the construction of the skid. Scratching his whiskered chin, he smiled at his own ingenuity. Construction had never been one of his strong points. In fact, he hated it. He was a cattleman through and through. The only things he took pleasure in building were corrals, fences, and the odd wooden trough. A builder he never was. Turning, he walked back to the fire and warmed his hands one last time. Then, loading his rifle, he retreated to the skid. Curling up in his bedroll, he sought solace and peace, but most of all sleep.

Back at the cave the following morning, long before a rooster crowed, William and Shileen were making final preparations for their search for Hank. They packed two gunny sacks with extra blankets, tea and clothing, then strapped them to the mare. There wasn't much food, so they packed only a small amount, enough to last two people for a few days.

"Are you sure both of you will be all right?" Renee asked with concern.

"I don't see any reason why not. We all know what direction Pa and Eli travelled," William trailed off as he brushed his bangs out of his eyes. "Besides, I reckon Eli's trail will be easily followed. You ain't got nothing to worry about, Ma," he assured her.

"Yes, Renee, we'll be fine. I'll keep my eye on Willy, don't you worry," Shileen said teasingly.

"Thank you, Shileen… " Renee smiled, "Just be sure that you all come back. And William, be careful."

"Come on, Ma. It ain't like I'm off to war. Pa can't be far. You keep forgetting that we have a ride now. I assure you that old mare is ready and willing to make tracks. She ain't never let us down before. I don't reckon she's about to start.

Less than a week, Ma; that's all it's going to take." William looked his mother in the eyes, and he could see the tears well up. There was no denying the way she felt. Traipsing over to where she stood, he gave her a hug. "Ma, it's going to be all right," he said as he kissed the top of her head.

"I know. I… I just don't want to lose another son. You understand, right?" Renee asked.

"I do, Ma. I do, but remember this as well: you lost a son, and I lost a brother. We can't bring Trent back." William shook his head. "All the worrying we do today, Ma, will never change that fact."

His mother's face suddenly radiated with a smile that only suited Renee Vanfell, and at that moment, William knew his mother had given him her blessing in what he was about to embark on. "William Vanfell, when did you become so wise and mature?" his mother asked, beaming with pride.

William chuckled. "I reckon I've always been wise, Ma. As for the maturity, well, now… it comes and goes."

"All right, William. Renee, are we forgetting about something?" Shileen intruded as she always did when she had a point to make. Usually, she was right.

"Yes, you are right, Shileen, and I reckon we ain't doing Pa justice reminiscing. Sorry, Ma. The sooner we get, the quicker we get back."

"Of course, of course, yes, sorry, son," Renee said as her voice cracked. "Godspeed." Turning, she walked into the shadows and wept.

William and Shileen traversed about fifteen miles by high noon. Stopping to rest the horse, they talked a bit. A question William had been meaning to ask for as long as he could remember wanted to jump out of his mouth like a frog jumping from one lily pad to the next. He was always curious to know why, in the few journals Beth Ann kept and shared, there was never any mention of Shileen or, for that matter, her daughter Honey. He knew, of course, that Honey was born out of a misalliance and that Shileen was only a teen when she gave birth. Perhaps that was the reason. Never wanting to pry, William learned to hold his tongue concerning other people's business, and that is how he thought about his relationship with his Aunt Shileen. She was not much older than he, that much he knew. It seemed relevant now more than ever that he ask her where her childhood went. Was it appropriate? Probably not, but he'd never know unless he asked.

"What's a matter, Willy? You look so distraught." Shileen asked as she beat him to the punch.

"What do you mean? I feel fine." William answered.

"Come on, we've known each other all of our lives, it would seem. I remember as if it were yesterday when I first met you. My only interests then were horses and boys." Shileen laughed that laugh of hers that always gave William butterflies. "It doesn't seem that long ago, does it?" she questioned.

"Not when it's put that way. No, it doesn't seem that long at all."

Shileen smiled. "So then, you agree we've known each other a long time?"

"Naturally, of course. How could I ever deny that, and why would I?" They looked at each other and snickered in unison.

"That's right, Willy, and that's how I know you look distraught. What gives?"

"Ah, it's nothing, nothing at all," William replied as he waved his hand through the air.

"Come on. I think we've already agreed that we've practically grown up together. I've always known when things have bothered you." She was begging him to ask the question, any question. It was typical of her. Shileen's entire world revolved around conversation, challenges, and knowledge. She was like a sponge and absorbed every word, every thought, every card played in a deck.

He swallowed deeply. "There is one thing that has kept me up on occasion."

"And that is what?" Shileen questioned ready to answer anything he may ask.

"Where did your childhood go? I've seen the journals and other stuff Beth Ann keeps and flaunts, but in all the years I've known about you, I ain't once seen a letter from you to her or any mention of Honey. Leads me to wonder sometimes." William exhaled. Finally, he had done it. He had asked the question.

"Actually, Willy, Beth Ann is only my adopted sister, or should I say, her father adopted me. I thought for sure you knew that."

"Nope. That never once even crossed my mind. I guess then, you ain't my aunt," he added with humour as he scratched the top of his head.

Shileen shook her head, "Heck, no. We're not related in any way. I feel so sorry that for all these years that's what you thought."

A smug look crossed William's face. "Well then, I guess I should've spied on you as we grew up."

"You mean to tell me that you didn't?" Shileen teased.

"Not exactly, I mean, leastwise not intentionally. On occasion, I might have passed by your bedroom window. You were my aunt back then. If I'd known what I know now, I'd likely have taken a better look."

"Yeah, well, since we're being honest, I admit to spying on you," Shileen jabbed back. Once again, they burst into frivolous laughter. Finally, catching their breath and wiping tears away, Shileen spoke. "There is more to the story. Would you like to hear it?" she asked.

"I don't want to seem as though I'm prying. I was only ever curious to know why there weren't any letters and such from you to Aunt Beth Ann. You answered that question already; not sure, more needs to be said, unless, of course, you feel a need to tell me?"

"I do. I do, Willy. I do want to tell you."

"I'm all ears," he replied as he brushed the bangs away from his eyes.

Shileen took a moment, then, inhaling deeply, she began. "My father and Beth Ann's father were partners on a trap-line and a few other unruly ventures. The trap-line, though, was their bread and butter." There was a pause as Shileen contemplated. "I never knew my mother; she died when I was born. I do remember, as I grew, being in the arms of an Indian squaw, a beautiful Indian squaw. I can't place her name now with certainty, but I think it was Running Rabbit or something like that."

There was another pause as Shileen reached back in time. "She raised me as her daughter for the first while. Then, for reasons never explained to me, she left. Later on, my father was murdered. No one knew for sure, but there was always speculation that it was a tribe of Indians that killed him. I don't know… that part of my life seems long ago."

Shileen smiled at the memories as she averted her eyes to William. "Anyway, after all that, Beth Ann's father took me in. I guess he felt compelled. From then on, I knew her father as my own. That's my story, Willy," Shileen said as she began to rise.

"Quite a story too, I might add," William responded as he nodded. "I reckon we've sat long enough. We'd best get gone. Pa is still out there." He squinted in the direction they were travelling. It looked and was, William knew, as rugged as ever. "What do you say, Shileen? Should we get?"

"Yes. I think we should. We still have a few hours of sunlight left." Shileen walked over to the old mare and took her by the reins. "I fear tonight is going to be chilly, though. Oh well, we'll have to have a big fire," Shileen responded with spirit. "So, shall we double or lead the old mare?"

William thought for a moment, "I suppose we could double a ways. Once the snow gets too deep for her to hold riders, though, we'll have to lead her," he pointed out as much as suggested.

In agreement Shileen swung up onto the mare, and William swung up behind her. Then, flanking the old mare with her heel, Shileen commanded her to 'giddy-up'. They travelled for another three hours before deciding it was time to settle. The temperature was already starting to drop, their breath rising like steam every time they exhaled.

"Over yonder looks like a good enough place as any to settle for the night," William said as he pointed toward a stand of large cedar. "We'll be able to gather boughs and such and likely put together a bit of a lean-to, might even get us out of the wind."

Shileen looked over her shoulder and nodded. "You're right. It will do. We're going to need a fire real quick, too, because my ears and face are frozen."

"I hear you. Warmth is good." Hurrying, the two dismounted and tethered the mare to a small sapling.

While William got a flame going, Shileen fed the mare some oats, making sure the old horse was content. "You've done a great job, old girl. For now, you can rest." Shileen patted the horse's neck. "Tomorrow you'll need all your strength again. Tonight I'm going to spoil you. After we get a lean-to built, I'll give you more oats, okay?" For the next two and a half hours, her and William worked diligently at gathering wood and erecting a shelter. With the task done, the old mare received her oats as promised.

The horse settled now, William and Shileen sat near the fire, reminiscing. It would be marked as the first night they spent together alone without the presence of others. It was also the first night that William knew who Shileen really was. His aunt she was not. With this knowledge, things got a little complicated when they finally bedded down. One thing led to another, and before either knew what hit them, the little shelter filled with the scent of sex and the sound of heavy breathing. Finally, their bodies smouldered as did the fire outside; they were spent, as was the outside flame, but a flame within had been ignited.

Chapter 3

A distant ten miles away, Hank was noting the smoke he saw on the horizon; *probably Indians,* he thought to himself. He had travelled that day for a solid six miles, near the same distance he had travelled the day before. It wasn't an easy feat, especially considering his wound, the amount of weight he was pulling and the lousy, rugged terrain he traversed. He had no idea that William and Shileen were looking for him. Tonight, he had wanted to sit by his fire, wrapped up in his bedroll. The thought of curling up in the skid for sleep was out of the question. It had been very uncomfortable when he had, and his back ached when he pulled himself out. He didn't want to go through that again.

Tonight, his every intention was to sleep near the fire. Now, however, with smoke rising in the distance, that too was out of the question. The last thing he wanted was to be approached by unknowns. He loaded both rifles and accepted the fact that he would have to face the elements without a fire of his own. Only his thick woollen blanket would keep the chill off that night. Not a problem for Hank, though. It was something he was used to. Inhaling deeply, he sighed as he tightened the grip on each corner of the thick, grey, woollen bedroll draped over his shoulders, his back against the skid. A rifle to his right and a rifle to his left gave him the assurance that he would sleep on occasion during the night, regardless of how fitful the sleep might be.

Morning came quickly, bringing new aches. He felt too old for this. Still, his family back at the cave depended on him. He wouldn't let pain slow him down. The tight ache in his chest was different from his wound—hot at times and sometimes making his breathing feel shallow and strained. He knew why his lower back and hamstrings throbbed that was from the effort of pulling the skid. The chest pain was new and came and went, unlike his other aches.

Making his way northwest, he saw a horse in the distance. The sun reflecting off the snow made it hard for him to make out who the strangers approaching were. Hiding, he waited, sighing in relief when the rider came closer, and he recognized his son. Obviously, one of their horses had found its way back. Scrambling out of the bush, he yelled out William's name. Waving his arms frantically, he fired a few shots from the rifle.

William, startled, looked in his direction and then sped up the horse. "Well, now, you don't look worse for wear. How are you feeling, Pa?"

"A lot better now that you're here. How'd you manage passing this little excursion off to your Ma?" Hank chuckled. "It doesn't matter none. Now un-strap me from this skid, build us a fire and let's have some food. I ain't spared a minute since heading back and ain't eaten a thing in the past while. Now I'm hungry."

William hurriedly removed the strap from the skid and half-chuckled as he did. "Quite a little contraption there, Pa. You come up with the idea all by yourself?"

Hank was rubbing his hands together to warm them, and he began to smile. "Never mind, boy. Reach in there and grab me my pipe and tobacco. They should be near the top. You wouldn't happen to have your flint on you, would you, son?"

William reached into his pocket and tossed his dad the flint. "Thanks, son. Shileen, you wouldn't mind grabbing a couple of them sticks over yonder, would you?"

"Not at all, Hank. Renee is sure going to be happy to see you. She's been out of sorts as of late. I don't think Eli's condition is helping," Shileen mentioned as she returned with an arm full of sticks.

"What do you mean by Eli's condition? Is there something wrong with Eli?" he questioned as he knelt and put a flame to some birch bark he always carried. Adding the sticks, he looked back at Shileen.

"Yeah, Pa, there is," William spoke out as he handed over the pipe and tobacco. "He's got a sickness of some kind or another."

"Is he going to be okay?" Hank questioned. He was standing now, his eyes big with concern.

"I reckon so. Ma and Aunt Beth Ann have been giving him some kind of serum from that black bag of his. He looked a lot better the day Shileen and I left than he had the day we found him. Eli claims you were both jumped by wolves. Figures, that's where he picked up the sickness."

"Indeed, we were, but I ain't sick. You mean to tell me he didn't make it back? Y'all found him?" If it were as they claimed and they found Eli, chances were he didn't carry the hundred pounds of moose meat.

"I wouldn't say that. He was only a few hundred yards away. What's the big concern about whether we found him or if he found us?" William questioned.

"The second night out, we had a visitor, a moose to be exact." Hank fidgeted with the pipe in his hand. "It stumbled into camp half-dead as it were. Eli headed back with about a hundred pounds of the meat. The rest of it lies back a good ten, fifteen, maybe even twenty miles back the way we came. It ain't no good, though. The rest of the animals in these parts will have feasted on it." Hank rubbed his whiskered chin. "Ah, it doesn't matter, we'll manage. I'm glad Eli will mend." He added tobacco to his pipe and, using one of the sticks from the fire, took a long puff.

"Come on, now," he began, "let's sit by the fire for a while. Maybe we'll get some beans or something cooking in a bit. I packed plenty of those, I reckon, lots of flour and sugar too. How many days are we from the cave, Will?"

The flames from their midday fire were as welcoming as their conversation as they found places to sit. "Today's only our second since leaving. We were able to double, of course, and I reckon we did at least fifteen miles yesterday and nearly ten this morning. Easily twenty-five miles to go, Pa. By the look of that skid or sled and what it likely weighs, I reckon it should take us maybe three or four days to get back. Of course, that all depends mostly on how far each of us can walk in a day. We could always take turns doubling. The old mare won't put up a fuss. The only thing is that one of us would still have to walk."

"Hold on a second, MEN," Shileen started, putting emphasis on the men part, "Hank has been pulling that contraption. Why can't the mare? We might even be able to ride with the gear he has packed, or at least one of us could, while the other two ride bareback. What do you think of that?"

Hank raised an eyebrow and inhaled a big lungful of pipe tobacco. "I had no doubt in my mind that the old mare wasn't going to pull the skid. Never once, though, did it cross my mind that we could do it that way. By God, you might be onto something, Shileen."

"Hold up a minute, Pa. How much do you figure you weigh? Over two hundred, I reckon. Maybe even closer to two and a bit. I'm close to one eighty myself, and Shileen, well, I reckon one thirty-five. Already, that's a lot of weight. If we factor in the skid and supplies, the old mare would be hauling a lot of weight. We could be running the risk of injury to her."

"That is a good argument, son. I say we play it by ear. Always best to play things safe. Since that's settled, how about we rummage through the food I've packed and see if we can't come up with something hot?" Standing, the three of them walked the short distance to the skid. It was packed solid with everything one could imagine, even tools for Christ's sake.

"Pa, you got everything in here, even a wash tub." William said as they looked through it all.

"Yeah, and then some," Shileen commented.

They settled on beans.

Things back at the cave weren't going nearly as well. Eli was convulsing again and going through a great deal of pain. Beth Ann ran to his side to comfort him. While Renee quickly looked through his medical bag, flustered and helpless, she found some morphine. Adding a small amount of powder to a glass of melted snow water, she forced Eli to drink it. Within a few short minutes, he became silent.

"Do you think Eli will be okay, Renee?" Beth Ann asked.

"He is doing as well as can be expected, Beth Ann. Yes, I think he will be okay. We have to believe that," Renee turned her gaze to the children, her mind fluttering with past memories. *The Double-U will never be worth all that we have lost...* she thought. *In fact, I already hate the place.*

Finally, leaving Eli's side the two women sat with the children near the fire wrapped up with blankets. As evening approached they prepared a watery stew and bannock. It might not have been much, but it was hot, and all they could manage with their dwindling supplies. The children didn't seem to mind. Food was food, and they were thankful for the little amount they had.

Checking on Eli, once more, Beth Ann dribbled some of the broth from the stew into his mouth. For a moment, she thought she heard him mumble. Bringing her head closer to his, she waited and hoped that he would mumble once again, but he did not. The only noise she heard other than her own breathing was Eli's. Sitting with him for a few minutes longer, she patted his forehead with a damp cloth, then rose and joined Renee.

The two women sat in silence, their eyes glazed and staring into the flames of the fire. Outside, they could hear the wind as it stormed past, causing the bear hide at the entrance to flap ferociously like a flag on a flagpole. "Sounds pretty bad, doesn't it?" Renee questioned.

Beth Ann nodded. "I'm afraid it does. I hope the kids and Hank will be okay."

"Not as much as I hope. I don't know how I could go on if anything more happens to my family. I've lost one son already. I'd die if I lost my husband and another son. Every night since Trent died, I've had dreams about how things would have stayed if the Double-U never existed. It tears me apart." Renee began to weep.

Beth Ann put her arm across Renee's shoulders and rubbed them. "It's okay, Renee. Things will get better once Hank and the kids return. I know God won't let anything happen to them. Come on, Renee, smile. I know it's hard. It's hard on all of us, but sooner or later we have to live for today." Beth Ann stared into the fire as she continued to rub Renee's shoulders. Her own mind now darted back to better times.

"Hank and William tell me the same thing. It's hard to let go of what used to be, though," Renee said as she wiped the tears away. *No one knows my pain,* she thought, selfishly.

Having travelled for about five miles, Hank, William, and Shileen stopped to let the horse rest. Noting the sky, Hank realized that they were in for a winter storm. It took them by surprise how quickly it transpired, first an arctic wind, then the snow. "We're going to have to call it quits," Hank hollered above the wind. "This cold will freeze our lungs if we don't stop and get a shelter and fire built." He pointed to a stand of large cedar and pine. "Over there is where we'll set up for the night. The trees will block most of the wind. Come on, let's go," he said as he waved them on.

By the time they made it to the cover of the trees, their pant legs and parkas were frozen stiff. The first thing they did was light a fire. They were painfully sore from the cold and freezing wind. Their fingers ached mercilessly as they warmed them over the orange flames. Next, they built a shelter and gathered more wood. Finally, all tasks done, they huddled close together around the fire, hot tea in hand. "I was always told the weather up in these parts gets rough at times.

I reckon this is one of those times," Hank commented as he tilted the tin cup to his lips.

"If this ain't one of them times, I'd hate to see it when it is. By the way, Pa, I noticed you were having a bit of trouble with your left leg earlier on. You okay?"

"That depends. I stumbled a while back, shortly after Eli and I split up. Ended up on my rump with a branch sticking out of my cheek. Not a little branch, neither, son; nope, this one was the granddaddy of all branches." He trailed off as he half-chuckled at how the story must sound. The truth was, it was no laughing matter. They had no idea how serious the situation was until he continued. "I sealed the wound tight two times with the hot blade of my knife." That was all he wanted to say about it. "Rest assured, son, it ain't nothing to concern yourself with. I'll be fine."

"I didn't like the way you said that you sealed it shut. What did you do, Hank? Don't tell me you cauterized it," Shileen, always the curious, questioned.

"Yep."

"Without sterilizing it first?"

"Yep," Hank said as he rolled his eyes.

"My God, Hank, do you know the risk you took. You could have ended up with gangrene," Shileen sputtered out in disbelief.

If you only knew, he thought. "Ah, could've, but didn't." Hank waved his hand through the air. He didn't want to tell them straight out that, indeed, that was what happened. There was enough on their plates to worry about. The wound was healing. He wasn't going to worry about it, and he wasn't going to let them either. "No need to worry about that. I've lived through worse, so don't get your feathers ruffled. Anyone want more tea?" Hank added as a decoy to get them talking about something else.

"I could put down another cup, Pa." William handed Hank his cup.

"Count me in, too," Shileen said as she held out her cup.

Hank filled Shileen's cup first, then poured the rest into William's cup and handed it back. "Well, looks like that's it for the tea. Guess this old man might as well head for bed." His plan worked. No more questions. "Night, kids," Hank said as he stood and walked to the shelter.

"I think your Pa just blew us off," Shileen smirked as she sipped on her tea.

"Seems as though he has. Fancy that, humph. Pa usually does that when Ma's been nagging him," William looked over to Shileen and winked.

"Are you saying I nagged him to sleep?" Shileen asked with witticism.

"Nah, I reckon he's tired. A man of his age shouldn't be dragging a skid that likely weighs more than his own self, and especially not through weather and terrain like this. Pa, though, has always been a sucker for punishment. Never knows when to call it quits; hates to give in. As my Ma says, he's as stubborn as a mule." William chuckled as he thought about that.

Shileen looked deep into the flames, searching for a memory of her own father, not Beth Ann's father, but her own. There was nothing. There never was, and that always frustrated her. She had learned to live with it and to take the good with the bad. Her life was far from easy. She was an unwed mother and as far as she knew, had no living kin, except, of course, her daughter Honey, her precious daughter Honey. She was the lifeblood, the sunshine on Shileen's face, the air that Shileen breathed. Honey was everything and more to Shileen.

William glanced over and looked at her; the flames from the fire illuminated her face. He could tell by her steadfast expression that she was in deep contemplation, perhaps even a little distraught. "Looks to me like you're the one who seems a bit distraught now. What gives?"

She looked up and into his eyes. "I was trying to conjure up a memory of my father, and like always... I can't."

Inhaling deeply, she kept her emotions in check. *Bereavement* never played a role in her life. At twenty-five and a mother of an eight-year-old, there was no time in her life for sadness. "Other than that, I feel fine. Perhaps a bit chilled and a little tired, maybe, but good nonetheless." She felt good, all right, in more ways than one. The longer she looked at William, the better she began to feel and the harder her nipples became.

A quick roll around the fire on one of the blankets curbed her urge and satisfied William's as well. The two of them lay there staring up through the trees that surrounded their camp. Every now and again, the odd snowflake would meander through the thick mass of branches and touch down on their skin, melting instantly. The wind, on occasion, tousled their hair, blowing snow onto them from all directions. It was an experience neither one would soon forget.

Taking up places around the fire once more, they sat close. Hand in hand, speechless, spent. All that resounded was their breathing and the odd crackle from the fire. Even the old mare lulled in silence. *What were they going to tell the others? How could they explain it? One moment they were kin, then acquaintances, then mad hat lovers.*

William was the first to speak, as he ran his hand through his hair. "Up until two days ago, Shileen, I always thought of you as kin, leastwise through marriage, not blood kin, of course, but kin nonetheless." He fell silent as he searched for more words, more ways he could use to tell her how he really felt. Straight up always seemed best. "I guess you can tell I've had feelings for you for some time, probably since we were kids. Until yesterday, I thought I'd never be able to tell you, but I have some deep-seated feelings for you. This thing, though, this... this." Again, he fell silent.

"This, this, what Willy?" Shileen coaxed. She knew what he was trying to say, and she was glad that he was the first to say it. "What were you going to say? I'm all ears."

"Well, you are aware that there's an age *thing* between us, ain't you? Fortunately, for me, I happen to be the one who is younger," William replied with a twinge of sarcasm and a lot of humour as he tried to buy himself more time.

Shileen snickered at the remark. "That's a good one; real sweet of you to bring that up now. By the way, I'm still twenty-five, so you're only five years younger. Besides, what does that have to do with anything relevant?"

Still lost for words, William sat there nodding at her as he grinned from ear to ear. Finally, the words came. "What I mean to say, Shileen, is that our relationship has undoubtedly taken a turn."

"That's obvious, but remember this also: we are both adults. Do you feel somehow unattached because of the intimacy we've shared?" Shileen questioned, perturbed it would seem.

William shook his head. "I wouldn't say that, just bothered about how we might explain it to the others, is all."

Shileen shrugged, it wasn't anyone's business other than theirs, still, it would have to be explained eventually. "That's the easy part. We won't say a thing. We'll wait until we've made it to the Double-U."

"I ain't sure about that," William looked into the flames of their fire, "I hate the thought of trying to hide from something like this."

"It does seem pretentious, but even Hank says it's better to be safe than sorry. If we told the others, who is to say what that might accomplish? I doubt the *Vanfells* would welcome more drama. If it'll make you feel better, Willy, I promise to keep my distance," Shileen responded with sincerity, longing, and respect.

"No. I wouldn't want it that way either. We'll tell the others when the time is right. Let's play it by ear and see where that leads."

Shileen spoke one word. "Done." It was settled. Feeling a chill as the wind picked up, they stood in unison and walked the short distance to the shelter, their bedrolls draped across their shoulders. Inside, it was dark and warm, a lot warmer than one might expect. Finding appropriate places to lie down, they curled up side by side. It took only minutes before the wind outside lulled them to sleep.

Back at the cave while Renee and Beth Ann gathered wood for the evening, a sudden, quick movement from some bramble caught Beth Ann's eye. On a second glance, a wolf pup darted out from behind. Alone, cold, and hungry, it tried to hotfoot past her, but she was able to block the pup's exit. It dashed to her right, then bailed to her left as it tried to escape her clutches.

In a final effort to escape its foe, the wolf pup stopped, raised its haunches, curled up its top lip, and threatened an attack. As fierce as the show was supposed to be, Beth Ann knelt down and cooed. "It's all right. I'm not going to hurt you. You must be cold and hungry." Averting her eyes to the forest around her, she made certain that the wolf pup was indeed alone. Satisfied, she continued talking softly until finally she was able to approach closer.

She reached out an open hand. Slow and easy, she held it out for the wolf pup to sniff. Her voice remained soft and constant. Finally, when it seemed as though she was making progress, a rustling behind her caught her off guard. Her heart sped up a beat as she turned to look. It was only Renee.

"There you are," Renee began.

Beth Ann brought her index finger to her lips. "Shhh… " she responded as she pointed to the small wolf that was now cowering at this new intrusion.

"Oh my God, it is soooo cute," Renee said in a whisper as she slowly approached. "Is it an orphan, do you think?"

Beth Ann nodded. "I think so. Look how skinny and cold the poor thing is…" Suddenly, a fluttering of wings as an owl took to flight startled the young wolf. With a burst of get-up-and-go, it darted headlong into Beth Ann, almost knocking her over in its haste to get away. Struggling, she got a hold of it and clutched it in her arms. "It's okay, it's okay; settle down, little guy." The pup, still frightened, fought to get away as it urinated all over Beth Ann's front. "Hey! Hey, quit that," Beth Ann responded lovingly as she held the pup out at arm's length.

Finally, it relented, whimpered, and then wagged its tail. Beth Ann brought the pup close to her bosom, snuggling it. It licked at her with fondness, relieved it would seem that something could love it back. Snuggling the cold and hungry wolf, Beth Ann and Renee returned to the cave. The children, awakened by the blustering wind, saw the pup in Beth Ann's arms, and abruptly they ran towards her. The pup sprang from her clutches and bound straight for cover under one of the pole-framed beds.

"Aw, you guys scared the poor thing," Beth Ann said as she knelt down and looked under the bed.

"Is it a puppy or a rabbit?" Sinclair questioned with concern.

"It's a puppy, silly, probably a wolf too, right Aunty Beth Ann?"

"That's right, Honey. It is a wolf pup. Come over close, Sinclair, so you can see it. You too, Honey. Just walk really softly," Beth Ann replied.

The two children tiptoed over to the bed and knelt next to Beth Ann. "Will he eat us, Mommy?" Sinclair looked at his mother, his eyes big with curiosity.

"Oh, I don't think so." She tried to coax it out, but the pup remained steadfast, shaking with fright. "We'd better leave him alone for now. He needs to get used to us first. Come on, like little mice, let's tiptoe back to the fire."

Tying off the bearskin that closed off the entrance to the cave, Renee took notice that it was beginning to snow. She shook her head. *Where are they? Where are Hank and the kids?* she wondered as she gazed out at the vast wilderness. It was dark, rugged, godforsaken. Turning, she walked back to the warmth of the fire and joined the others. "We're in for another storm," she stated as she sat down, relieved to see that Beth Ann was boiling water for tea and was adding the leaves. "Oh, that smells so good. A nice hot cup of tea and then off to bed. How is our little friend coping?" she asked, referring to the wolf pup.

"Silly puppy is still hiding under Aunty Shileen's bed... he's probably really hungry, I bet. Hope he doesn't eat me," Sinclair responded with weary eyes.

"He won't. He's a baby." Honey began to laugh. "He's too small to eat us."

"But he could, right? If he were bigger, he could gobble all of us up."

"That's enough, Sinclair. You're going to give yourself frights," Beth Ann responded firmly. "He's not going to hurt any of us, you'll see. Now, I think it's time for both of you to head off to bed. Tomorrow you can feed the puppy, and I bet you that if you are nice to him, he'll give you a big, sloppy puppy kiss right across your cheek." The two children laughed and giggled as they sleepily found their way to their beds. Only a few minutes passed before soft snores were heard.

"How is the tea, Renee?" Beth Ann asked, now that the children were asleep and the two of them were alone they could have adult conversation.

"Fabulous, Beth Ann, thank you." Renee brought her cup to her lips and blew gently. "It's hard to take knowing it will be another four months before we'll be able to walk away from here, isn't it?"

"In a lot of ways, yeah. I do admit that I miss the normalcy," Beth Ann responded as she added wood to the fire. "I also admit that nothing good has come of this journey so far. In life, though, we have to take our bumps and grinds, struggle with our men, our families. I think this is one of those times."

"True enough," Renee spoke out as she took a sip of tea, "but whatever awaits us at the end of this journey is far less valuable than what we have lost." She added.

Beth Ann nodded with skepticism. "I like to believe that something marvellous awaits us, though it could never be more marvellous than if all of us were together again. The reality is that our dead are lost to us forever. We have to accept that and move on." They continued with their talk through another cup of tea until finally deciding it was time for bed.

Chapter 4

The following morning, a day's ride to the northeast, Hank and the kids were well on their way. They'd been in a constant battle with the weather since starting off that morning. They continued on for nearly three hours before having to stop. The weather remained cold, unrelenting, and miserable. The freezing temperatures, it seemed, froze every limb. Sitting behind the skid, protected somewhat from the wind, William managed to light a fire. Their faces felt frozen as they huddled close, absorbing the heat from the flames.

"We're getting close, Pa. I reckon we can rest up for a couple of hours. I'm sure the old mare could use the break."

"You got that right, boy. This weather ain't safe to be wandering around in, no sir," Hank answered as he flipped up the collar of his heavy felt parka. For two hours, the day stood still. Now rested and ready, they were once more on the move. It was near dusk when the first scent of smoke wafted their way. Stopping, they looked on. Sighs of relief resounded, and smiles crossed their faces. Up ahead was home. "Now ain't that the most pleasant smelling smoke," Hank chortled as he inhaled deeply. Minutes later, they tethered the old mare, pulled the skid up to the entrance of the cave and called to be let in.

The old bearskin had never come down so quickly. "Hank, William, Shileen, oh, God bless! Hurry up, get in here, it's freezing out." Just as quickly, once all three were in, Renee closed it off. "God, how I've worried, Hank. How are you? I've missed you like crazy." Renee kissed his mouth.

"I've missed you, too, doll. I'm here now, though. We're safe," Hank responded.

"Mommy," Honey yelled as she darted past and into Shileen's arms. "Mommy, you're okay. Yippee. I knew you were coming soon."

Shileen's entire face lit up. "Oh, Honey, I've missed you so," she sang out as she twirled her around. "God, how I've missed you."

"What about me? I've missed you, too, you know," Sinclair said as he stood there, his hands on his hips.

"Oh, Sinclair, little Sinclair. I missed you as well. I missed all of you," Shileen responded.

"I don't know about the rest of you, but I'm kicking off my boots and heading for a bed," William commented. "I tell you, I never thought I'd ever welcome a dank, dark cave as much as I welcome this one right now." Before he could make it to a bed, the wolf pup that had not yet been mentioned dashed out from beneath Shileen's bed, jetted across the floor and headed for the cave entrance. "What the… " William blurted as he took a double-take.

"Oh, no! The pup," Beth Ann called out.

"No worries, Beth Ann, the bearskin is up," Renee answered. The pup did a quick turnabout and darted back to the safety of the bed. "You've all just been introduced to the new baby of the family."

"Well, I'll be," Hank responded. "I had no idea anyone was expecting."

"Nor did I, Pa. Is that what I think it was?"

"Depends on what you think it was. To me, it looked like a wolf pup," Shileen said with intrigue.

"We found him half-starved, and as you can see, he likes it under your bed, Shileen. He remains nameless and seems to have a crush on Honey," Renee joked.

"What are we supposed to do with a mangy wolf pup? Give him some time, Ma, and you'll wish he were a coat. Anyway, I'm still heading for a bed." William waved his hand through the air with little reverence in regard to the pup.

Next morning, well rested, Hank exited into the cool outdoors. They'd left the skid overnight, and he didn't want to waste any time in unloading it. Besides, he needed some time alone; he hadn't mentioned the devoured human remains he had come across. Now, back at the cave, it haunted him as never before. How could he tell the others that cannibals were in the area? He didn't even believe it himself. His eyes, though, knew the truth. Hank grabbed an armful of supplies; turning, he almost stumbled into Renee. "Well, good morning. A might early, I'd say, for a beautiful woman like yourself to be out and about. Don't want to sound rude, but if you'd be as kind as to step away for a moment, I'd get these items set down a might quicker." Hank jostled his wife.

"I'll grab something too," Renee responded as she stepped out of Hank's way.

"Thank you, much pretty lady." Entering the cave, he set down the things he had grabbed. He looked around at the others, still wrapped up in bedrolls and sleeping. Smiling, he banged two pots together and watched with humour as they practically fell out of their beds and dreams, as the clanking din echoed throughout the cave. A little humour to start the day. "Rise and shine, folks; daylight is upon us. We have things to unpack and things to go through. I reckon we'll all find something we've missed. So, come on, shake out the cobwebs." Hank turned and snickered as he exited for a second load.

Renee passed him, shaking her head and snickering to herself, "Couldn't you have at least waited until I was there. I would have loved to have seen their expressions."

"I reckon they still have them on their faces. It was darned funny, I'll tell you that." Hank nodded as he traipsed over to the skid.

"I can tell you all one thing for certain; I had nothing to do with that," Renee stated as she entered the cave. "On a lighter note, Hank darling has packed a lot of linen. We should use it, I think, for privacy around our beds. We'll all work on it together later. I'm sure we can convince William or Hank to gather poles and such that we might need. Anyway, I'm going out for another armful. Whenever you guys are ready, you could start going through this stuff. We're getting down to the preservatives, flour, and stuff; we'll have a nice breakfast-lunch meal once all this has been tackled. Here comes Hank now with another load, so I'd best get going," Renee commented as she turned and walked away. "Is there much left, Hank?"

"Yep. I reckon three or four more loads. The heavier stuff is near the bottom, so don't try to pack it. I'll get to it."

"I'll grab another load. Then, I'll start going through it all. How does that sound?"

"Suits me. Are the others up and about? Or do I have to throw snow on them?" Hank snickered.

"They're moving, so don't be mean."

"Who, me? I would never think of it," Hank responded as he pulled open the bearskin at the entrance and entered. *Seems to me, I brought along some tools. Should consider fixing things up, get rid of that darn stinky bearskin,* he thought as he looked at it for a moment. Turning, he walked the short distance to where their sundries were accumulating on the cave floor and added what he carried. Beth Ann sat cross-legged on the floor, sorting things out. "A couple more loads, Beth Ann, and that'll be the end of her. Seems as though I've packed a lot of unnecessary whatnots."

"I wouldn't say that, Hank. These linens and toiletries will keep us healthy, clean and warm. The trinkets, well, they are good for the kids to play with. I wouldn't say any of it is unnecessary. You did well, Hank, really, you did."

Hank stroked his chin. "All right then. I guess if you women can put it all to use, then it wasn't such a bad thing to grab. Maybe it's a good thing that I didn't look either, cause I'd have left it. Anyway, I'll finish up now," Hank said as he waved his hand through the air.

Finally, it was done. The skid was unloaded. All except Hank and Eli gathered around the semi-circle in the middle of the floor. Hank lay on the bed, his hands behind his head, and looked on, watching satisfied as six pairs of arms sorted this out with that and vice versa. The six voices echoed and shrilled with elation as the sorting took place. The sound to Hank was as peaceful as a warm, sunny day in July, and he smiled. The Vanfell legacy lived on. Sighing, Hank lazily closed his eyes. Sometime later, the smell of coffee wafted up his nostrils. Opening an eye, Hank looked. There hadn't been any of that in months. Tea had been the choice, not by preference, though. Hank shuffled in his bed. "Is that what I think it is?" he asked in delight, as he sat up.

"Sure is, Pa. We found it amongst everything else."

"Pour me a cup, boy," Hank replied as he stood and traipsed over to the fire. "Been hoping for this; missed it as much as my pipe and tobacco." Hank extended his arm as he took the cup from William. "Thank you, boy. Thank you very much." Hank brought the tin cup to his lips and blew. "Ah, that makes a man feel blessed," he commented after taking a swallow. "What does the weather beyond that bearskin tell us today, boy?" Hank asked, referring to the outside. "Any changes since sunup? I seemed to have dozed off for a bit." Hank rubbed his eyes.

"I suppose. Looks like we're due the same as yesterday. Early morn was calm. Near noon, though, old Mother Nature decided we needed another spanking. We got the old mare sheltered, fed, and watered beforehand."

"Guess I dozed longer than I expected."

William chuckled. "Not at all, Pa, an old folk like yourself should turn around and go back to bed, after all, it's near dusk now."

Hank nodded and took another swallow of coffee. "I guess your old Pa is getting old, huh?" Hank teased.

"Could be. I figure it has to do with that wound on your leg, which you keep favouring. I've been watching how you hobble about. You ought to have Ma take a gander."

"Before too long, I reckon she'll have to. In the meantime, now that we're all present, leastwise those of us fit enough, there are some things I neglected to mention on our return yesterday and for good reason too." Hank paused for a minute. "The children don't necessarily need to hear," he said, looking over to Renee. "Do you suppose you could get the youngsters occupied over yonder? I'll wait."

"Yes, yes, of course, Hank." Renee could tell the seriousness of the situation by Hank's tone. "It'll only take a minute." Scooting the children over to their beds, Renee handed them a couple of glass figurines. "You two play nicely with these. The adults need to talk."

"Oh, thank you so very much, Aunt Renee. We'll be extra, extra careful," Honey commented as she looked over the figurines.

"Good," Renee turned and joined the others. "There, that should occupy them for a while. What is it, Hank, that you need to tell us? You are okay, aren't you?" she asked with concern.

Hank raised his hand. "We'll get to me in a minute. First off, I want all of you to know that we ain't alone out here."

"How's that, Pa?"

Hank extended his arm, gesturing for another coffee. "Ten miles north of our first camp, I came across something of which I still ain't able to comprehend. I've been sick about it since." William poured him another coffee. "Thanks, boy." Sitting down on one of the few blocks of wood they used for seating purposes, Hank took a swig. "As I was saying… I came across a butchering ground of sorts. Five dead men in all, chopped up and half eaten, some of it. Hard to swallow, ain't it?" Hank took another swig from the coffee in his hand.

Renee gasped. "What are you saying, Hank? Are you saying there are cannibals around here?"

"There ain't no other way of putting it. Plain and simple, that's what I reckon. It's hard to imagine, I presume, without seeing it firsthand, but I ain't about to head back and double check."

"If that didn't ruin everybody's day, I don't know what might," William commented.

"Well, it ruined my day," Beth Ann offered.

"Mine too," was Shileen's response.

"I figure we've been here this long already, and been fairly safe too. As long as we know of the possibility, then I reckon we'll continue to be safe," Hank assured, as he gazed into the flames. Inhaling deeply, he reached for his pipe and tobacco in his shirt pocket. The wound was the next thing he had to address. He hated the thought of having to cut at it; this time, at least, he wouldn't have to burn it close. As for the pains he suffered in his chest, that was something he'd bring up with Renee alone. For now, they seemed to have stopped. The leg was another story.

Putting tobacco into his pipe, he took a long draw from it. "Now about my wound," he started as he exhaled a plume of blue smoke. "I need your skilled hands, Renee, since Eli ain't able to take a look-see. Seems I contracted gas gangrene, leastwise that's what I suspect, so... well, you'll have to cut the rot away."

A hush fell over the cave, and mouths gaped open. "What would be the meaning of that?" William asked with revolt.

"Actually, that is exactly what has to be done," Shileen spoke, "if you have contracted gangrene, the rot will have to be removed. Isn't that right, Renee?"

"Most likely, yes," Renee said with surprise, "my God, Hank, I pray you haven't got gangrene, I have never cut away rotting flesh from any wound, ever!" Renee brought her hand up to her forehead and wiped away a small bead of sweat. "It's not like a sliver under your toenail, Hank. This is way different," she trailed off.

"It's only different if you think it's different, Ma." William chortled. The instantaneous look he received from Renee and Hank told him there was no room for humour. "I'm sorry, Ma. You too, Pa. I didn't want it to come out like I was making fun of the situation, but I reckon, Ma, you're Pa's only hope. There ain't no way I could do it." William brushed his bangs out of his eyes and scratched the top of his head. "Unless, of course, you weren't around, Ma. Least of all, Pa, I'd heat the blade for you," he snickered, "ever I need to tell someone something about you, Pa, this'd be it. I… I can't figure out why hot steel, maybe a little gunpowder, wouldn't take care of such an ailment."

"The rot would have to be cut away first," Shileen remarked, "the same is true for severe frostbite. You have to cut it away to prevent gangrene." Shileen looked over to Renee, her teacher, her mentor, and smiled. *See, I've learned something after all,* she thought.

Renee returned her smile. "Shileen and I have been reading some of Eli's medical journals; we've learned a few things."

"Well then, teach the rest of us," Hank said as he started to remove his trousers.

"You might as well be comfortable, Hank. How about swinging up onto our bed? I'll get a lantern," Renee intervened.

"I reckon I'm as comfortable here."

"That doesn't matter, Hank Vanfell. If you want me to help, then I will only help if you're lying on the bed. Where you're sitting now is where we eat for crying out loud."

Hank made a face at her. "Ah, for the sake of saving an argument, I reckon you're right." He looked over to William and gestured. "Come on, boy. Give your old man a hand in standing, would you?" William stepped forward and grabbed Hank underneath the shoulder. "That's it," Hank responded as he slowly rose. "Thanks, boy."

"Need help the rest of the way, Pa?"

"I don't reckon." Finally making the distance, Hank kicked off his boots, swung onto the bed and struggled with his trousers until they were past his hips. Then, he waited patiently for Renee to start the procedure. She laid out a cotton sheet next to the bed and made Hank roll over on his side, then covered him up. "What the heck are you doing covering me up, woman? Don't you need to see it to fix it?"

Renee slapped his good cheek. "Of course. I don't think everyone else wants to look at your hairy butt, though. Now, be still." Using scissors, she cut a slit in the sheet as near to the wound on Hank's buttock as she could. Satisfied, she tore it slightly so that the wound was visible.

"Ouch. That burn must hurt like almighty, Hank." For a moment, Renee thought she was going to throw up. As if the sight of the third-degree burn wasn't hard enough for her to take, the rotting flesh made her even more queasy. Renee inhaled deeply. *Don't falter now, Renee. It won't take long...* she coaxed herself. "This might not be as hard as I first thought. I think I can cut the rot away. It's going to hurt, though, Hank. We should probably mix you up some of the morphine that Eli has first."

"Never mind that. If the scalpel and catgut are handy, cut away." Hank took a deep breath.

"All right, here we go. Hold on, Hank, and hold on tight." Carefully, Renee made the first few incisions and gently pulled the pieces of rotting flesh out and away from the wound. "I'm cutting more of the flesh away now, Hank. Does it hurt? Yuck," she said as she briefly turned away.

"What's all the fuss about?" Hank resounded. His first instinct was to feel around with his hand.

Renee smacked it out of the way. "Don't put that dirty thing back here. You'll end up with a worse infection than you already have, Hank." Renee cut away more of the rotting flesh and, as quickly, dappled the wound with iodine. This time Hank hollered and cussed. "Quit being a baby."

"A baby! My God, woman, that hurt like a son-of-a-bitch, almost made me wet myself. What in the heck was the purpose of that?"

"The purpose of that, Hank, was to keep the wound clean while I cut away more of the rot. I'm almost done. There, there, is the last of it; now roll over. The catgut is next."

"Can you give me an idea of how the wound looks?" Hank wanted to know.

"Not very nice," Renee commented as she pierced the half-moon-shaped needle through Hank's skin, bringing the two sides of the incision together. Hank jerked and twitched slightly. "Did you feel that, Hank?"

"If that's all I got to look forward to, I reckon I can stand it."

"That was the needle, Hank. I'm pulling the catgut through now. All right, that's one," Renee said as she tied the two ends. "Still able to cope, Hank?" She swabbed at the wound, mopping up the blood that continued to ooze, and at the same time went forward with a couple more stitches.

"I can remember pleasanter moments," Hank paused as he shifted his weight. "I think the worst part was when you pulled the catgut through. It wasn't anything, though, compared to hot steel. Feel free to continue, wife, whenever you're ready."

"I've got two more finished since you started talking, Hank. I think it will take at least two more." And it did. "There. All done," Renee said as she washed the wound with a solution of rubbing alcohol and water. "Another scar added to the old battle axe," she commented as she stepped away. "You're not going to like what comes next."

"Next? What's that?"

"More iodine."

"You're right; I ain't going to like that. Is it even necessary?" Hank could already feel the quick, painful sting.

"Maybe not," Renee shrugged, "regardless, we all know Eli wouldn't hesitate to dab it with more, and he's the doctor. It can't hurt, Hank. You do have a high-risk infection. You're not out of the woods yet."

"No kidding, wife, in more ways than one, too. I assure you."

"Make all the jokes you want, Hank. You're still getting an iodine wipe down."

"I can't wait. Been looking forward." Hank turned his head toward the cave wall. "Whenever you're ready." His mouth went dry as he waited, bracing himself. The pain he knew would only last a couple of seconds. He was certain he could handle it.

"Count to three, Hank." With the bottle already opened, she wasted no time giving the lesion a healthy dose. Inhaling deeply, Hank clenched his teeth as the quick sting permeated the wound. The others winced in pain as they looked on from the fire. They knew all too well the stinging pain iodine caused.

"I reckon that stung a bit," William remarked, shaking his head as he looked on.

Hank shuffled on the bed, pulling up his trousers. "It did. I tell you, though, there ain't no pain as compared to red-hot steel. Although I hate the iodine, I'd much rather be swabbed with it than bring hot steel to my flesh. That, boy, I can tell you from experience." Hank winced as he traipsed over to the fire. "She's still a wee tender, I reckon. Feels better though. Is any of that coffee left?" Hank questioned as he sat. "Wouldn't mind some if there is."

"Sure is, Pa." William poured Hank a coffee.

"Thank ya, son. Did y'all get an eyeful of that procedure?"

"I watched for as long as I could," Shileen commented.

"Me too, I reckon."

"Well then, what did you learn? Anything valuable?" Hank took a deep swallow from his cup.

William snickered, "You start counting long before Ma tells you to. That's what I'm able to walk away with. Wasn't close enough to see what her hands were doing."

"Not to worry, Willy. That is about what I learned, too."

"What's a matter? You both got weak innards? Should have been right there in the blood with your Ma. There ain't nothing wrong with learning. Could be what you might have learned could save you some time."

William lowered his head and thought for a moment. "I reckon you're right, Pa. Hey, Ma, want to show us what you did to Pa. We'll watch this time." William chortled as he snickered.

"Always the wise guy, huh, boy," Hank commented as he looked at his son. He loved everything about him, even his humour. He smiled and shook his head. "Should've known you'd have come up with something like that."

"Yeah. It's just like me... ain't it?"

Hank snickered. "Yep. Don't know where the humour comes from; must be from your Ma's side of the family. Seriously, though, boy, I'd hope the next time something comes about, you'd do me the favour and learn what you can from it. Might need to use that knowledge before we get to civilization." Hank downed the last of his coffee.

"All right, Pa. Consider it done," William responded in all seriousness. Hank was right; the knowledge of medicine was indeed critical, especially way out there. It couldn't hurt.

The next morning, Eli insisted he get up and walk around before he forgot how to use his legs. With Beth Ann's assistance, he took his first steps since he had returned. Still not 100% healthy, he was improving daily. In the evening, he read aloud from his medical journals to the others and began teaching them medicine. It became a family ritual. Nightly, they gathered at the fire waiting for Eli to deliver the next vital paragraph, page or chapter from whatever medical journal he was reading.

February came to a halt, and March brought a touch of spring, but not enough for the Vanfells to continue onward to the Double-U. Eli recovered completely and, except for the scars on his back, was in good shape. The young wolf became known as Friend. He seemed to grow in leaps and bounds with each passing day. As wild as he remained, he was content to live with the family. They sheltered him and fed him. More importantly, they loved him, and for that, it was Friend's instinct to protect them.

Chapter 5

It was mid-March when the Indians came. It was late in the evening when Friend warned them. The women fought alongside their men. Shileen was knocked unconscious by one of the Indians and fell to the cave floor. Renee and Beth Ann were raped and bludgeoned to death. What saved Shileen from the same barbarism was that the Indians believed her already to be dead.

The men were subdued and murdered. They stood no chance against the onslaught of the dozen or so Indians who attacked. William, too, was knocked unconscious and thought to be dead. After the slaughter of the Vanfells, the Indians retreated. In their clutches, they held the screaming children, Honey and Sinclair.

"Can we not kill these screaming white skin pigs and eat their livers? They will slow us down," spoke Black Crow, one of the Toukia's most heartless braves. Young and handsome, Black Crow cared nothing about the white man. He'd rather slaughter them and drink their blood. "They scream and stink like white men. I say we kill them."

"Chief Bloodwater said we must return with the children. New blood is needed in our tribe. As these children grow, they will offer us that. The fair-haired girl will bear us children at womanhood. The boy will breed with our woman when he reaches manhood. These children, along with the others we have gathered, will make our tribe strong again. They must live," responded an elder brave, "and I, Ti-Cheaka, will see to it."

"I'm thirsty for their blood."

"You will not hurt a hair on their heads, or I will slaughter you." Ti-Cheaka raised his hand in the air. "That is all, Black Crow."

"Perhaps I will eat them when you sleep," Black Crow commented as he looked at the children under discussion.

"No more talk of that, Black Crow. We do not eat children. Grab the white man's horse; they will have no need for it now," Ti-Cheaka demanded as he strode ahead to where Black Crow released the children. "The children will ride with me." Ti-Cheaka looked at the young girl and boy. "Climb up." The children, traumatized, followed the Indian's instructions and got on his horse. "Do not be afraid. I will not hurt you, nor will Black Crow. You are safe." Into the darkness the Toukia rode, leaving behind the battered and bloody bodies of the children's kin.

Hours passed. Finally, Shileen was the first to come to. Revolted by the blood pooling on the floor, she screamed for her daughter, became hysterical, and passed out from fear. A friend crawled to her side; wounded himself, he kept vigil. Alert now to the horror around him, William hurried to Shileen's side and checked for breathing. There was no use checking the others. The blood on the cave floor already showed their fate. Scrambling, he looked frantically for the children. Finding no remains, he realized that they were gone. His only thought was that *the Indians must have taken them.*

Distraught tears of horror and hate towards those who had committed the assault streamed down his bloodied face. The wound to his forehead made him dizzy, and he vomited. The cave began to spin, and he fell to the floor once more unconscious. First, he felt his shoulders being shaken, and then he heard her voice. "Willy, can you hear me? Willy, say something, anything. Please, William, say something. Don't leave me; don't leave me, Willy," Shileen sobbed as she banged her fists on the floor.

Opening his eyes, he looked at her. "I'm okay; I'm okay," he mumbled. "Give me a minute; my head hurts something bad, but I'm okay, Shileen. I'm okay." He gripped her hand and squeezed it, giving her the assurance she needed.

"Thank God. Thank God, you're okay. Honey and Sinclair, where are they?" Shileen questioned, hoping he knew.

William shook his head. "I think the Indians have taken them. They're alive, though, Shileen; they're alive. I didn't find them… so they have to be alive." His throat went dry; how he hoped that was the case. In all the books he read and all that he had been taught, Indians did not kill children. Children were the lambs of the flock. The Indian needed them. They were the future.

"They can't have my daughter! They just can't," Shileen sobbed.

Slowly getting to his feet, William tried to comfort her. "Shileen, they ain't got no intent on hurting them. If they had, they too would be lying amongst the dead. No, they have no reason to kill children. They'll raise them like their own. They're alive, and so are we. We'll fight to get them back, I assure you."

"What can we do, the two of us against all of them?"

"Whatever it takes," he said with conviction.

Moments of silence passed as Shileen stared at the floor. Her eyes full of tears, her heart beating a mile a minute as adrenaline coursed through her veins, hot and unrelenting. It was then that she decided that if the children were alive, they would find them. "Yes, we will find them no matter to what degree or extent of our lives it may take." She wiped her tears away.

William only nodded in agreement as he continued to stare at the bodies on the floor. Taking a deep breath, Shileen stood. She wanted to see for herself what had taken place. Removing the sheet William had put over their kin, she looked at her sister's battered body. It was evident what had happened. She had been brutally raped, then bludgeoned to death, as had Renee. Both men were decapitated, their heads scantily hanging on to their lifeless bodies by only a few tissues. Horror, disbelief, and vengeance were only a few of the feelings Shileen and William shared at that moment. The fact that they had come so far, endured so much, only to be slaughtered and left for dead, made the two of them now more determined to see the end of the journey with Honey and Sinclair at their sides or not at all.

"There ain't nothing we can do for them, Shileen. Please, please cover them back up," William said from the dark shadows of the cave, his eyes welling up with tears. Sitting in the shadows, he stared at the blood-soaked sheets that covered his kin. The Vanfell bloodline now concluded with only him and Sinclair. William inhaled deeply. They were all that remained of a family once strong, proud, and undaunted; now there were only two.

Shileen rose and made her way over to him. Sitting in silence, the two survivors joined hands. Together, they made a pledge to withstand the mountains until the children were found and they had their vengeance on those who attacked. To no end would they stop looking. Friend also seemed to respond to their pledge as he whimpered in pain and then wagged his tail. He was strong, and from his strength, they drew theirs. The three of them would remain together. Together they would fight. Together, they would win. The Vanfell Legacy would go on.

After prayers and a few moments of mourning, they embraced each other in their arms and wrapped the bodies in linens and woollen blankets. The ground was frozen. It left them with no choice but to give their kin an Indian burial in the big evergreen that shadowed the cave. Raising the last and heaviest body to the platform made of poles and rope, tears welled up in William's eyes as he secured what he knew to be his father's corpse. "Until we meet again, Pa; until we meet again." For what seemed like eternity, he could not avert his eyes. He looked on at the enshrouded bodies, transfixed, saddened. *I will never hear their voices again,* he thought. Shileen, too, looked on, her heart remaining strong. In the end, they said farewell to their kin one last time, then entered the cave. *The dark, dismal cave...*

Chapter 6

As the days progressed, so did their relationship. Things couldn't be better considering their situation. They were finally beginning to heal from both the physical and mental state the barbarous Indians bestowed on them weeks earlier. Friend, too, was healing. No one knew how deep his hatred burned for those responsible for both his wounds and the demise of those he had grown to love. No one, that is, except Friend himself, and it burned deep and unrelenting. He was only beginning to realize the intensity of his survival instinct. His ability to hunt and kill, the power of his jaw, and the cunning of his breed were all gifts bred into him. He was unhindered, vicious and loyal.

Finally, spring arrived. They buried the deed to the Double-U, as well as the entire amount of money the family had set aside, totalling fifteen thousand dollars and some change. The family had raised the amount after selling everything they owned back in Greenfield. William and Shileen knew exactly where it was, should they ever need the cash or deed. It was in a place they could never forget, a place where they had struggled, faced death, and survived.

They loaded the most important things into the skid, which they hoped they could pull across the thawing terrain. Things of no use were burned. They did their best to destroy any evidence that they had ever been there. They had lost eleven family members in less than a year. Now their efforts called for them to find the children; the Double-U would have to wait. With one last glance at the cave and the surroundings, they slipped into the early morning, the skid strapped to William's shoulders and Friend nipping at their heels.

By evening, they had travelled well into the mountains. They guessed the date was sometime in late April, in 1826. As they set up for the evening, they heard wolves howling in the distance. Friend only perked his ears, unafraid. "You're a good boy, Friend. You'd best stay close. I wouldn't want you getting tangled up with those howling."

The wolves circled them unannounced, unknowing, invisible to them, but not to Friend. Instantly, Friend's ears perked up, his sight transfixed on something a short distance away. With a full head of speed, he darted out of Shileen's grasp, uncontrollable, unstoppable. "Friend!" she called out as she tried to restrain him.

The sound of snapping jaws, whimpers and growls echoed in the silence. A brief struggle ensued. Finally, Friend persuaded the rogue wolves to disembark. A little sore from the few nips and bites he received, Friend traipsed back to the fire, his tail raised in victory. He walked leisurely up to Shileen and licked at her face. "How did you manage to get out of that alive? How many were there, Friend?" Shileen asked with praise as though he could tell her.

"I reckon they were all rogues. Good job, Friend," William commented as he knelt next to him and scratched behind his ear. They had never seen eye to eye. "I recant all those times that I threatened you, figuring you'd make a better coat than a friend. No, tonight, Friend, you made me change my mind. From here on in, I reckon I'll treat you better," William said as he put out his hand.

Friend tilted his ears, wondering why William's hand was empty. He looked into his eyes, and William gestured again with his open hand. Finally, Friend raised his paw and set it into his palm. A smile crossed William's face as he looked over to Shileen. "I guess that means we're friends." Looking back at Friend, he nodded. "Besides, you ain't big enough yet to be a coat." William chuckled as Friend tilted his head. "Just funning with you, Friend. You'll never be a coat, honest."

Rising, William walked back to where he was working on their evening lean-to and added the finishing touches. He stood back and looked at it. It wasn't much, but it would certainly be better than sleeping outdoors in the elements.

Sitting next to the fire, he helped himself to some hot tea and honey. "Going to be a cold one again this evening. Wonder if the weather around here will ever let up?" he asked as he took a sip of tea.

"I'm sure spring will decide to show up sooner or later, hopefully sooner. Until then, we have enough blankets to keep us warm, and we have each other," Shileen responded. William looked at her and smiled.

They were bedding down when the first few snowflakes began to fall. As they slept, the wind entombed the lean-to in a snowdrift, sparing them a very uncomfortable, cold night. The temperature settled at –20 that evening. When they awoke the next morning, the creek they followed now had a rim of ice around its banks.

During the day, the wind whistled relentlessly. They were definitely going to be stranded for a day or two. Settling in for the duration, they made a fire pit inside the entrance of the abode. William built up snow around the shelter to prevent the freezing wind from penetrating the walls. They brought inside with them only the rifles and dried food. The lean-to was beginning to look more like an igloo with a wooden frame than anything else, but it was comfortable.

Friend lay at the entrance. It was not so bad for him. He knew that if he were to get cold, he could make his way into the shelter or dig himself into the snow. William and Shileen sat inside, peeking out on occasion to check the weather and to make sure Friend was present. Other than that, they read from one of Eli's medical journals. They told each other stories about this, that, and the other thing. It was a long and tiring day.

Around suppertime, they decided to take a breath of fresh air. Exiting, they noticed that the moon had already risen. The scenery was beautiful. The moon illuminated the fresh snow, and it glowed like a thousand coal oil lanterns. "Would you look at that. Now don't that make you feel alive?"

"It's beautiful. I've never seen such a beautiful sight. The snow and moon light up the entire wood." Shileen inhaled deeply. "Serenity." Catching a chill, they returned to the comfort of their leant-to. It could only have been 7:00, but it seemed much later. Inside, it was warm, cozy, and romantic. Shileen slowly removed her clothing. "Make love to me, William." Looking at her with excitement, his manhood sprang to life, way ahead of everything else. Wrestling, he removed his boots and woollen pants. Their lovemaking lasted well into the evening. The shelter warmed up with their steamy breath and body heat. The scent of their frolicking lingered. Spent, Shileen lay her head on William's chest and, without strain or anxiety, slipped into a deep slumber, followed closely by William's snoring.

The next morning, low on wood, William set out to gather more. He walked a short distance, and Friend bounded close behind. They were gone for less than an hour, long enough to load the skid with as much wood as he could comfortably pull. Returning, he spotted a wolverine thirty yards away. Luckily, it did not seem interested in them. Holding Friend, the two slowly continued the short distance back to camp.

He looked in the direction they travelled, making sure they were not followed or stalked by the cagey wolverine. They weren't. "That's a good sign. It doesn't look as though that skunk bear was interested in us," he commented as he unloaded the wood. Friend nearby was looking once again intently at some undergrowth. William looked on as well but saw nothing. "What are you seeing over there, Friend?" Friend remained steadfast, looking. In the end, he curled up and fell asleep. *Well, whatever it was, it doesn't seem to be bothering him much,* William thought to himself as he continued unloading the wood.

When he finally entered the shelter, Shileen was sitting on the floor reading from a medical book she had taken a fancy to. They had only begun a conversation when they heard the ruckus outside. It was the wolverine. William knew it!

Quickly, he loaded the gun and peered out, seeing Friend defending them once again, this time against the deadly skunk bear. He fired the rifle, and it echoed like a thunderclap, frightening the animal away. This time, Friend had taken a beating. His legs and ears were torn, and a cut to the top of his head bled thick and unrelenting. His coat now crimson, Friend sauntered back to the camp, hungry for blood.

"Looks like you took a beating this time," Shileen spoke with concern as she looked his wounds over. "That is a nasty cut to your head. It will heal, though, as will the rest of the battle scars you have. God, Friend, you are the bravest of the brave," Shileen cooed as she patted him.

"Maybe he ain't all there," William commented as he snickered. "You figure he'll be okay?"

"I believe so. There's nothing falling out; he's got all his legs and ears. Although they are tattered, he'll be fine."

"Good. If he'll be fine and that skunk bear is pulling lead out of his behind, I reckon it's time for some coffee. What do you say?"

"Coffee or tea, either works for me."

William added wood to the early morning fire. Then, setting the pot of snow onto the flames, he spoke to Shileen. "I've added enough water so that we might get some bannock or griddle cakes whipped up. I'm a might hungry, yourself?" William asked.

"Oh, that sounds stupendous. Are you making them?"

He looked at her, raising an eyebrow. "Heck, Shileen, I boiled the water, gathered the wood... "

Shileen cut him off. "Right, you couldn't make them if you had to. I'll do it."

"But, that ain't what I was saying. I've cooked a little... " William looked into the flames. She was right.

"How about this morning, I'll teach you how? It could be fun. There really isn't anything to it." Shileen gathered the items she needed. "When the water is hot, bring it inside. I'd rather mix it all up where it's a bit warmer."

William was about to respond when she ducked into the lean-to and out of sight. "What do you think of that, Friend? The female species, they sure seem to know how to make or break a man's day." He looked over to the uncaring wolf. Friend beamed back, panting as though he were laughing. His eyes grew dreary then slowly closed. "Yeah. I know your world is fine. No smooth-talking woman can make a fella like you follow their example. In the human world, that's all backwards," Williams snickered as he warmed his hands above the flames.

Looking to the sky, he squinted. The sun was winning its battle. It penetrated the dark clouds, casting shadows throughout the ominous forest, only a few paces from where he sat. "Might turn out to be a half-respectable day after all, especially if the sun keeps beating back those clouds. Ain't any use heading out today, though. Can't be sure how this weather is going to turn out." He took note of the boiling water. "Oops, almost forgot about that. Best get this inside and take my first cooking lesson like a man." After tossing more wood onto the fire, he got up, pot in hand, and entered their shelter. "She's all boiled and ready, I reckon." He handed the pot to Shileen.

"Thank you very much. Now sit." The lesson had begun.

The rest of the day was spent sipping tea. They talked around the fire, nibbled on the freshly cooked bannock and waited for dusk. The sun remained warm and promising. With luck, the weather would cooperate, and the following morning, they could once again begin their search for their kin.

Their luck held out. The following morning, when they awoke, the blue sky boasted a yellow rising sun. It was hot and real, the first in days. "I reckon today is a good day to travel." William inhaled the warm spring air deeply.

"Should we have a fire first or just go?" Shileen questioned as she took in the beauty of the spring day herself.

"The embers tell me we should have a fire first. Warm up our extremities. We'll start off soon enough. We'll give ourselves enough time to swill a hot tea or coffee, then we'll go." He added birch bark to the embers and gently blew at the coals. The fire sputtered as flames laid waste to the added bark. Tossing a couple of sticks onto the flames, he sat. "That'll take off in a minute; be able to warm up our hands and such momentarily."

Shileen handed him the pot. "Can't have tea without water."

"Yeah, yeah," he waved his hand at her as he set it in the flames.

"Also, Willy," she began, "we can't have water without snow."

He looked into the pot. It was empty. "I guess we could have imaginary tea," he responded as he plucked it out of the flames and scooped snow into it. "Then again, that was when we were kids." He was referring back to their childhood when they used to play house.

"That was so long ago. I can't believe you actually remember that. Those are some long-lost memories, aren't they?"

"A lot of things are lost. Memories are one of them." He looked at her and winked. "That doesn't mean we're trodden and worn. We're a long way from that."

Shileen nodded. "Could say that we are provoked and heartbroken, though."

"Yep. We could say that." William agreed. They sat in silence, both drawn back in time. Their memories now filled with despair as they thought of their kin. In the end, the tea was served, and once more, they were traversing the terrain, only guessing in what direction their search should begin. During those first few nights of travel, they heard drums in the distance. Instinctively, they followed the thumping din, drawing closer to it by each passing day. They travelled for another three days, convinced that the beating drums that led them were the drums of those who held their kin captive. They set up a camp. Nightly, the drums pounded. Somewhere, out there, their kin waited to be rescued.

They needed a more secure shelter, a place where they could bring the children to recover before finally making their way to the Double-U. It was in these mountains that they were certain they would find their kin. They found the perfect spot to construct a cabin. The creek was only a short distance away and would provide them with water. The forest, all except for that one peculiar spot some fifty yards away, was dense and secluded. It was perfect for concealing their presence.

Labouring for two days, they constructed what, for now, they would call home. It was built on the thick, heavy branches of three full-size cedar trees that grew as precariously as the big rock that happened to jut out of the ground below their drooping branches. "There's home," William said as he stood back and looked on.

"Yeah," Shileen stated. Somewhat disenchanted, she averted her eyes to the dark wood. "What if it turns out that those drums aren't the drums we're hoping they are? What if the children are miles away? I know that sounds pessimistic… but we aren't sure otherwise."

"Yep, that's pessimistic all right, but it's appropriate to admit. We ain't never going to know until we find out where those drums are beating from. It could be anywhere, North, East, South or West of us now. That's why we need to search them out. It's going to be a heck of a lot easier without having to drag that skid every which way. Having a place we can return to will make a difference, also. We'll start in the morning." William nodded as he gathered an armful of the goods they had stocked in the skid. "I reckon this sticks out like a sore thumb. I'd best unload it. I'll drag it out yonder somewhere and cover it up with branches and bramble."

He inhaled as he looked on at the skid. It was the last and likely best thing his Pa built. Somehow, it meant something to him. "I might consider it firewood if I were certain we wouldn't need it." He brushed the bangs away from his eyes and tucked them into the scraggly red bandanna that he began to wear some days earlier. "Could be we find those kids in the next week, in which case it'll come in handy; otherwise, it might be firewood soon enough."

William set the armful down near the ladder and loaded up again. It took four trips to empty the skid. "There we go; empty as a nut shell. I guess now we rig up a couple of lengths of rope and get this stuff tucked up and out of prying eyes that might see it."

He looked at the array of this, that, and what have you that lay before him. There were rifles, reloading kits, easily a pound of gunpowder, gun oil, blankets, clothing, canned goods, dried goods, some frilly pinks this, and whites that. He saw soaps, medical supplies of all kinds and medical books. They had a few maps, gardening and building tools, a spade, hoe, axe and hatchet, the head of a broken rake, two hundred feet, maybe more, of one-inch thick hemp rope, a couple of burlap bags full of nails and spikes. The list went on. William scratched his head. *Huh, packed everything, even a dang washtub. No wonder it was so awful, dragging it about... Need all those things though, I reckon,* he thought for a moment.

"Quite a load. I had no idea we packed so much," Shileen said.

"No. Me neither," he replied as he raised an eyebrow. "I reckon our haste to leave the cave might have hindered our good judgement. No matter, it'll all be used one way or another." He ran the thinner piece of rope that was used for the skid's harness through the rifle's trigger guards and bunched them together. "I'll climb up and pull these with me. I'll throw the end of the rope back down. Bunch up what you can, and I'll pull her up. Should take a few loads, but we'll get her done."

Shileen nodded. "You bet. Those rifles aren't loaded, are they?"

"Already checked them. No worries there." William climbed to the hut entrance, the rope ladder swaying this way and that as he pulled himself up, one step at a time. "That wasn't bad," he called down. "Hang on, and I'll toss the rope to you." Three heavy and well-packed loads later, the task was done. The gardening tools, including the big, heavy axe, were stuffed into a rotted-out log behind the big cedars. The hatchet found its way upstairs with them.

Next, they spent some time coaxing Friend into the hut. They showed him that from the big rock, he could, in one well-placed leap, straddle one of the thicker tree branches and, easily enough, follow it to the entrance. It took some practice, but by the end of the day, it had become second nature. "Atta boy, Friend, good for you. Way to go," Shileen cooed as he sniffed out the hut and even urinated on the wall in one particular spot. "Friend! No," she said in disgust. "Do that outside."

William chuckled and shook his head. "Ah, he's marking his territory, I reckon. Ain't that right, Friend? No harm in that, no sir."

"Please, Willy. Don't encourage him." Shileen punched him on his shoulder. "We have to live here."

"He needs to live here too, I reckon. It's like a den to him. Heck, that ain't such a bad way in describing this place, a den." He looked around at all the poles and branches they managed to weave or tie together that made up the walls, floor and ceiling. "Now that we've come across those few pounds of nails and spikes, we should spend some extra time making sure this place is as well-built as we'd like. Come spring, if we're still in need, we could add grass and mud to the outside walls to make this place really cozy. For now, we'll add a nail here, a spike there; eventually, she'll come together. It's dang sturdy as she is now, I reckon. A few nails will only make her that much *sturdier*, if that's such a word."

"It is, and it means exactly what you want it to. We wouldn't want to be blown out of *our den* in the middle of one of those wild windstorms that seem to plague us every now and again. I think the idea of grass, moss, and mud, come spring, providing we still need to be here, is a good idea. It would last for a long and seemingly endless time then. Like our commitment to find Honey and Sinclair… " Shileen trailed off as her mind drifted.

William finally broke the silence. "Well, now that all our stuff is tucked away. Feel like taking a short jaunt? Still got a skid we need to dispose of. Out of sight, out of mind. Better to be safe than sorry." He rose and reached out his hand to help her up.

"Yeah. Some fresh air and a brisk walk will cheer me up. Thank you, Willy," she responded as she took his hand. They walked out on the branches of the big tree and waited for Friend to make the jump back to the rock. Then, following suit, they tested the exit for themselves. It added some fun to a rather dull and boring day.

William went first, almost slipping on the rock as he landed. He held his composure as he shuffled his feet, avoiding what might have been a nasty fall. "Whoa! That was different. Careful when you jump, Shileen. The rock is a tad slippery, I reckon."

"Maybe I should use the ladder?"

"Nah, you'll be fine. Come on, I'll catch you if you slip. Besides, it's a good idea to get used to both ways. Two exits are always better than one." He stood, waiting.

Finally, Shileen made the jump, landing on the rock as gracefully as Friend had. "That wasn't bad at all. In fact, I kind of liked it, kind of thrilling." Shileen looked back and nodded. "I guess only an exit is all it can be. There's no way we could jump back that way."

William looked on. "Yeah, for us, it doesn't help as a way in. Brings me to my next thought. Did we let down the ladder, or am I looking at climbing up once we get back?" William asked as he ducked and looked under the branches up to the hut. "Looks like I climb. The ladder is rolled up," he reported as he shook his head. "No matter. That's easy enough. Come on, let's get rid of that skid." It pulled easily now that it was empty.

In an area not far from their hut, the skid found its new home. Covered in branches and a few old logs, it was camouflaged from the naked eye. It could be found, of course, if one knew it was there or if one inadvertently stumbled upon it. "That ought to do." William looked the area over, taking mental notes of the terrain in case he forgot where they had stashed it.

The big thorn bush he would remember, as well as the two birches a short distance away. They stood out like white horses in a pen full of black ones. He inhaled deeply. "All right, reckon we can turn back now. It'll be dusk soon enough." Turning, they coursed their way back to *their den*.

Chapter 7

By the end of May, they had thoroughly explored the forest within a five-mile radius of the hut. Beyond that, it was more of the same, a forest thick with evergreens, thorn shrubs, swamplands, ravines and more forest. That was it. There was no reason to go any further. Plenty of game, lots of water, and everything they needed could easily be obtained within the five miles of forest that they explored.

The sounds of the drums faded as days went by, and soon they were no longer heard. They didn't discover in what direction they sounded from. The dense, unrelenting forest and terrain disallowed any confirmation. It was, they knew, possible that whatever the Indians were celebrating over the course of that first week had now ended. It could be that they would never hear the drums again. Whatever the reason for the drumming, they were certain that Honey and Sinclair would be found in the mountains where they now dwelled.

It was early evening when they heard the voices. Silently peering to the ground below, they saw two braves. Friend caught their scent. Without mercy or pity, he attacked. His every purpose was to kill them. The braves' screams of pain and surprise echoed with eerie dread. Blood-soaked and unrelenting, Friend lunged at them again and again, like a wolf from Hell, stopping only when the last mangled body quivered and the Indians' souls escaped into the night, death the only outcome. Silently, William and Shileen watched with both worry and recognition as the horror took place. *What had happened with Friend? Was he suddenly completely mad?*

"I ain't ever seen anything like that before. I can tell you that much. He ripped through them like a hot blade through lard. They didn't stand a chance. What do you make of it, Shileen? Think he's gone mad?"

Shileen, though, recognized one of the Braves, and she shook her head. "No. They're the barbarous men who attacked us. I recognized one of them. Friend also recognized them. That's why he attacked. We can't scold him for that."

Friend looked up to the two faces peering down at him from the hut. The fur on his chest was deep crimson with the braves' blood. Proud and victorious, he looked away and then rolled on the ground where the untamed attack had taken place.

"I'd hate to be them if that's how it is. Obviously, Friend ain't forgotten their scent. Hell waits for them," William commented, referring to the Indians below and their unknowing tribe.

"Why shouldn't it? An eye for an eye, right?" Shileen knew that wasn't the Christian way, not always at least. This time, though, from her point of view, that saying meant something.

William stroked his chin, his eyes still averted to the ground below. "Yep, I won't disagree. Of course, though, that means we have a couple of dead Indians to bury." Descending from the hut by way of the branches, keeping the rope ladder hidden in case others were near, they looked at the disarray scattered on the forest floor. The Indians had lost the battle before it even started. Looking over their weapons, they decided that they could use them. The bows and arrows were made with regard. A lot of time had been put into making them.

The arrowheads, oddly enough, were of different sizes, skinny ones, fat ones, long and short ones, all piercing and sharp. The arrow shafts were straight and flawless. Other well-crafted tools included tomahawks. Stripping the corpses naked, they carried the lifeless bodies deep into the forest and disposed of them as one disposes of scraps. Again, not the Christian thing to do, but it mattered little to them. *Religion, Faith, what was that… ?*

Returning, they looked over the weapons. Each quiver held 26 arrows. The bows were made from a very hard wood that William believed to be walnut. It made no difference, really, what the species of wood was. What mattered was that they were alive, alive and well, protected by Friend, the spirit wolf who months earlier had led Eli back to the safety of the cave. However, only Friend knew that history.

Shileen insisted that William try on the cleaner of the two rawhide vests, which one of their attackers wore. Surprisingly, it fit him nicely, as did the loincloth. The buckskin pants, however, were another story. They fit Shileen and formed to every curvaceous curve of her legs and buttocks. She looked stunning in them.

"Yep. I must admit those look good."

"Thanks. They do, don't they?" Shileen looked over her shoulder at her lower extremities. "I think I like these. Can't wait to wash them up."

"I ain't sure we have any saddle soap to wash them. I reckon that's what you're supposed to use on buckskin. Could be wrong though, that's happened a time or two before."

"Not this time. You are right. Of course, one could rub them down with oil and pat them dry. That, too, I think, might work. Whatever it takes." Shileen shrugged. "I'm keeping these buckskins."

"No complaints from me." William looked at the vest he was wearing. He didn't like it. "Might as well take this vest too. I reckon it'll go well with the pants. These other ones, though, they're too darned blood-soaked to do anything with, especially this second vest." He thought for a moment, *it does seem like a waste.*

"Maybe we could use them for leather lacing. It wouldn't take much to cut them up into different-sized strips, patches, or what have you. Yeah, I reckon that's what we'll do. Nothing wrong with having strands of leather at our disposal. Sometimes a man needs things like that, and there ain't no mercantile out here." He looked again at the blood-soaked clothing, deciding the vest was too far gone even for laces. He removed the debris that hid the fire pit and tossed the vest in. The not-so-blood-soaked buckskin pants that Shileen wasn't wearing, he placed over his shoulder. "I'll climb up and toss down the ladder. We'd best get up and inside," he gestured toward their hut. "Out of sight, out of mind. Can't be sure if there are others out and about, leastwise not as dusk settles."

"Lead the way, Willy." Shileen looked over to Friend. "Up, Friend, up. Come on, get into the den," she coaxed. In a quick, stealthy leap and hurdle, he followed her command, nearly beating William to the entrance. "Atta boy, Friend. Stay. I'll be there as soon as Willy lets down the ladder. Hang tough. Good boy."

"Are ya ready down there?" William asked as he looked below.

"Fire away." Shileen responded.

"All right, here it comes." He kicked the ladder out the door. "I'll climb down and gather those bows and such once you make it up." Shileen tugged on the ladder to make sure it was secure, then ascended. It took only moments for her to make the top. He winked at her as he turned and climbed down to retrieve the bows, arrows and tomahawks, which he tucked into their sheaths, then tied around his waist. The quivers and bows he slipped over his shoulders, then once more, he ascended into the trees above. Bringing up the ladder, he rolled it up neatly and slid it to the corner of the entrance.

Earlier that day, they had transformed the wash tub into a fireplace of sorts, and now they lit it for the first time. Surprisingly enough, it heated the inside comfortably. The smoke, on a rare occasion, offered little escape as it lost its way through the hole in the roof. It was something they'd have to work on; a small price to pay for the comfort.

Bored, William loaded one of the arrows, pulled back the bow-string and let the arrow fly. Embedding the far wall with a solid *thud,* it passed through, leaving only the feathers visible. The two marvelled. *How ironic,* he thought. *We could use these to hunt rather than giving ourselves away with the rifles.* Pulling the arrow out until the arrowhead was butted up against the outside wall. William looked at the shaft, half expecting to find a crack. The shaft remained flawless. "Ain't going to be pulling that arrow out. I reckon it'll work to hang something from. Hard to believe that the shaft didn't suffer any. A lesser-made arrow would've cracked or snapped from the impact. Those who built these knew what they were doing."

That night in her sleep, Shileen dreamt about her daughter, Honey. In her dream, Honey was a young woman. Not the Honey she remembered. Her golden hair was past her waist, and she held in her blood-soaked hand a beating human heart. Her face was contorted in a demonic smile, her teeth crimson with fresh human blood. Shileen awoke screaming, calming down only when William comforted her. He reassured her that Honey was all right. Somehow, he was sure of that.

At dawn, with Friend at their sides, they set out searching for signs of the Indian tribe. They travelled in the direction from which the Indians had approached the night before. It was a southeast direction. They searched high and low from dawn until dusk. Their search was fruitless. Discouraged, they turned and headed back the way they came. Walking the last few miles, William stopped abruptly.

"Shhh, listen. Can you hear that? Drums." He was positive that that was what he heard.

Shileen tilted her head, cupping a hand behind her ear as she listened intently. "I do hear them. They seem so distant. How far away do you think they might be?" she asked with hope.

Friend heard the drums long before they did. Antsy as he was, he stood steadfast at their sides, protecting, guarding, ready to pounce at any given moment.

"I ain't able to say for sure; couldn't even guess. The mountains hinder that. Leastwise, we know that there are Indians about." William looked at Shileen and gestured for them to keep moving. "It is going to be dark soon; we'd best keep heading back. Hate to get lost."

"We'd never get lost, not with Friend at our sides. Isn't that right, boy?" Shileen questioned with confidence. They continued on around a bend up a little knoll and across a small wetland. There it was, their den, now only a few paces away. "There's home. Come on, Friend." Shileen and Friend raced the distance, leaving William in the dark. Friend didn't even second-guess his footing as he bound from the rock to the thick branches. Shileen struggled as she climbed the ladder, laughing the entire time. Friend had won. He stood at the entrance panting as Shileen finally pulled herself the rest of the way in.

"You beat me. Good for you, Friend. Good boy." Shileen snickered as she scratched him behind his ears. Turning, she squatted at the entrance, looking out for William. He was only now making the distance to the ladder. "Did you happen to see that? Friend didn't even look when he jumped up."

"I saw. Ain't that something. It was only the other day that he learned that. Smart wolf, I reckon." He continued his gaze at her. She looked stunning as she squatted above. Butterflies danced in his stomach as thoughts of her nakedness, touch, scent and feel fluttered his mind. He felt himself grow semi-hard, and a smile crossed his face. "You know," he started, "the way you're squatting up there puts me in kind of a peculiar spot."

"How's that?" she asked, a smile of her own crossing her face.

"Well, from down here. The view is quite something else."

"Would you like the view to be naked?" She knew that's exactly what he wanted.

"I wouldn't complain none."

"How fast can you make it up the ladder?" Shileen teased.

It took him only a few seconds. "Guess I'm a pro now, too," he commented as he pulled himself in.

There she was, naked and squatting. Her long, dark blond hair draped over her firm breasts. "How's the view now?" she purred, waiting for him to take her to limits unknown.

"I hope I can get these pants off quick enough," he chortled as he slipped them off, his manhood full and erect, throbbing with desire.

Shileen licked her lips. "I have a very nice view now, too." An hour later, hot and sweaty, they lay on the floor, their bodies drained, their urges curbed. As dawn beckoned, they headed outside, a bow and quiver each across their backs. Walking only a short distance, Shileen noticed a flock of geese resting in a little clearing. Nudging William, she pointed at them. "Over there," she whispered.

They each loaded an arrow, took aim, and then let their arrows fly. With a stealthy *thud,* their arrows hit the designated targets. The remaining geese took to flight. In quick succession, William re-strung an arrow, took aim, and let his second arrow fly, adding a third goose to their kill. Call it beginner's luck or perhaps fate; whatever it was, they seemed to be natural bowmen.

"For our first time out with these bows, we seemed to have done okay, I reckon." He looked on at their kills. "Three kills, three arrows. Seemed simple." William stroked his chin as he squinted at the rising sun. "I ain't sure about you, but I ain't ever drawn back an arrow before to try and kill something."

"That makes two of us. You're right; it did seem simple." Heading back to the hut with their kills in hand, they dreaded the gruesome task of disembowelling them. Friend, lulled around, waiting for some handouts. William grabbed a handful of the guts and tossed them on the ground. Friend wasted no time in devouring the bloody mess. When all the geese were finally cleaned, Shileen roasted two of them directly over the fire. The other was cut into strips and hung to dry, neither one knowing for sure whether that was how it was done, but what better teacher than experience?

Setting out to gather more wood, William came across a lone Indian. It startled him and frightened him all at once. Silently, with trepidation, he loaded an arrow and drew back the string. He noticed right from the beginning that the lone brave did not dress as the others nor was he armed. Stepping back, he snapped a twig; the sound echoed in the stillness of the moment. The Indian, alerted, looked in his direction. Crouching, William tried to slip deeper into the forest. Too late, he was spotted.

The Indian stared at him, neither afraid nor threatening. Raising the bow, William took aim. Ready, willing, and able to let the arrow loose, he did not falter. Adrenaline, fear, hate, and uncertainty were all feelings he felt at that moment.

Noticing the quality of the weapon, the Indian shook his head and pointed at himself. "I'm not from the same tribe. Who are you?" Looking closer at the bow, the Indian smiled and added. "You are brave. You have killed Chief Bloodwater's best hunter. In my tribe, you would be a great warrior."

"Who is Chief Bloodwater?" asked William, the arrow still drawn back and pointing at the Indian's heart.

"He is bad medicine. He belongs to the Toukia tribe; they are flesh eaters," said the Indian. "My name is Bearfox. I belong to the Wakashan tribe."

"I am William, William Vanfell. I am searching for my kin, two children, taken by renegade Indians with blue feathers in their hair. Do you know of any tribe in this area donning blue feathers and who might do such a thing?" he asked, the bow still sighted on this fellow named Bearfox.

"Yes. It would have been the Toukia. Their blood is faltering; they search for new blood. They steal children and young ones for this reason. They have hunted and killed many men. They take the children and young women. They are the ones hunting me now. However, by the look of that weapon in your hand, one less tracks me. I am forever in your debt. I can help you in your quest to find these children you speak of."

"How do you reckon on doing that? And why should I believe you?" William asked.

"I can only answer that with my word and solemn oath. I am a Wakashan. We have been wearing down the Toukia for many years. Our battle with them will never end until Bloodwater's scalp is in the hands of Wakashan. As each year passes, they grow in numbers. Let me live, and I will guide you to the Toukia tribe. There you will find what you are looking for. Otherwise, let the arrow fly, and I wish you good luck in your quest."

The sincerity in the lone brave's voice is what convinced William to let him live. The ultimate test would be when they arrived back at the hut. If Friend didn't attack the stranger, then the brave was telling the truth. He lowered the bow and signalled to the Indian to follow. They walked in silence back to the hut. Friend bounded out from behind some bushes, startling both William and the brave named Bearfox. "It's all right, he's mine," William commented.

Bearfox looked at him, bewildered but relieved. Friend sniffed the Indian and then began panting. That's all, just panted. *Bearfox spoke the truth.* If he hadn't, they'd be disposing of another body, that much was certain. William introduced Bearfox to Shileen, reassuring her that he wasn't there to hurt them. "It is a good day for Bearfox. I am pleased to sit with you as friends."

"Please then, sit." Shileen gestured toward the fire pit where the geese she was roasting continued to sizzle. The cooking meat made their mouths water as they sat and conversed. As the day progressed, Bearfox told them his father was a white man for whom his mother worked. It was then that Shileen felt a kinship. *Could it be that her memory of the Indian squaw was this man's mother?* As she told William many months ago, she could faintly remember an Indian squaw who looked after her while her father worked his trap line. "Is your mother's name Running Rabbit?" Shileen asked with apprehension.

"Yes, Running Rabbit is my mother's name," Bearfox said with confusion. *How was it that this woman knew his mother?* "How can you know such a thing?" Bearfox asked with apprehension. At first, he thought she might be a witch.

Shileen explained to him how she knew of an Indian squaw named Running Rabbit. As they continued to converse, they pieced together the puzzle, and all the pieces fit. *The same blood coursed through each of their veins.* "This is good. You must come and reunite with my mother, Running Rabbit. My tribe is five days' walk to the north. Can we leave now?"

"No," said Shileen, "We must make you well again first. You haven't eaten in a long time, I'm assuming. You must eat and rest. These geese will feed us tonight. In a few days, when you have your strength back, you can take us to them."

"So it shall be," said Bearfox.

During the next few days, their friendships grew. Then, finally, their journey began. They took with them only the clothes on their backs, their bedrolls, and a small bag of food, coffee, and a stitching kit, as well as their bows and arrows. They hid the rifles and two pistols in the same rotted-out log as their tools, deciding that the stealthy bow and arrow would suffice in their search for Honey and Sinclair. They would return with their kin once they found them alive and safe. Then and only then would they gather up what they left behind and head for civilization and the Double-U.

Chapter 8

For days, the children were starved by the Toukia until the brink of sickness. Then they were fed pungent human flesh, berries, and bread until their health was restored. They hated the taste of the meat; however, young as they were, they knew that their survival depended on it. They were unaware of its origin. As their strength and health were restored, Honey's desire for the flesh deepened. Sinclair had reservations and ate only small amounts, trading the meat with Honey for her bread and berries as time went on.

By late afternoon, the first day that William, Shileen and Bearfox left in the direction of Bearfox's tribe, they managed to traverse ten miles. Sitting by a mountain stream, they quenched their thirst and ate some dried meat. Rested, they walked into the early evening until finally deciding to set up camp. Bearfox took it upon himself to build them a wigwam while William fetched wood. Shileen voluntarily made coffee. It was something Bearfox had never tasted. At first, it seemed bitter to him, but he soon grew used to it.

Sitting around the fire that evening, he told them stories about Chief Bloodwater. He had not always been bad medicine. Since being exiled from the Blackfoot for practicing cannibalism, he banded together with other renegade Indians and began the Toukia tribe. Now, Chief Bloodwater was a killer feared by others.

In between stories, Bearfox asked questions regarding Honey and Sinclair. He told Shileen how proud he was to have met the girl his mother had spoken of on occasion. He had never met their father; he died before Bearfox was born. It was rather odd meeting each other as they had. Bearfox believed it to be the work of the *Good Spirit.* The three of them conversed into the dark of night, the flames from the fire spitting sparks until finally sleep beckoned.

The next morning, the threesome woke with the rising sun. Setting the coals of their fire alight, Bearfox warmed his hands above the flames. Without rhyme or reason and in an instant, Friend darted into the forest. Shileen called for him, but her call went unheeded. As they prepared to set foot again, Friend had not returned. This was not like him. They waited and called for him. Nothing, Friend was not responding. Deciding finally that he would find them, they continued on.

They walked only a few short miles before they heard Friend's panting. Something dangled from the side of his mouth. They held up and waited. They were shocked to see that dangling from his mouth, ragged, torn and blood-soaked, was a human arm. At first, they gagged at the horrible sight. Friend's fur was matted and grossly saturated with blood, but he was unharmed.

"It is not so bad," Bearfox stated. "This bracelet is that of Toukia. Their sacred sign is carved into it. Friend is a good name for you, wolf. Are there others following?" He questioned the wolf as he knelt and patted him. Friend wagged his tail, *how he hoped others were...*

"I reckon it is darned lucky he picked up the scent. Could be he might have been a Toukia scout, likely checking us out," William spoke as they continued on.

"Yes. It is likely, William. The Toukia are uncertain where *we,* the Wakashan, are. My tribe moves from here to there. Our land is vast, and we use it. The Toukia live in only one place, the dark, forbidding forests of dead souls, a place where only the Toukia desire to live. There is a place near there that is known to only a few white men as Eerie Lake."

William shrugged his shoulders. "Ain't ever heard of Eerie Lake, an odd name, I reckon. What could be eerie about a lake? You ever hear of that place, Shileen?"

"Can't say as I have. There must be a reason it's named that. So, what's the reason, Bearfox?" Shileen asked with curious titillation.

He seemed to know but replied evasively. "I cannot tell you what I do not know. I can only tell you what I do. I do know it is good that the wolf has killed another Toukia. If they have sent one, they will send two, but they will not find us. We are lost to them now, for my land is near," Bearfox continued as he changed the subject.

"Sounds to me like you're a little sore about Eerie Lake. You must know something. Why can't you tell us?" William asked, as they continued.

"As time goes by, you will learn about Eerie Lake and the forest of lost souls. It is not my place to tell you. I would ask both of you, as friends, not to speak of these places around my tribe. I perhaps spoke when I shouldn't have. I apologize. Sorry."

"Darn it! Now you got me all curious, but as a friend to a friend, I won't ever mention it," William responded with wit and sincerity.

Shileen nodded. "Yeah, me either, Bearfox. Our lips are sealed."

"Thank you." Bearfox smiled.

Although they thought Friend had killed the Toukia brave, he had merely maimed him. If he didn't die from the wound, he would serve as a warning that *Hell* was on its way in the form of a *vengeful wolf*.

After walking for hours, they rested on the other side of a wetland, then proceeded for another eight miles until deciding it was time to set up for the evening. That day, they made good progress. It was a warm evening, and they decided no shelter would be needed; instead, they'd sleep under the stars. Their fire was warm and absorbing as they watched the flames dance this way and that. Weary from the day's travelling, they soon found sleep.

The following morning, the rising sun glared down on them, a sight all its own, and stirred them from their slumber. They welcomed it; they praised it. By midday, when the sun was at its hottest, they stopped to rest. "Smell that freshness, that's spring. Don't it smell good?" William inhaled deeply. "How far, Bearfox, to your people?"

"Tomorrow at this time you will meet my people," Bearfox responded.

"I can't wait. Running Rabbit was so kind and gentle. She made the best wild berry muffins I ever tasted."

"She still does," said Bearfox with a smile. "The white man has taught my mother many things, except cooking," he chuckled.

"Funny," said Shileen, "are you saying we don't know how to cook?"

"You decide," said Bearfox.

They carried on joking back and forth, and William realized that Shileen and Bearfox did share some traits. Humour was one of them. He also noticed the resemblance Bearfox and Shileen shared. It was obvious in certain shades of light. They were definitely brother and sister.

Rested, they headed again northward in the direction of the Wakashan tribe. Crossing three creeks, Bearfox explained that they were the runoff from a great glacier that sat high up in the mountain valley. "It is said that anyone who crosses over it will find emerald green forests and will have everlasting peace," Bearfox explained. In silence and contemplation, they trudged on.

The sun, now slipping behind the western mountains, signalled it was time to stop for the day. Again, they had managed ten miles easily. Tomorrow at noon, their journey to the Wakashan tribe would be complete. Building a fire, they ate. pemmican and drank hot tea. The sun vanished for another day, and the western horizon grew crimson. They knew it was a telltale sign that the next day would be as beautiful.

In the early morning before the sun rose, they began their trek. They walked continually, not stopping until they were standing on a ridge looking down. "This is my home," said Bearfox, and he welcomed them. As they walked the remaining distance, the entire tribe greeted them. They had presumed Bearfox to be dead. As Bearfox introduced his companions, Running Rabbit approached, very excited about her son's arrival. Looking at Shileen, a tear ran down her cheek. Shileen's eyes told the story. She was the daughter of Bearfox's father. She spoke tenderly and, with open arms, hugged her. She explained to Shileen about a dream in which a warrior came to them seeking their help. "You are that warrior, Shileen. What is it you need help with?" They told her about how the Toukia had killed their kin and had taken two family members, Honey and Sinclair, captive. "We will help," said Running Rabbit. "First, you two should rest. We will talk about this matter tonight." She led them to an empty tepee. It was clean inside. There was a fire pit in the middle surrounded by rocks. On the walls of the tepee were drawings of battles, animals, the sun and the moon. They tossed their stuff on the dirt floor, removed their bedrolls, then slept.

Running Rabbit, Bearfox and the tribal council met to discuss what part the Wakashan could play in helping the two desperate and desolate travellers rescue their kin. It was decided that the tribe's best warriors would join their fight.

Wakened by the sound of beating drums and Indian voices, Shileen and William rose and exited their sleeping quarters. Approaching the fire, they were greeted by an Indian wearing a mask. Draped over his shoulder was a cougar skin. "I am your spirit guide. Take this knife and cut open the palm of your right hand." As William reached for the blade, the Indian grabbed Shileen by her hair and slit her throat from ear to ear. Blood gurgled and gushed from Shileen's throat as she fell to the ground, her body limp. Her dead eyes filled with shock and fear as they looked to the sky. William screamed her name. Shaking and sweating, he sat up. *It was only a dream,* he realized, as he wiped the sweat from his brow. The sudden movement woke Shileen as William sat up.

Outside, flickering flames danced in the darkness. The Wakashan were gathered around a fire, and at one end sat the chief. William, Shileen and Friend ambled over as the chief stood and introduced himself. "Hello. My name is Chief Black Cloud. We did not meet earlier as I was detained by our medicine man, Oowatchy. Come, sit. I have heard of your troubles. The Toukia have murdered many. The Toukia also took my own son, Black Crow. They poisoned his mind; he is only the shell of my son now. His soul is Toukia, but that is Wakashan trouble." Chief Black Cloud paused as he reminisced. "While you rested and the story on how you came to be here amongst us was told, we held debates and have decided that the Wakashan will send a band of our greatest warriors with you on this quest. They will engage in battle with you."

"The Wakashan's help in this regard is greatly appreciated. We'll be indebted to your people," William made oath.

Black Cloud looked deeply into William's eyes. "We know that the Toukia are growing weak. It is why they capture the young. This time, when we battle, we will battle until their demise. They have slaughtered our friends, the Painted Face to the north, the Blackfoot to the east. This time, we, the Wakashan, will fight in darkness, taking them by surprise. Their evil must end. The first to die must be Bloodwater and his woman, Death Dancer. Bloodwater's soul must be released. Then and only then will his reign end. Over many moons, we have sent braves to kill him. None has succeeded, and none has returned. This time, we, the Wakashan, will be guided. This time we mustn't lose." Black Cloud returned to his seat and signalled for the war dances to begin again. The stage was set.

Chapter 9

The Toukia war party of five was only a short distance away. Friend caught the scent of them. He exited the tepee silently and bolted into the nearby forest. The first and second fell quickly to Friend's rage. The remaining three fell as easily, their bodies strewn for the animals of the forest and worms to enjoy. Blood-soaked, Friend circled the Wakashan village one last time. Satisfied there were no more, he returned. *The Toukia would see his wrath. In the wolves' world, you do unto others what others do unto you, or you do it first.*

On the next full moon, the Wakashan war party would set out. Their mission would be to kill, maim, and disable the Toukia tribe. Bearfox would lead the party as he had the knowledge and endowment to be cunning and abrasive. As evening approached, the tribe gathered around the fire. Tonight they would celebrate once more. Chief Black Cloud stood, and a hush fell over the tribesman. He raised his hand, and the flames from the fire shot high into the air. He spoke briefly about their upcoming war. "I have spoken with the great spirits. They will help us win this battle against the Toukia. You have all been blessed with the spirit of the great wolf and bear. The dark spirit wants the souls of our enemy, the Toukia. I know this because the dark Chimera spoke to me. He said bring forth the souls of Bloodwater's infernal tribe." Chief Black Cloud bowed his head and began to chant.

The great medicine man Oowatchy appeared next. He circled the members and splashed each with the blood from all four great spirits: the fox, the wolf, the deer, and the bear. Then he vanished into the darkness. The tribe stood in unison and joined in chanting with their Chief. The flames from the fire now burned red. "That, my brothers and sisters, is the blood of the Toukia," Bearfox said as he danced.

Black Cloud passed around the pipe of battle, and each warrior inhaled a lungful of the sweet smoke deeply. They danced and feasted on wild boar that roasted over the fire.

They drank a fruit punch that consisted of wild berries and a potent root that caused hallucinations. It tasted like the white man's wine. As the evening stars began to shine, the warriors chanted a few more chants and danced a few more dances.

The following evening, when the full moon shone, the war party began their journey to the forest of lost souls. There were a total of ten in the war party: William, Shileen, Bearfox, his three cousins, and three more braves whom Black Cloud handpicked. Friend would bring the total to ten. For six nights, they journeyed until in the distance they could see the smoke from the Toukia village.

Keeping Friend under control was difficult. He could smell the scent that drove him to kill. In the distance, they could see dark clouds approaching. They settled behind a crop of rocks hidden in a grove of aspen. There they rested until dusk. The storm seemed miles away. It would come, though. When they set out on the final leg of their journey, the early evening sky darkened with clouds, and a deadly calm followed. They walked relentlessly until the sun again rose. They were perhaps a quarter of a mile from the village. In the pitch of night, they would attack.

Settling in and hidden from sight, they rested. Friend anxiously lay beside Shileen and panted impatiently, waiting to strike. Red Feather, one of Bearfox's cousins, climbed a cedar tree and looked at the village where he counted twenty-three tepees. That was more than the Wakashan expected. It meant there were at least 46 Toukia. Descending, he quietly told the others what lay before them. If only half of the Toukia were warriors, then they still outnumbered the Wakashan two to one. The odds were in the enemy's favour. The Wakashan would have to outwit them. Under the cover of darkness, they would stage their attack. The clouds now glided across the sky, moving closer with the blowing wind. Lightning cracked in the distance, starting a dozen fires. By early evening, the fires had spread. Unhindered by the rain and wind, the Wakashan crept closer to the village. It was not quite dark enough to attack yet, and they grew impatient. From that distance, they could see exactly what they were up against. They watched with vicious intent until dark.

Finally, in the silence of darkness, Bearfox dashed to the Chief's quarters. Listening with purpose, he heard the voice of a man and a woman inside. Without hesitation, he entered quickly, knife in hand. He grabbed the chief and, in one sweep, slit his throat. Blood spewed from the jagged wound, foaming red. Bloodwater gasped for air, a look of shock upon his now contorted face; then, he fell silent. In one motion, Bearfox threw his tomahawk, hitting the woman behind her ear. Her lifeless body crumbled to the floor as her steaming blood covered the tepee floor.

Holding the chief's corpse up by the hair, he drew his knife and removed the Indian's scalp. The corpse fell to the ground, joining the dead squaw known as Death Dancer. Exiting, Bearfox signalled his kill to the others. Chief Bloodwater's reign had ceased. No longer would he spread his evil; no longer would he be feared.

Peering through the small opening she had ripped in the tepee, Shileen saw her daughter and Sinclair for the first time in months. Her eyes welled up with tears, but she knew she must stay strong. Stringing an arrow, she approached the entrance with Friend at her side, startling two braves as they reached for their weapons. Friend lunged at one, crushing the brave's neck and spinal cord. At the same time, Shileen let her arrow fly. With a solid thud, the second brave fell to his death. Entering the tepee, Shileen ran up to Honey and the two embraced. She told both Honey and Sinclair to sit quietly and not to stir, that she would be back to take them home.

Exiting, she spotted another brave approaching. Stringing an arrow, she carefully took aim. Before Shileen could set the arrow loose, Friend attacked from behind some bushes with savage retribution. Blood from the dead brave covered his grey coat. Not stopping there, he continued ripping and tearing at the Indian's throat until the head was grossly severed. Shileen moved on, killing two more braves. William, too enraged, killed the first three braves he came across with his Dad's knife, up close and personal. Another five he killed with his bow and arrow. Still, the Toukia were unaware that they were under attack, their gaze and thoughts diverted to the fires in the distance.

Bearfox spotted another brave, and as he raised his bow to shoot, the sting of a blade sank into his back. Spinning around with the arrow ready for flight, he saw his attacker, a young Indian boy. The boy darted into the forest and disappeared. *That was brave,* he thought as he lowered his bow and reached around to check his wound. The blood already soaked through his rawhide vest. Catching his breath, he found the strength to stand. *Poor child,* he thought. *We will probably kill your entire family, leaving you alone to fend for yourself. I should have killed you only to save you from suffering.*

As he stumbled through the darkness looking for members of his war party, he spotted two single braves. Loading an arrow, he took careful aim and let his arrow loose. Like a gust of wind, the arrow hit its target. The other brave, now alerted by the whistling sound and solid thud, jumped behind a growth of mountain ash. Bearfox saw the gleam of a metallic object behind the shrubbery. Drawing another arrow, he focused on the silhouette he could now make out. Concentrating, he took aim. It took only a second before he heard the solid thud he was expecting. The arrow had been true.

Walking to where the braves lay dead, he looked at his kills. Sitting down, he noticed how badly he was bleeding. The blood soaked his back and was streaming down his legs. Looking around for something to slow the bleeding, he noticed a string of porcupine quills around the neck of one of the braves. Ripping it from the dead brave's neck, he reached around to the wound, grimacing in pain as he did so. One by one, he pieced his flesh together with the quills to slow the bleeding.

Two braves, undaunted and full of rage, had cornered Shileen. She prepared herself for what was to come and took a stance with her knife in hand. Her eyes were full of hatred, and she showed no fear. As they began their charge towards her, Friend bounded out of the undergrowth. This diversion gave Shileen enough time to lunge forward. With the blade tightly in her hand, she grabbed one of the remaining braves and thrust the knife deep into his stomach, ripping the blade upward. The Indian's internal organs seeped out, making a grotesque sound as they bubbled outward. Frightened, the other brave began to run. His thought of escaping was short-lived. Friend leapt through the air and caught the back of the Indian's skull in his jaws. The brave man was dead before he hit the ground.

Picking up her bow, Shileen stayed hidden in the shadows. She spotted a circle of about six Toukia. The blazing fires in the distance held their gaze. Stringing an arrow, she took careful aim; the arrow whistled in the wind and dropped its target. The others looked around quickly, then, as if by some miracle, three more fell silent. Focusing her eyes, she spotted William and two Wakashan standing in the shadows. Stringing her second arrow, she dropped another as he tried to escape. Friend wasted no time in attacking the last one, killing him with satisfaction. His fur glistened with cold Toukia blood.

Big Weasel, another of Bearfox's cousins, lay silently on the ground waiting for three braves to approach. When they were standing almost directly in front of him, he stood up. Armed with both a knife and a tomahawk, he slaughtered them. His killing instincts were quite remarkable, and he invariably liked to kill with his knife. *'Man to Man'*, he always said. Looking at the three dead braves who lay before him, Big Weasel smiled, untied his buckskins, and urinated on their bloodied bodies. "Take that with you to Hell," he blurted with hate and vengeance.

By now, the remaining Toukia realized they were under attack. Quickly, they gathered the women and children and sent them running. Shileen ran frantically towards the tepee where Honey and Sinclair were. To her dismay and fear, they were gone. Falling to her knees, she began to cry uncontrollably. "Why, why, why," she sobbed. Finally, taking a deep breath, she stood enraged and exited. Spotting her foe in the distance, she quietly approached. Pulling back the arrow, she set it aflight, wounding the brave.

Loading another just as quickly at close range, she drew back the string and cursed. The brave pleaded for his life. His eyes were big with fear and shock as he stared at the woman standing above him like a she-devil. Shileen felt no remorse as she let the arrow go. It penetrated the brave's skull between his eyes with a sickening bone-splintering thud. Instantly, blood shot up in a stream like that of a canteen being pierced.

Red Feather, spotting one of the Toukia braves, strung an arrow and moved cautiously toward him. Approaching from the rear, he laid down his bow. Pulling his knife from its neck sheath, he vaulted over the bush and held it to the Indian's throat. "Nice of you to be waiting for me. How does it feel to know your life is in my hands?" In a single swipe, Red Feather slashed the brave's throat from ear to ear. Blood streamed from the wound, misting Red Feather's front as the dead brave fell to the ground. Picking up his bow, he crouched. Seeing the Wakashan war party in the distance, he stood and quickly approached.

Friend appeared from out of the bush, and at his side were both Honey and Sinclair. William threw his weapons to the ground and embraced the two children. "Where are Shileen and Bearfox?" William asked with fear and concern. No one knew the answer, and they shook their heads. Bearfox finally ambled out of the bush. His staggering told them he was injured, and they hurried to his aid.

Then, from out of the shadows, Shileen emerged, dazed and confused. Realizing that the children were standing next to William, she ran towards them with her arms open. "Honey, Sinclair," she said with relief as she embraced them. Tears of joy streamed down her cheeks. It was finally over. They were together again.

After gathering the dead, they built a funeral pyre. They counted thirty-seven corpses. Oddly, Black Crow's body was not amongst them. "Black Cloud's son, Black Crow, is not amidst the dead," Big Weasel commented as he lit the pyre.

"There is nothing we can do, cousin. Perhaps he ran off with the woman. When he is found, he will die. His reputation is acknowledged by all. Death awaits him by our hand or by others," Bearfox responded as Shileen looked over his wound. The Wakashan watched as the flames from the pyre began to spread. The stench of burning flesh lingered in the air as the Wakashan war party listened to Bearfox's tale of how the little Indian boy wounded him.

Big Weasel strode into the forest where the party stored their supplies. He returned carrying what he could in his big arms. "Let us drink some tea, eat plenty and then rest," he suggested as he lit a fire a distance away from the burning corpses of the Toukia. The air was stagnant with blood and burning flesh. The buzzing of insects, especially flies, was obnoxiously loud.

Looking to the distance, Soaring Eagle, one of Black Cloud's handpicked warriors, noted the devastation the fires the night before had caused. Turning to walk back to the war party, he stumbled upon two young Indian squaws. They were huddled beneath a big cedar. He guessed their ages to be around eighteen or nineteen. Oddly, they were dressed in prismatic colours. From this, he could tell they were not Toukia. He walked towards them in plain sight. "Why are you here?" he asked.

The older of the two spoke softly. "My name is Raven. I once belonged to the Painted Face tribe. The Toukia took my little brother Aquilla and me captive two winters ago. Aquilla warned me of this attack. Now he is nowhere to be found. I do not blame your war party for this, but the filthy Toukia."

The younger one seemed evasive. "I am Clea. My tribe was also the Painted Face."

"Come with me. You are now amongst friends," said Soaring Eagle. With Raven and Clea trailing behind, they walked the distance back. Friend greeted them and sniffed the two newcomers, then turned and walked alongside. Soaring Eagle introduced the two. "Friends," Soaring Eagle began, "these are Raven and Clea. They are Painted Face taken captive by the Toukia, as so many others. There is one more, a boy named Aquilla. Raven is his sister. She is saddened that Aquilla has not been found."

"If your brother Aquilla is the one who wounded me, you have no worries, Raven; he is feisty. I am sure he will be fine until we find him." Bearfox pointed out.

"What did the child who wounded you use?" Raven asked.

"Something sharp," said Big Weasel, smiling at Bearfox's misfortune.

"I did not see what he held in his hand," said Bearfox, as he tried to hit his cousin with his walking stick.

"Is the wound deep?" asked Raven.

"No," replied Shileen.

"It was probably Aquilla. Where did you see him last?"

"West of Chief Bloodwater's tepee," replied Bearfox.

It was then that the young boy Aquilla walked out of the undergrowth. "Aquilla!" cried Raven, picking her little brother up. "Come," she said, "you must meet the ones who have saved us from this wretched place." Walking hand in hand, the two approached the Wakashan. "This is my little brother, Aquilla," said Raven.

"Why did you attack me?" Bearfox asked forgivingly.

"I thought you were here to kill us all. I was only trying to protect my sister. Would you not have done the same?"

"What did you use, Aquilla, to cause my wound?" Bearfox asked, now aware that Aquilla wore no knife.

Reaching into his pocket, Aquilla pulled out a talon from an eagle. "This is what I used," he said, holding up the weapon. "I was going to use this to kill the Toukia myself," Aquilla replied.

Low chuckles from the Wakashan resounded. "Welcome to the Wakashan tribe. For a little cuss, you sure have big colochies," Big Weasel said, grabbing himself between the legs.

The young women blushed and turned their heads. "Don't worry," said Shileen, "Big Weasel means well."

The girls were sensuous and intelligent, as was Aquilla, handsome and bright. Raven's smile could light up anybody's day. Her face glowed every time she smiled. Clea was shy and quiet. This only added to her personality and demure nature. Many young braves would want her for themselves. Raven's personality was mature and somewhat hostile for a young woman. Her body was full and curvaceous, her breasts ample. There was a unique scar above her left eye where the hair from her brow did not grow. Both Raven and Clea had long, dark, well-groomed hair; their skin was clear of blemishes, their teeth as white as snow. Both of them were very desirable.

As the stars began to twinkle and the young children were tucked away in bed, Bearfox reached into his gear and pulled out a pipe. It was called the pipe of *Unity*. This pipe, in particular, was handed down from generation to generation. It was used after a young Chief engaged in battle with his warriors and became victorious. It was sculpted from soapstone with jade and turquoise beads carved into it. The substance smoked in it was black and sticky. Bearfox himself did not know what it was or how it was concocted. Black Cloud had given it to him the night they left and told him how and when he was to use it. He passed the pipe around for everybody to admire.

Putting some of the substance on the blade of his knife, he held it in flames. It needed to be heated slowly over the fire until it hardened and dried. When it was ready, he removed it and gently blew on it. The colour changed from black to brownish-red. The odour it produced was sweet and floral. Soaring Eagle handed him the pipe, and he crumbled some of the essence into the bowl. Lighting it with a twig from the fire, he drew in a lung full of the tasteless smoke. He passed it on down the line. It was only a matter of minutes before they all began to feel the effects. Each felt a rush of warm air, and holding hands, followed Bearfox in a chant. Their minds slowly filled with visual hallucinations as they danced and chanted, hands entwined around the fire.

Chapter 10

Waking at dawn, Big Weasel added wood to the glowing embers of what was left of the fire. He cooked some Indian bread for the children, and he added wild berries to the dough. He brewed a strong pot of tea and made cakes fried on a flat rock. A good breakfast would give them energy for their return trip to the Wakashan. Looking over at the sleeping children, his mind began to churn with a devious ploy. He ran over to them, screaming in his deep voice. "Bear! Bear! Bear!" Not only did he scare the children, but the entire entourage jumped as well. "Just wanted to get your blood pumping," he said as they threw things at him.

With breakfast now out of the way, they packed up their gear and headed for home to the Wakashan village. Some distance later, while they rested, Aquilla jumped up and pointed into the backwoods. "I see a horse. I see a horse." Looking in the direction, William recognized it was their old mare. He tried to approach closer, but the mare darted deep into the forest. If she had managed to survive, then maybe the horses that had gone missing from the Wakashan over the years lived too. It was decided that they would stay put. Perhaps the mare would return, and they would get another chance to capture her.

As evening drew close, the women gathered wood while the others made shelters. It looked as though it might rain again. The children sat with Big Weasel, whittling wood. He told them stories and joked with them. Kids had always taken to him, yet most men feared him. When the first raindrops began to spit, and the thunder began to roll across the darkening sky, they found evidence of more than one horse being in the area. The rain had washed away any tracks that would have been visible. Noting a large cedar tree, Lightfoot put a notch in it. This would be where they would begin their search at first light.

Lightfoot and Big Weasel would accompany William, while the others carried on. Lightfoot was the tribe's best tracker. He relished the thrill of the chase. He'd faced mountain lion, bear, and wolverine— the greater the danger, the greater the thrill. He'd trained under Cloud-Talker, Black Cloud's younger brother, who had died three years earlier in a rockslide while hunting mountain goat.

The next day at dawn, the three men bid farewell to the twelve-member party returning to the Wakashan village. "If there are horses, we shall return with more than one," Lightfoot commented as the threesome turned and descended the embankment where they had spotted the mare the night before. They were pleased to find the scat of what looked to be that of three or four more horses.

When tracking was difficult because of the amount of shale the horses had crossed, they relied on other telltale signs. They travelled about five miles down the mountain before they were able to pick up the horses' trail again. Near sundown, they found a brook, its shore laden with horse tracks. It was where the horses gathered to drink. Setting up an evening camp nearby, the three companions settled for the evening. With luck, the horses would return.

Bearfox and his crew had an eventful evening. They'd been stalked for at least three hours by a wolverine. They decided to stand watch that night. Bearfox's watch was uneventful; not even Friend flinched. During Soaring Eagle's watch, he and Friend spotted the hunter. Now the wolverine was the hunted. In a blink, Friend attacked. The fight was relentless until Friend was victorious and the wolverine was left a ragged pelt. But this time Friend wasn't as lucky. When the attack ended, he wobbled, collapsed, whimpered, and fell silent as Soaring Eagle rushed to help.

Tears welled up in Soaring Eagle's eyes as he listened for the wolf to breathe, but Friend ceased to move. The only hope for Friend was if he could breathe for him. Holding

Friend's mouth tightly closed. He blew air into the dying wolf's lungs through his snout again and again. Still, Friend did not respond. The wolf had succumbed to his wounds and now lay dead. Returning to the wolverine, Soaring Eagle skinned it and removed its teeth. These, he would lie beside Friend's head as a monument to his last kill. Turning to walk away, he heard Friend whimper. Somehow, the wolf had returned to the living. Soaring Eagle dropped to his knees and listened. Friend was breathing although unsteadily and laboured. There was a chance that he could survive. Cradling the wolf, Soaring Eagle carried him the distance back to camp. He laid Friend down as near the fire as he could, then woke the others with the dreadful news.

Shileen was aghast at the wounds. It was hard for her to believe that Friend was even alive. His broken leg would mend. As for the gouge in his stomach, that was for time to tell. Shileen mended it as best she could while the others fitted him with a splint. It was all they could do for now. In the morning, they would have to make a skid for him. It would be impossible for him to walk. A minimum of eight days' travel lay ahead of them, and if Friend could live that long, then he would survive. Helping him to get comfortable, Shileen remained at his side. Through the course of the night, Friend's bleeding slowed. Although not enough, it seemed to make a difference. His wounds still trickled blood. There was no way of knowing the damage sustained to his intestines that were exposed. Only time would tell.

Back at William's camp in the early dawn before the dew dissipated, the three of them picked up the trail. In daylight, it was easy for Lightfoot. It was around midday when the trail broke up again, and they lost the trail for a short distance. Eventually, Lightfoot found the tracks, and he smiled. Between here and there, another eight or so horses had joined the mare. Lightfoot took note of their location. They were in a valley the Wakashan called Jagged Peak because of the rugged territory. The valley was scattered with rock and poison sumac. It was not a place the Wakashan favoured. *Why were the horses going in that direction...* There was nothing there, as far as they knew, that could sustain a horse's appetite. The nearest source of water was where they had last seen the mare.

By dusk, they walked to the end of the valley. The horses' trail led them up a gorge, where, at the top, looking over, they spotted a marshland. Surrounding the marshland as far as the eye could see were green rolling hills. "Look at that. There's enough pasture down there to support twenty or thirty horses. Ain't that something. A place like that way the heck out here." William said as the three continued their gaze.

"I've never seen this place before," Big Weasel commented as he looked on.

"Perhaps our forefathers knew of this place, but not the Wakashan that live today," Lightfoot pointed out.

"I can't imagine a place like this going unheeded by your people." William said as he looked at his friend.

"The Wakashan do not venture this way often. It is too near the forest of lost souls where the Toukia reigned. We had no reason to risk coming here." Lightfoot looked on.

"Remember, Lightfoot, the Toukia are nothing but ashes now. This land can offer many promises to the Wakashan," Big Weasel spoke, as he squatted and watched the horses in the distance. It was too late to round any of them up, and so the threesome set up camp overlooking the pastureland they discovered and horses that freely used it.

The others managed a good day as well, considering their situation. Friend was coping with his pain, and his bleeding stopped. Shileen cleansed his wounds three times a day, carefully trying to prevent any dirt from infecting them. He showed his appreciation by trying to wag his tail every time. Around the fire that evening, Honey sat on her mother's lap, and Sinclair sat beside them. "Mommy, will Friend be okay?"

"I'm afraid I can't answer that, Honey. I guess it depends on how badly we want him to live and get well."

"What if we pray, Aunt Shileen? Will Friend lick my face again?" Sinclair asked, saddened with grief.

"Let's try," Shileen responded. Honey slipped off her mother's lap. Kneeling next to Friend, Shileen led them in a prayer. For the first time, Friend managed a low whimper, assuring everyone that he remained strong.

Chapter 11

"You must rest now, Shileen. You have been by Friend's side from dusk to dusk. Tonight, I will lie awake with our wolf guide. If there are any changes, I will wake you."

"Thank you, Raven. Your help is appreciated. I will take you up on the offer; I'm wiped." Shileen rolled out her bedroll close to Friend. Weary from lack of sleep, she closed her eyes.

The stars illuminated brightly in the sky, and Raven smiled at their brilliance. It was a beautiful night, and she gave thanks. Bringing water to Friend, she patted him on the head and smiled. "Grow strong, Friend, and get well." Standing, she turned and sat at the fire. She was grateful to the Wakashan for rescuing them, but how could they, the Painted Face, mix amongst the Wakashan tribe? Their pagan religions and customs were different in many ways.

Raven daydreamed as she tried to imagine how it would be that a Wakashan brave might father her children. In the past, such an act meant immediate exile from the tribe, not because of the act alone, but because of the different customs and pagan religions. There were no choices now. All that remained of the Painted Face were her, Clea, and Aquilla. Their whole tribe had been annihilated by the bloodthirsty Toukia. For whatever reason, the Toukia had spared only them. Raven's mind fluttered with memories of her home, the people she loved. They were all lost forever, and a tear rolled down her cheek.

Lying awake, William listened to the distant neighs of the horses as they called out to each other. It would be only a short while before the sun would rise. Closing his eyes, he attempted to sleep once more. This time, the sandman won, and he slept, although fitfully.

In the early twilight, they devised a plan on how to capture the mare. It would be simple. They would build a corral across the well-beaten trail, then coax those they could into it. The best place for the corral would be about a quarter mile from where the trail exited into the horses' grazing grounds. Lightfoot estimated the herd to be less than thirty by the amount of damage done to the surrounding vegetation. Climbing an adjacent rock bluff, he got a good view of how much further they had to go. "Not far from here, my friends, we can build the corral. The grazing ground is less than an hour's hike."

They made good time. The trail they followed at worst was overgrown only slightly with mountain ash. While hiding in the brambles of the forest, they counted twenty-seven horses. The mare and what was obviously her newly born colt were being fussed over by the dominant stallion. His muscles rippled around his ribs and down his hind side in all directions. He was a magnificent animal. His sleek black coat shone like a black pearl. A tuft of white marble design in his mane was barely visible.

If the stallion were the father of the mare's colt, then William and Shileen would have a strong breeding horse once the colt reached stud status. Before the sun began to set, they gathered enough poles to build half of the corral. They stood and admired their work. In the morning, they would complete the pen, and by early afternoon, they hoped to put it to the test.

Bearfox, Shileen and their crew travelled a good distance. Deciding to take a break, Shileen checked Friend's wounds, pleased that they were finally scabbed over. They bled a small amount as they drained, but that was expected. All in all, Friend was mending. She checked his leg and tightened the cloth that was wrapped around the splint. His leg was grossly swollen, but the bone remained straight. Rested, they set off again and travelled until dusk.

William, Big Weasel and Lightfoot sat huddled around their fire talking about the stallion they saw. They wanted him. It was not one of the Wakashan horses, although they did see a bundle of those. This horse was not from any other neighbouring tribe either. The Indians in that area all rode Indian ponies, which were not as tall. Likely, the stallion at one time belonged to a white man who passed long ago. The white man was always cutting through Indian Territory, and some were killed for that reason.

Tossing the skeleton of his well-eaten ptarmigan into the fire, Big Weasel spoke. "We must catch that big stallion so my big, jolly rump can ride." He was never really keen on horses. His big body always made the horses they rode tire quickly. Now, in his mid-thirties, *his* body tired easily. They would indeed make an effort to catch it. If nothing else, it would be fun to watch the big Indian civilize it. Lying out their bedrolls, they retired for the evening. Tomorrow they would rise at dawn, finish the corral and round up the horses.

The next day, Big Weasel woke a couple of hours before the others and started working on the pen. He thought of nothing else except that stallion, and he was determined to have it. When the others finally woke, it took them only three hours to finish. They walked the short distance to the grazing field and circled the herd. First, they singled out the mare and her colt. When William approached, she came to him willingly. He slowly tied a piece of rope around her neck, and as he led her to the pen, the black stallion, another young stud and three mares followed her without as much as a neigh.

Lightfoot couldn't believe how simple it had been. He expected a stampede of sorts or at least some difficulty in restraining them. The black stallion seemed friendly enough until he was approached. Big Weasel liked that about the stallion. He said it showed spirit. With the exception of the stallion, the others were quite docile. They decided that rather than jump on the animals and start for home, it would be better to let the animals get to know them for a day or two.

They took turns riding the mares. The stallion, of course, needed work. William and Lightfoot left that to Big Weasel. After all, it would be his horse as the others were too small for a Wakashan his size.

By early evening, it appeared that the stallion and Big Weasel had an understanding. He would get on, and the stallion would toss him off. Finally, on his last attempt, Big Weasel whispered in the horse's ear, jumped on its back and the stallion didn't move. He heeled the stallion's flank, but the stallion stood still. He jumped off and took the animal by its rope halter so that he could lead it.

Getting discouraged and muttering to the stallion, he let go of the lead. Sitting on the top railing with his back facing the animal, the big stallion approached him and nudged him off. Big Weasel stood on the other side of the makeshift corral and shook his head. "This relationship is going nowhere."

Deciding he would try one last time, he jumped back on the stallion, and before his right leg was over the animal, it bolted. It cleared the fence in one leap with Big Weasel holding on for dear life and cussing at the horse. William and Lightfoot burst out into laughter. "That's spirit for you," they yelled behind as Big Weasel and the horse took off.

The horse and rider returned about twenty minutes later, and Big Weasel seemed to have won the battle. The stallion now obeyed his commands. Sliding off and tethering the animal to the pen, he raised his arm in victory. Nevertheless, as he walked behind the horse, it kicked him in the stomach, not hard, just enough to startle him. Big Weasel slapped the horse on the rump. "Do that again, and I will cut off your colochies with a dull knife."

The horse offended, snorted, and huffed as though he were going to mule-kick him. Jumping back and losing his footing all at the same time, Big Weasel fell backward and landed on top of a pile of horse scat. The others laughed so hard that tears trickled down their cheeks, and even Big Weasel chuckled. "See, he and I have an understanding," he said sheepishly, as he looked at William and Lightfoot.

As the others travelled the last half-mile of the day, they came across a new source of water and decided they would spend the evening there. The water meant that spring runoff had begun. This was good news. The winters had always been long, spring and summer so short. It was usually the spring runoff that told the Wakashan it was time to start preparing for winter.

Soaring Eagle estimated that they would be back at the Wakashan village in two days. Friend was in good spirits, and he wagged his tail as Aquilla came to him. Patting the wolf on the snout, Aquilla gave him a drink of water. Friend lapped it up and licked the Indian boy. He was finally able to lie on his stomach rather than his side. He still couldn't stand, as he had not yet completely healed. He was mending, though, and that was good news.

That night, they fed again on ptarmigan and ate biscuits. The children gathered near the water's edge, trying to catch some small trout, unsuccessfully, of course, but it was fun. Returning, the children sat near the fire while Bearfox told them stories about Indian legends and animal spirits. Soon, the children fell asleep, followed closely by the others. Shileen stayed awake and sat with Friend, petting his soft coat.

Suddenly, Clea woke up sweating and heaving. Shileen dashed to her side and consoled her. She had taken ill earlier that day. Shileen gave her a drink of water and checked her temperature again. It seemed to be rising. Using a damp cloth, she blotted Clea's forehead to try to break the fever, but Clea continued burning up. Shileen had seen the symptoms before when Eli had been attacked by the wolves. However, Clea had not been bitten by anything. *Perhaps it was an infection, a lot like what Eli had suffered?*

Chapter 12

Early next morning, William's crew set off on their trek back. The horses they didn't ride followed quite nicely. Big Weasel and the stallion were getting along considering their differences. By lunchtime they traveled the distance they would have made in a complete day if they were walking on foot. At this rate, they were probably only one day behind the others. While they rested, Big Weasel wondered what he would name his new friend. It had to be a name that fit his disposition. He thought of many offensive names, but none really suited him as did *Black Thunder*. Big Weasel would call him *Thunder* for short. Rested, they jumped back on their mounts and set off.

The others were stopping more often than expected due to the extra weight of the skid. Travelling for them was slow and tiring. Still, they traveled eight miles, which was not bad considering the terrain. Clea had not regained consciousness since the night before. Her temperature throughout the day continued going up and down. By nightfall, when they decided to set up camp, none of that had changed. She was in a trance, it seemed. On occasion, she muttered words but they were unclear.

Standing high on a ridge, Soaring Eagle looked to the distance. He was hoping to see smoke from the Wakashan tribe. *There was none.* In the opposite direction though, when he looked he could see smoke. He smiled. Obviously, the others, Lightfoot, Big Weasel, and William were close. With luck, they would have horses.

The three companions sat around their fire, eating pemmican and drinking herbal tea. The horses were behaving well and as long as the ones they were riding remained tethered, the others stayed in close proximity. Lightfoot estimated that it would take two days to reach the Wakashan village. Mac

Henry, a well-known mountain-man and trapper, a trusted friend to most Indians in the region except for the Toukia. He alone had scalped a dozen over the years and was almost captured a few times himself, stumbled upon William and his companions' camp late that evening as the threesome slept. He recognized Big Weasel and nudged him awake. "Snuck up on ya again, Buck," Mac said as he winced in pain.

"Mac Henry! How have you been? We have not seen you in a long time," exclaimed Big Weasel.

"I got myself into a bit of trouble, old friend. A dang polecat jumped me a few miles back. Killed my best darn packing mule. Son-of-a-bitch, did I have words with him, but not b'fore he thought my leg was a drumstick," explained old Mac.

When Big Weasel's eyes focused, he saw the wound to Mac's leg and it wasn't pretty. He woke the others and they tended to Mac's wounds together. Survival for him depended on stopping the gaping wound from bleeding. Tying his bandanna as tightly as possible above the wound, Big Weasel reefed on the ends as he tied the knot. Mac squinted in pain, but did not move. The blood flow slowed to a trickle. For now, they would have to keep it clean and under observation. In the morning, they would get a better look at it. Having done all they could that evening for Mac's wound, they covered him up and he fell asleep in a feverish state. By early morning, his wound stopped bleeding, but he couldn't feel his leg.

Big Weasel asked if he could ride. "Can you ride a steed, my friend? We can get you to help in a short time if you can?"

"Goddamn it, Buck," he always called Big Weasel that, "do fish shit in the water? You're Goddamn right I can ride," replied Mac. They put Mac on the mare that Lightfoot had ridden. After travelling for five hours, they stopped and rested the horses. They came across one of the camps the others made beside a creek.

Once rested, they mounted again. If they traveled until dusk non-stop, they would be able to finish the journey by dusk the next day. They traveled another two hours when they finally stopped. The terrain became too rugged for the horses to have riders. Their only choice was to lead them, slowing their pace down. By 4:00 p.m., the smell of smoke from a distant fire wafted their way. Whose fire it was they couldn't know. Heading to higher ground for a better view, they spotted smoke rising above the trees. The direction from which it rose told them that it was likely Shileen and the others. The distance was not even five miles and so they continued onward.

Raven got a peculiar feeling that they were being watched. Looking into the brambles, she spotted the men and horses. Pointing excitedly, she called to the others. "It is William and the horses!" she exclaimed.

Approaching, they were greeted with open arms. Bearfox was saddened at the sight of their friend Mac. He helped the man off the mare. Mac put his arm around Bearfox's shoulder and told him not to worry. "Hell, Bearfox, don't you go worrying about this. I've pulled teeth that hurt worse. B'sides if I lose this old leg, I still have another. It ain't gonna stop ol' Mac, no siree."

"Come, my friend, there is a white woman who can look at this," Bearfox said referring to Shileen.

Loosening the bandanna around Mac Henry's leg to get a better look at his wound, the only thing Shileen could think of was to stitch it. Out there, though, in the middle of nowhere and almost home she decided it would be best to wait until they arrived back at the Wakashan tribe. Re-tightening the bandanna, Shileen used a stick to make it extremely taut. She twisted it until Mac hollered in pain. "Goddamn it, woman. You almost made me soil my pants. Ain't your type supposed to be gentle?" old Mac commented.

Loosening it half a turn, she tied a leather lace around the knot to prevent the stick from unwinding and loosening. The wound, however deep, was clean and there was no sign of infection. There was hope that the old codger would recover.

As the new and old acquainted friends reminisced about days gone past, the horses became nervous. They picked up the scent of a bear. Big Weasel picked up his quiver and bow. He spotted the grizzly before the others and pointed at it. Looking in the bear's direction, Soaring Eagle focused his eyes. Black Thunder broke his tether and charged the grizzly with his hooves in the air. Crashing his front hooves into the large bear's cranium, the bear stood up on his hind legs swatting at the horse with his huge paws missing by only inches.

Thunder again rose and crashed his hooves for a second time into the head of the bear. The bear turned and high tailed it into the undergrowth. He was no match for such a cunning and agile stallion. Watching in disbelief at the horse's heroism, the party shouted in excitement. Big Weasel looked at the others. "I taught him that," he said with a grin.

Black Thunder approached his harem the mares were impressed with him. He strutted around each with his head held high. Big Weasel took it upon himself to round up the horses that went astray. He returned with even a bigger grin on his face. "You must come see what I have found." Grabbing a torch, the others followed. They walked a short distance into the brambles and there in front lay the grizzly, dead from injuries inflicted to him by Thunder. Big Weasel gloated. "I taught Thunder that too," he said. The others shook their heads and laughed.

Being as the bear was fresh, the entourage decided to butcher it and skin it. The meat and hide would come in handy. Cutting off some steak, Big Weasel threw it on the embers. *We will eat well tonight,* he thought. They feasted and conversed around the fire until their eyes grew weary. Tomorrow they would reach the Wakashan village. Tomorrow, they would be home.

Rising in the early predawn light, they made final preparations and began their journey. Before dusk that day, they made it back to the Wakashan as predicted. However, all that remained were the ruins of what used to be their homes. A massive slide had destroyed the many tepees that once stood there. Soaring Eagle spotted a pile of rocks, which showed that the tribe or the survivors had moved in that direction. Showing it to the others, they sighed in relief. It lifted their spirits knowing that someone survived.

Chapter 13

The full extent of the devastation that occurred while they were gone became clear the next morning when they awoke. The mountain face where their village once stood had collapsed. Years of deterioration and previous rainstorms had taken their toll. Mud and rock bulldozed through the tribe like a moose in rut. Trees that once stood tall were now splinters. Those remaining, forced by the slide, leaned precariously as if to fall at any moment. Disastrous as it was, since they found no bodies, there was a glint of hope.

Deciding to send a search party for survivors, Bearfox enlisted Lightfoot and Soaring Eagle. The others stayed behind to re-establish their village beyond the rockslide, where trees still stood tall. As Shileen prepared to treat Mac, she paused to check on Friend and Clea. Friend was recovering swiftly. Clea, meanwhile, was not; her temperature remained unstable, and a rash bloomed around her ankles and wrists. Shileen would consult Eli's old medical journals for clues to the symptoms. First, she treated Mac, whose wound had started to bleed during the night.

Removing his outerwear, Shileen looked over the gaping wound. She retrieved the stitching kit, which contained a scalpel, a set of small stitching needles, and a pair of forceps. Requesting help from William and Bearfox, she began stitching Mac's leg. He bit down on the wooden handle of his hunting knife and winced in pain, but did not flinch, as Shileen meticulously stitched the wound. The leg bled around the stitches, as expected. It took only seconds to see the results; Mac's leg instantly gained colour. Ten stitches may have been an overkill, but it was always better to be safe than sorry. "All done, Mac. How does it feel?"

"Leg feels warm. Stings a bit. I reckon it ain't as sore as it was. I thank you kindly for being as gentle as you were. When can I use her?" Mac spoke, referring to his leg.

"Easily two weeks."

"What are ya sayin'? Are ya crazy? I ain't got two weeks to be laid up in bed."

"Listen to her, Mac. Your wound needs to heal. It was very bad. You would have bled to death if you hadn't come across Big Weasel. If the white woman says two weeks, two weeks it must be," Bearfox commented.

"God dang it, Bearfox, we got a lot of buildin' to do. I saw what was left when we strode in last evening. The mountain finally gave in, didn't she? I've been telling the Wakashan that was gonna happen for years. I ain't gonna be much help if I'm laid up, now am I?" Old Mac was a cranky sort. Claimed to have been born under an evergreen and raised in the mountains, he was a big man with muscle and brawn, fearing nothing. He scraped out his living prospecting and trapping, undecided which one he was going to give up when the time came. He also liked gambling and drinking whiskey, again unsure which of the two he was going to give up. They both got him into trouble equally.

"No worries, old friend. We will save some work for you," Bearfox responded. "Rest now, Mac. I will see you again soon."

"Yeah, yeah. Go on, get," Mac replied as he waved his hand through the air.

Checking on Clea for the second time that day, Shileen looked at the peculiar rash, and it dawned on her to look for wood ticks. The symptoms were those of Rocky Mountain spotted fever. She searched Clea's scalp and underarms. In the end, she found the culprit embedded in the crease where her hip and her pubic area came together. Shileen shaved away the hair so she could remove the tick completely. It was large, about the size of her thumbnail. Likely, it had fed on Clea for days. Shileen scolded herself for not noticing the symptoms earlier.

Carefully, she gripped the tick by its head and heated up a sharp needle over a candle. The hot needle, when impaled into the tick, would cause it to release its jaws from Clea's skin. Then, she could gently remove the diseased tick. It took only a few short seconds. Putting disinfectant around the area, she covered the girl up and proceeded over to Friend. He was cheerful and managed to crawl a short distance from his bedding. Shileen coaxed him back, and he wagged his tail. Giving the wolf some water, she patted him on his head.

"You're doing wonderful, boy. Let's take a quick look at that wound to your stomach." Shileen helped Friend roll to his side. "Looks good. It's healing nicely. You're still going to need rest, though. Your leg looks good, too. The swelling has gone down a lot." Shileen patted him. It had been a busy six hours, and she needed a rest. She exited the tepee into the late afternoon sun. The wind blew gently in her hair. Smiling, she surveyed the work: two new tepees were erected, and a corral for the horses was being constructed beneath some trees. Things were beginning to take shape. Now, if only the others were found safe and sound. On the lakeshore, the children played. Shileen inhaled deeply and sighed. *What a beautiful place,* she thought.

Hearing a child scream, Big Weasel dropped what he was doing, and in what seemed like only a few short strides, he was soon standing next to the crying child. Aquilla had spotted some maimed bodies. Big Weasel picked the young boy up and walked away, gesturing for the others to come quickly. Swiftly, the men approached. The rock and debris covering the dead were large and impossible to move. They were able to count sixteen bodies. Instead of digging and searching for more remains, they sadly decided to build a monument and proclaim it holy ground. It would be the final resting place for all those who perished. A beautiful day it was no more.

Finally, the dead Wakashan's resting spot grew to a ten-foot-high burial mound. Every member helped build the tomb. On top of the mound, they affixed a plaque that read: *Here lies our kin. Lost forever are their bodies, but their souls will have no end. In the sky tonight, more stars are shining bright. Dated June 19, 1826, Wakashan.* They built a fire around the tomb and decided to keep it lit until Lightfoot and Soaring Eagle returned with the survivors. Only then would they know how many had perished. Saying one last prayer for their dead, they turned and walked away.

Lightfoot and Soaring Eagle were setting up their evening camp when, in the distance, they heard the chatter of voices. Realizing it was in their native tongue, they looked on and could see the flames of a fire not far away. Once they were sure their fire was out, they mounted their horses and approached. They were saddened to learn that only 12 survivors remained. Soaring Eagle's entire family had perished. Lightfoot's only remaining kin was his twelve-year-old niece, Sky. Bearfox's family, too, was annihilated.

Early the next morning, Lightfoot set off to bring the news back to the village. The others would follow on foot. He arrived late the following evening, having ridden nonstop. Tired and hungry, he dismounted and called the members together. He spoke quickly, telling the others what had happened to their kin. Then he put down his bedroll and was soon fast asleep. The others sat in mournful silence around the fire late into the evening.

Dawn's early light brought with it a red sky. This meant bad weather was to be expected. Around midday, the storm hit with vengeance. Tending the fire while Shileen checked on Clea and Mac, William noticed the young Indian girl Raven staring at him. He wondered what she was thinking and smiled at her. For a brief moment, he lusted for her. Any young man would if he were alone with her. Raven was extremely desirable. Finally, breaking eye contact, he added wood to the fire.

Looking outside, Raven thought of her home. This would be her home now. She marvelled at the beautiful rainbow that hung magically in the sky and decided that it would be a perfect night for a walk around the lake. She had walked around almost the entire lake when she felt as though she was being watched. Stopping for a brief moment, she listened to her surroundings. She heard nothing except the crickets and frogs that were orchestrating. Picking up her pace, she began the trek back. She took only a few steps when a young Indian brave stumbled into her path. Jumping back, she screamed. The brave raised his hand and spoke with a native tongue or bad English, Raven wasn't sure. "I cannot understand. If you can understand me, my tribe is in that direction. Come, follow me," Raven responded as she gestured for the brave to follow. The brave stepped forward, then collapsed to the ground. Raven ran to his side and checked his breathing. Satisfied, she turned to get help.

Minutes later, she entered the tepee and spoke quickly. She and William darted back to where the young man lay. Picking him up and putting him over his shoulder, William returned with Raven. The young, brave couldn't have been that old. He was different from all the other Indians. His fair complexion and crazy blue eyes meant he was either a half-breed or a white man. Entering the teepee, Raven helped lay the young brave down. Before long, she was patting his brow with a damp cloth. "What do you think is wrong with him, Shileen? Will he die?" Raven questioned as Shileen made her way over and checked the young brave.

"There are no wounds," she said as she looked for signs of bleeding through his clothes. "He will recover, I think. Until I can speak with him, there are no answers, Raven."

After breakfast that day, the young children, Aquilla, Honey, and Sinclair, played at the lakeshore. Big Weasel promised to take them fishing in one of the canoes later in the day, provided the storm stayed away. Big Weasel was like a great big teddy bear, and the children adored him. Early that afternoon, the young brave whom Raven had stumbled across awoke. He was confused as to where he was, but when he saw Raven, his fear subsided. He spoke to her, but Raven could not understand. Calling for Shileen, Raven stood, walked over, and knelt at his side. When Shileen entered the tepee, the young man looked on with nervous apprehension as she approached. Raven calmed him down. Shileen asked how he was feeling. When the young man spoke, she smiled. He did speak English, but with an accent.

They discovered that the young man was from Australia and that his family simply vanished one day while he was out scouting. His father was a prospector with a gold claim not far from where he believed he was now. His name was Adam Stershca, and he was eighteen years old. Adam's story didn't end there. His father was definitely a prospector, but his mother had been dead for over five years. His father had killed her. The senior Stershca fled to Australia with his son to avoid prosecution. They lived amongst the mountains ever since, prospecting here and there. They made a good living at it until the Indians came.

Adam's father hadn't touched a drop of whiskey in five years, but the Indians had plenty. All the Indians wanted in return were a few gold nuggets. When they saw exactly how much the Stershca's had, suddenly, they wanted it all. Both the boy and his father were beaten and left for dead. Weeks later, they met up with the Toukia, and the Chief welcomed them into his tribe with open arms.

They were extremely friendly to Adam's father, and soon he trusted them enough to bring a select few Toukia around to his gold claims. He even reluctantly brought them to a place he staked out over a period of one year, where he knew there was a mother lode. The vein of ore that was beneath the surface convinced him of that. He called the claim *Aquarius One.* The Toukia worked alongside Adam's father only to learn what he knew about minerals and precious metals. Then one night, the chief called upon him, and Adam's dad became a victim of the Toukia.

Chapter 14

The following morning, Adam felt a lot better, as did Clea. It was good to see them up and about. Old Mac was in the background, cursing again regarding the fact that he had lost his best packing mule to a darn polecat. One thing about Mac was that he was not afraid of anything. In the white man's world, he was Big Weasel's maker plus a couple of years. After his bellowing stopped, Big Weasel piped up. "You sound like an old woman. You'd better check to see if that polecat took your colochies."

"I have bigger balls than any Wakashan, past, present, or future. If I could walk, I'd prove it to you, Buck," Mac retorted in fun. Big Weasel shook his head and laughed. The day had just begun. Everyone was introduced to Adam except Mac. He was grumpy, and Bearfox figured the introduction should wait. Around dinnertime, the remaining Wakashan arrived. It was decided that the mourning for the lost members would begin the following evening. It would be a five-day pow-wow after which Bearfox would address his new role as tribal Chief.

On July 3 1826, everyone gathered in a circle around Bearfox. Only twenty-two full-blooded Wakashan remained. Their populace, Bearfox knew, would feel the impact of this tragedy. "Remember, my people, the Wakashan, have lived in worse times. When the white man's army went through, they brought with them sickness and disease. When they left, the Wakashan had fewer than seventy brave men and women. From only a few full-blooded Wakashan, we came back stronger in both wits and brawn. What has happened here is history speaking to us. The Wakashan are strong, and with our latest victory of destroying our enemy, the Toukia, we will be stronger," proclaimed Bearfox. Looking over to William and Shileen, who sat next to him, he smiled and inhaled deeply. "My sister, my friend William, your life begins when you get to your Uncle's homestead. It is many miles away. Your destiny, I believe, is at that place. The Wakashan will promise you the safety of our land anytime and for many miles in all directions. Our land is your land."

"We will leave here in time, Bearfox; for now, we will stay here. We will help rebuild the village and help with the ailing," Shileen said as she looked around.

They continued to converse until all that could be said about their plans had been said. In agreement, and with a smile on his face, Bearfox retreated to his tepee. Shileen and William watched as the tribe members began preparing for the evening's events. The array of wildflower scents overpowered the usual pine scent. The air was filled with the sounds of Indian drums and tambourines. Indian dancers were putting on their headdresses and dancing shawls. The Wakashan women, Terae, Sparrow Hawk and the others were preparing breads and traditional stews.

Shileen marvelled at how the Wakashan were so proficient and peaceful. She wished for the same serenity and proficiency when they finally arrived at the Double-U. Her daydreaming was interrupted by the silence that now fell. Turning, she saw Bearfox wearing the traditional Chief's headdress. He looked proud, and a tear welled up in Shileen's eye. She smiled and bowed.

Bearfox stepped forward and called for the others to gather. "From today, the month of the sun and the fourth moon, until thirty moons have risen, I will be your leader and chief. I will serve you well. After the thirty moons have risen, my headdress will be worn on Soaring Eagle." He raised his hand so no questions would be asked. With that said, the tribe began to whirl. Bearfox returned to his tepee, leaving the tribe with no explanation. As the preparations continued, Shileen entered his tepee. She asked him why he chose to hand over his reign.

Bearfox looked at her with admiration, "Sister, I'm a mere twenty-three. I want to see your land. I want to help my only living kin. You have many miles ahead of you, and the terrain has freed many souls. I do not want my only sister to lose hers yet. I am also keen on white women, if I may admit. My dream, sister, is to help you in your quest for this place you call the Double-U. I want to help you for a few seasons. Then, I will travel as a half-breed. I would like to see some of your cities, study your people and perhaps find a wife. Then I will return here once again and wear the chief's headdress."

Shileen couldn't find the words to thank him and instead burst into tears. Bearfox cradled his older sister. "Who is supposed to be the baby of this family anyway?" That was the only question he asked, as he continued to cradle her close.

At 4:00 p.m., as on every other day, Shileen began her rounds. Checking on Friend, she was pleased to see him as he came sauntering over on all fours, walking with only a slight limp. "Terrific!" she exclaimed, "you're fine." Friend pawed at her in his playful gesture, and the two continued onward. Her next visit was with Mac Henry.

Mac seemed to be in better spirits today and spoke softly with Shileen. "Hey, little woman, I thought I'd take this opportunity to thank you. Sorry if I seemed like such an old coot. I want you to know that I'm indebted to you, you know, for putting up with this old man's crap. If ever I had a daughter, I'd want her to be like you."

Shileen smiled, "Funny you should say that, you old coot. You remind me of my father. If he lived to be as old as you are, I'm sure you and he would have a lot in common," she chuckled as she moved on over to check Clea's condition. Shileen gave her a clean bill of health. Clea was elated and quickly exited the tepee. Inhaling deeply at the floral scents, Clea admired the beautiful day. Adam would also receive a clean bill of health.

The days went by swiftly with prayers, dancing, chanting, and feasting. During the course of the five-day pow-wow, not a tear was shed. The Wakashan did not celebrate death that way. Instead, they looked upon the lives that the dead lived. Death was only a rebirth into something else. To the Wakashan, that could mean the next butterfly one saw or the next hide one might skin. *Perhaps it was good to look upon death like that.*

Bearfox's reign ended without incident. Handing the headdress over to Soaring Eagle, Bearfox stepped back and wished him well. He told the Wakashan that he would return in two years. It was August 10 1826. In a few days, the Vanfells, Shileen, Honey and Bearfox would begin their journey to the Double-U, their first destination, the cave.

Adam thought that he should travel with the Vanfells. Maybe he could make a deal with them. Perhaps if he helped them, he could convince William to help him. He knew it would take at least two men to work the *Aquarius One,* perhaps more. He really didn't want to try to work it alone. There were many marauders and bandits who would shoot him for the information without hesitation.

Before dusk that day, Mac Henry finished packing up his belongings, he had a couple of claims that needed to be worked, not to mention all his trap lines. Mac knew he had a lot of work to catch up on. Besides, he was aching to get back to where he belonged. The Wakashan gave him one of the mares bred by Black Thunder. In return, he promised to come back in the late fall for a visit. Said he would bring with him fifty or sixty of his best furs and maybe a nugget or two. Bidding farewell to the Wakashan and others, Mac headed north.

When the first stars began to shine that evening, Adam approached William about joining them. "Ma'am, William, how are you this evening?" Adam started.

"Hi, Adam. Come sit," Shileen gestured.

"Thank you, ma'am. I'm not intruding, am I?"

"Not at all, Adam. In fact, we were talking about you," William replied.

"Oh, huh. I guess I'm flattered. What would you be talking about me for?" Adam questioned.

"We were going to ask you if you might want a job as a hired hand. I reckon there'll be enough work for easily ten men at the Double-U. If you want to join us, we can start your pay thirty days after we get to the damn place. Interested?" William cut right to the chase.

"Yes, yes. Actually, I was going to inquire about that just now, this evening. I'd certainly like to get out of the mountains, even if only for one or two seasons. I'd be greatly appreciative of the opportunity. Thank you both," Adam responded with sincerity.

"You're hired, Adam, welcome aboard," William nodded and smiled. "There are two towns between here and the Double-U. We're hoping to hire a few more men from one or the other, but you're the first besides Bearfox."

"I heard you talking to him. I knew, yes. Thank you again for the opportunity. Thank you very much."

"Can't thank me yet. We still ain't come to a wage agreement." William stroked his chin as he thought for a moment. "Don't know if it's fair, but how does twenty-five dollars a month to start sound? Room and board are included. Depending on how things go, I reckon I could pay you a little more."

"I accept that." Adam held out his hand, and William shook it. So it was settled. Adam Stershca joined the Double-U as a hired hand. Clea also requested to join them. She felt as though she owed an obligation to Shileen. She had already spoken with Raven, and Raven reluctantly gave her blessing. There was no skepticism at all, and William agreed. However, Shileen made it clear that Clea owed them nothing.

Chapter 15

On August 12 1826, packed and ready, the Vanfell party was on the move. They waved their goodbyes to their friends and promised to return with Bearfox in two years for a visit. They travelled for five days. Finding one of their earlier renditions of a camp, they settled in for the evening. Friend remembered this place, and he eagerly sniffed the air. Everybody was in good spirits. Travelling was easy with the addition of the horses, the wagon, and companionship. Adam was surprisingly helpful. He knew the woods well and showed them a few shortcuts. Before long, they were in and around the area near the cave. Not wanting the children to see the disarray they knew the place to be in, they decided only William and Bearfox would go forward. In a couple of days, they'd return with the deed in hand.

During their excursion, Adam and Clea struck up a friendship. They spent a lot of time in each other's presence. It was heartwarming in the sense that when they first met, they only nodded at one another. The past nine days changed all that, and the two were now quite close.

Bearfox and William trudged back into camp a few days later as promised. They had with them the deed and money. By the following morning, everyone was again on the move. Reaching the small creek that would lead them to their tree hut, the travellers rested. It took another three days before the hut came into view. Friend paid a visit to every tree that circled the perimeter. William went to the hollowed log where he had stored the rifles. They would need maintenance after all this time to make them safe.

Bearfox was amused by them. The one with two big barrels got his interest. "What kind of a white man's weapon is that?" he asked quizzically.

"That, my friend, is a double-barreled shotgun, one of the first of its kind, I reckon. There ain't many of these around."

Bearfox insisted that he shoot it. William loaded the rifle with two slugs. Handing it to him, he told him to be careful, to hold it as tightly as he could and to stand firm. They walked a short distance from the hut and found an old log to shoot at. Bearfox raised the weapon. Trembling, he looked down the barrel and then slowly pulled the trigger. The blast from the big gun echoed in the forest, turning the log into splinters, and Bearfox was knocked to the ground. The recoil from the gun was like being kicked by a mule. Standing, he dusted himself off and handed the big gun back.

William smiled and told him that he needed to hold it tighter. He convinced Bearfox to shoot the last slug. "It's like riding a horse. If you get bucked off, you get back on, right?"

Smiling, Bearfox nodded, took the gun and fired. Again, he was knocked down and landed on his behind. Getting up as quickly as possible, he tossed the gun back. "I can see the damage this big gun causes, but it is useless if every time you shoot it, you get tossed on your ass," he pointed out as he shook his head.

"Bearfox, you sound like an old woman. You better check your colochies," William teased with a smile.

That evening, sitting around the fire, they cleaned and oiled the guns. They talked amongst themselves and told stories. They would stay there for a week and harvest the vegetables that Shileen had planted weeks earlier, before meeting Bearfox. Besides, everyone needed a long rest. Honey and Sinclair were beginning to feel the effects of the trip. A rest was in order.

Looking at the map that William retrieved from the cave, they realized in shock that they were two hundred miles off their route, at least according to the map. Spreading the map out on the crude tabletop, William lit an oil lamp. They calculated the distance to the Double-U from where they were to be about eight hundred miles. If they were able to travel twenty miles a day, they might make it to the Double-U in forty to sixty days, longer than they expected. It was close to the end of August, and they decided that at the beginning of September, they would begin their final trek out of the mountains and into civilization, with luck arriving at the Double-U near Christmas.

For two days, Shileen and Clea weeded the garden and harvested the few vegetables that had grown. The men practiced heartily with the rifles. Bearfox, on the other hand, proved that he was able to hit more things with his bow. He was not sure that he even liked the rifles. They were too loud and bulky in his opinion.

On September 1 1826, they loaded up the last of their gear and headed towards the Double-U. They travelled for three days until they were finally back on the route that was outlined on the map. What lay ahead of them was Elk Ridge. Beyond that were the eastern Rockies. Elk Ridge was known for the many lives that had been lost there. The Wakashan knew about this ridge, and they always claimed that the missing were victims of the Toukia. However, the stories circulating about Elk Ridge in the civilized world portrayed something more sinister.

Setting up for the evening, they gazed at the mountain that they would soon be crossing. They discussed other routes, but Elk Ridge was the most direct. On the other side lay a pint-sized gold town called Hinterville, population sixty. The people living there were prospectors, merchants, and trappers. There was a Trading Post and a small Saloon that housed fifteen guests. The town's buildings, including the Saloon and Trading Post, were made roughly, and they contributed to the town's rustic look.

That evening, as their fire crackled, the distant howls of wolves echoed in the eerie silence. It was peaceful but haunting. Friend too cried out. After all, these mountains belonged to him and the Wakashan. This was his home.

Morning approached, and as the mountain air became warm, they rose to meet the day. Today, they would be three days closer to Hinterville and one day closer to Elk Ridge. From where they stood, they could faintly make out a creek that they would have to cross. It looked intimidating even from a distance. They located the creek on the map. They guessed it would take them the better part of the day to get there. It would leave them with time to investigate the easiest crossing point. On the other side, not less than a three-hour ride, was the face of Elk Ridge.

Today, they would focus on getting to the creek before sundown. Their best approach was directly north, then east down a ravine. At one spot, they were left with no choice but to lead the horses and walk the wagon themselves. That was the hardest part of the trip. They arrived on the north shore of Taras Creek by midday. The creek's breadth, which was not nearly as high-risk as its current, would have to be traversed carefully. They tethered the horses and set up camp. The cool spray from the water felt good in the early evening sun. Shileen and Clea, along with the children, prepared some fresh vegetables and roasted a catch of fish.

The men sought out the best possible place for the party to cross. It had to be shallow enough for the wagon and not too swift for the horses or themselves. They ventured downstream for half a mile. Then found exactly what they were looking for. The creek slowed. The shallowest part may have been three feet deep . It was the perfect crossing point, and they marked it on the map for future reference. Trudging back upstream, they could smell the scent of food. "Smells like we'll be in for some eats tonight," William commented as he inhaled. "What do you think it is?"

"I say fish."

"I agree with Bearfox; I think bread, too," Adam responded as he too inhaled deeply.

"Yeah, I reckon fish for sure, bread and vegetables too. Leastwise, that's what I hope."

Finally, back at camp, they sat down to the food that waited. They sat close to the flames of the fire, enjoying both the meal and the misty spray from the pounding creek. As darkness approached and the air became silent, again they heard the howling of wolves in the distance. This time, Friend darted into the shadows and disappeared over a knoll. They called for him to come back, but he continued on his way, neither looking back nor stopping. "Ah, he'll come back, no worries," William assured.

Stoking the fire, Bearfox looked into the embers and thought of home. *Were they all right?* he wondered. Bearfox swallowed the last of the coffee in his cup. Looking south in the direction of the Wakashan village, he said a Wakashan prayer, smiled, then curled up in his bedroll and fell asleep. He was asleep for only a short while when the dream came: The journey they were pursuing led them to the Double-U, but what remained was only the bunkhouse and barn.

Then the scenario changed, and he was standing in an open field. In the distance, there was a beautiful house surrounded by corrals, fences and a magnificent barn. From the bunkhouse, smoke rose out of the chimney. There were a number of men, faceless men, branding and tagging a herd of whiteface cattle. Yet he stood transfixed, staring into the forest. There were eyes watching him, frightening and intense. The air was misted with a scent of fresh blood, and in all directions, ghostly chants echoed.

Waking in a cold sweat, he sat up and inhaled deeply. The fresh mountain air filled his lungs, and he gave thanks that he had only been dreaming. Wiping his brow, he wandered over to the creek guided only by its sound. He splashed water onto his face. Then, taking a drink, he contemplated what the dream could have possibly meant. No answers came.

Rising the next day as the sun began to shine, the travellers prepared for the half-mile hike downstream. It was while loading the last of their gear that Friend came panting out of the forest. "Friend, glad you've come back," Adam said as he patted him.

"I worry one day he may not," Shileen said as she knelt next to him and kissed him on his snout. "Today isn't that day, though, is it, Friend?"

"All right, everybody, we're all set. The gear's loaded, and the horses have been checked. Are we ready?" William asked as he looked around. "Let's go."

The shoreline was jagged with rocks, and leading the horses at times was treacherous. Nevertheless, they made the short hike within an hour. Crossing the creek was not as difficult as they had anticipated. Once on the other side, they checked over their belongings and the horses. All had crossed intact. Now the real work would begin. There were five miles to traverse before they would be face-to-face with Elk Ridge's northeast slope.

They travelled deep into the mountains, looking back only once. Approaching a swampy area at the base of Elk Ridge, black flies and mosquitoes overwhelmed them. In the end, they made it to the base of the ridge by noon. Suffering from the effects of being ravaged by black flies and what have you, they decided that they would continue the following morning, giving the horses a chance to recuperate from the many insect bites that covered their eyes.

The coming of dawn was a pleasant yet rich reminder that during these months, the mountains could be deadly. Sipping coffee, they looked at the face of Elk Ridge. It was immense, and they chose their route carefully. They would travel up to the summit in a diagonal direction, zigzagging. At the summit, they would have a better view of what lay before them. There was one shortcut Bearfox knew existed that he had heard the elders speak of from time to time. It was hidden by a large growth of mountain ash and hazelnut bushes. It was the quickest and safest way around Elk Ridge. For now, he kept this information to himself so as not to give false hope.

Towards the top, there was a heavy fog. It looked as though it was going to either rain or snow. Bearfox was mesmerized by the sheerness of Elk Ridge's face. With the oncoming rain or snow, he hoped that he would find the shortcut the Wakashan elders had mentioned. They travelled for three hours before resting. Their concern now, as they looked up and beyond, was that the clouds looked dark and dismal. Deep within them, lightning flashed. It hadn't started to rain yet, but the wind was cold, and it whistled down the ridge unrelenting and swift, making the small pines dance and sway. As luck would have it, the rain greeted them when they made the summit.

Bearfox looked to the east and, standing, he pointed. "I did not mention it earlier, but over yonder is a shortcut that leads around Elk Ridge," he said above the wind.

The travellers were taken aback, but relieved. "Why didn't you mention this earlier?" William questioned.

"I needed to be sure that I could find it. I didn't want to give false hope." They rested for a short while, catching their breath, then made their way to the entrance of the ravine. Friend stopped dead in his tracks, looking quizzically in the direction they were travelling. There was something bothering him, and he alone knew what it was.

Pushing the big mountain ash to the side, the crew entered the ravine. As the last member pulled ahead, Bearfox and William stepped aside and let the branches go, closing off the entrance. The trail went in a northeast direction, then wound around again to the northwest. By nightfall, they made it to the other side of Elk Ridge. Looking north, they could make out smoke rising from the shanties in the town of Hinterville. Finding an area where they could bed down for the night, they set up their bedrolls. The dead calm of the forest that evening aroused suspicion in the travellers. *Why was it so silent tonight?*

Unable to sleep, Sinclair rose and sat silently by the burning coals of the fire. Friend sensed there was something wrong with the child, and he approached. Sinclair patted the wolf on the head. He wrapped his arms around Friend's neck and hugged him gently. The emptiness he was feeling was something Friend knew too well. He and Sinclair both had witnessed the death of their parents. It was a lonely feeling that took Friend some time to get over. Friend nudged the boy and gently pawed at him. Tears welled up in Sinclair's eyes, and for the first time in months, he began to sob.

At the first sign of dawn, while the dew remained, William stoked the embers of the fire and warmed up the coffee from the previous night. Sipping the rich dark brew, he looked towards Hinterville. In only a few hours, their journey to civilization would end, and they would be entering the rustic town. When the others rose, they descended the mountain. On more than one occasion, they were forced to stop. They had to lead the horses down the steeper grades, constantly making sure that the horses wouldn't stumble. It slowed the travellers down considerably.

Making it to flatter ground, they stopped and rested. They hadn't counted on such delays. They rested only briefly, long enough to check the horses. There were another four to five hours of travel time ahead of them. After that, they would be only a short distance from the main wagon trail that led into Hinterville. The forest stretched for three miles until opening onto rolling hills. The moon glowed in the bright, starry night when the wagon trail came into view. It would lead them directly into Hinterville and civilization for the first time since leaving their home in Greenfield in 1826.

They stopped on the outskirts. Looking back in the direction they came. They counted their blessings. "Up ahead is Hinterville, folks. Listen real quiet, and you can hear the noises of civilization," William commented. "We've made it, we're alive."

The noises they heard filled their imaginations with hot baths, warm beds and friendly people. They had walked only a few paces when the town erupted in orange flames, smoke, and gunfire. They halted in their tracks, aghast, taken by surprise and shock. "Head back. Turn around; head for the

woods!" William exclaimed as he turned around. They darted
to the protective cover of the forest and hid beneath the
drooping branches of a big cedar. "I don't know what all that
was about, but something is going on. We'd best hang tight
here and wait for daylight before going any further. Wrap
yourselves up with blankets too, 'cause we ain't having a fire
tonight," William spoke out with apprehension.

They huddled close together as the sound of constant
gunfire, hoots and hollers, echoed for what seemed like
eternity. In the end, all was silent. The smell of smoke wafted
in the wind, and with it, the stench of death. The night was
cold and miserable, and as dawn approached, they listened
for unfamiliar sounds, but the forest remained silent. The men
decided that they would venture to the outskirts, scout out the
area and look for any signs of life. When it was safe, they
would return.

A soft wind began to blow, carrying with it the same
wretched stink that had plagued them the night before. It
could mean only one thing. Hinterville suffered. They stayed
hidden along the tree line and approached the town
cautiously. There was no movement that caught their eye or a
sound they could discern. Hinterville was hauntingly silent.
For three-quarters of an hour while they sat transfixed,
nothing moved. The only sounds were those of snapping
wood as flames fed from the rafters of the buildings that
smouldered.

Not a soul remained alive. It was devastating. Bodies of
young and old were scattered on the street. A couple of
horses were alive in a corral along with a cow and her calf.
Other than that, the town no longer existed. "What we have
here, Bearfox, is a heck of a mess, one I know we can't walk
away from. These bodies have to be put into the ground, and
the law needs to be notified," William commented as he
gazed.

"Yes. That is what needs to be done. It is too late to send
for help. The dead would ferment and rot long before help

arrived, and we would be short of the extra hand. We alone must do it."

William nodded, "That's what I reckon too. The body count is high. I reckon it'll take some time, at least a week, maybe longer. Once we're done, we'll have to head for the nearest town and let the law know, unless, of course, they're already informed. Help could be on its way. No use waiting to find out. We'd best get to it," William sighed as they turned their horses and headed back the way they came to inform and gather the others who waited patiently for their return. The news they shared was devastating and saddening, but they knew what they had to do.

As time went by, they were glad that the weather remained cool. It lessened the stench and prevented the rotting bodies from bloating. On the fifth day, they spotted a horse and carriage in the distance. Halting all work, they waited until it approached. They raised their hands, assuring they were not a threat. The passenger stood. "Hello, my name is Ned Buckley. My driver is Ben Horvath."

"Nice to meet you. I'm William Vanfell."

"I heard this took place. What a destructive lot the renegades must've been," Ned said as he looked on.

"Looking at these bodies, I'd reckon you were right. Now if you ain't here to help us. We got work waiting."

"Sorry about that. William, was it?"

"Yep."

"You must be Roy Vanfell's kin? I heard you folks were headed this way. Mac Henry mentioned it."

"Hold up a minute. You say you know Mac. How's that?"

"Mac overlooks a couple of my trap lines . He's also a good friend, as was Roy." Ned spat on the ground. "When I heard what took place here, I assumed Roy's kin was either close or maybe dead. You see, William, was it?" Ned asked again as though he were testing him.

William nodded. "That's right, Ned, was it?"

Ned chuckled at his retort. "Your Uncle Roy was a well-loved man, William. A lot of people from here to Medallion owe him for his generosity. When Roy lay on his deathbed, I promised I'd keep my eyes open for his kin. My condolences, by the way."

"Thanks, Ned. What else is it you want?"

"Well, Hinterville was founded by Roy. He owned the deed to the entire town, everything."

William's mouth watered, and he took a big gulp. "What are you saying, Ned?"

Ned reached into his carrying case and pulled out a legal document. "If you have the deed to the Double-U, I need to see it in order to make this transaction legal."

"What transaction?" William questioned, "I don't recall us talking about any transaction."

"You're Roy's heir. Hinterville is yours now, but I need to see the deed first. It's legal, a formality."

William walked the short distance to where his horse was tethered and pulled out the deed to the Double-U from the saddlebag. "Here you go," he said as he handed it over with nervousness. "Believe me, Ned, you try anything stupid, I'll kill you both and bury you with the rest of these dead."

Ned chuckled and shook his head. "No worries there, William. I respect the Vanfell name a lot more than you will ever know. I'm following Roy's wishes." Ned looked the deed over briefly. "All right." He signed the legal document and handed it back with the deed. William read over the document. It was true he had inherited what remained of the once little town of Hinterville.

The document was dated September 9, 1826. William was awestruck. Not only did he own the Double-U, but also the remains of Hinterville. "Don't know what to say about all this," he stroked his chin. He had never met Roy, but he remembered how highly his pa spoke of him. He had always said that Roy was the hardest-working man he had ever known. Not well-educated, he still knew how to run a business and always did well for himself. Roy was once married, but his wife and children died from undetermined causes. The symptoms were grotesque to say the least.

William remembered overhearing his father speaking to Eli years earlier and hearing his father mention that Roy's family had become violently ill. The doctors could not diagnose the problem. They told Roy that it might very well be a mental condition. Only a few months after hearing that conversation all those years ago, Roy's wife and children died. That is all William knew about his great-uncle. To be handed this made him wish he had met the man once. How was he to react? Inheriting a cattle ranch was one thing, but an entire town?

"Also, William. I took the liberty of hand-picking a few workers who agreed to help you folks out in rebuilding or whatever. They're following behind and should be in around dinnertime, I believe. Two of them once worked the Double-U. You might want to keep that in mind. All right, William, folks, my business here is done. I wish you great success, William Vanfell. Your uncle's boots will be hard to fill, but I think you have what it takes."

"Thank you, Ned." William nodded as he continued looking and reading what was in his hand.

"When I pass the men, I'll let them know you folks are expecting them." Ned tilted his hat, waved, and he and Ben headed back the way they came.

That evening, the five workers did ride in. There was one man whom William quickly lost respect for. He overheard him speaking to Bearfox and calling him a bloody redskin. Bearfox only looked at the man, smiled and walked away. The man's name was Hubert Wernhouse. William made it a point to tell Hubert that if he ever heard him saying anything like that again, he would introduce him to Big Weasel. Hubert lasted only two days. Then, he was beaten up by a young man whom he called a Pollock. The worker was younger and more fit than Hubert. He was somewhat surprised when the young man jumped up and flattened him. Hubert fell to the ground with one blow. He tried to stand, and every time he tried, the young man knocked him down again. Then he helped Hubert round up his stuff, holding him by the scruff of his neck, and escorted him out of Hinterville.

It took only a few days with the help of the hired men until the last corpse was buried and the stench slowly dissipated. Finally, they were able to move all their belongings into town; after all, the Vanfells owned it. The saloon would serve as their new home for now. The little shanties that once dotted the street were only piles of smouldering ash.

Chapter 16

Four days after the saloon's roof was repaired, the first snowflakes began to fall. Winter was on its way. Two of the workers returned to Ned's cattle ranch, while the remaining two, Lester McNeil and Brandt Lippinski, decided to stick it out a while longer in Hinterville. William decided that the Double-U would have to wait until spring. Hinterville was situated on 1600 acres. The deed stated that the town would always hold exactly 25% of the land. The remainder could be resold to homesteaders and the like.

The work in Hinterville continued throughout the fall and winter. One morning, spotting a herd of elk at the east entrance of town, William alerted the others. They were in need of meat, and two or three elk would certainly make winter a little easier. Loading two rifles, he tossed one to Adam. Bearfox packed only his bow. The three exited the saloon from the rear so as not to startle the herd.

They circled silently, picking out three of the biggest elk. Bearfox was the first to shoot, and his elk fell to the ground after running a short distance. William looked over at Bearfox and raised his brow in disbelief. Taking aim, he fired at the elk he had honed in on. The elk fell to the ground, then rose and headed into the brambles. Simultaneously, Adam fired his shot. His elk wobbled then fell motionlessly to the ground. The remaining elk charged into the woods. The men were pleased with their kills. The elk meat would feed them through until spring. Bearfox would tan the hides and use them to make clothing, winter coats, and moccasins. The meat was cured, smoked and stored in the saloon cellar.

It was only October, and still, there was a lot of hard work ahead of them. William was grateful for Shileen. She had a business sense about her and knew how to handle people. As the snow fell to the ground and the cold wind moaned, William added wood to the potbelly stove in the lobby. By dawn, the snow that covered the mountains and Hinterville was knee deep. Venturing outside, William fed their livestock and broke away the ice in the trough. He and Bearfox removed the wagon's wheels and added the skis. Now that it was emptied of all their gear, it could seat all of them comfortably.

They spent the afternoon sleigh-riding, then, at dusk, headed back into Hinterville. The saloon was cold and damp. Shileen added more wood to the potbelly stove and then hung the children's clothes to dry. As the fire spat and crackled, Clea prepared some Indian bread. The men bedded down the horses and fed them grain. When they came in from the night air, they each packed an armful of wood. Stacking the wood and removing their jackets, they eagerly sat down and drank hot coffee. The bread that was cooking smelled delicious, warm and inviting.

They had been settled only momentarily when a ghostly scream echoed, alarming them all. Moving outside, they stood spellbound as the sound grew distant. The men glanced in all directions, but saw nothing. Later that evening, the eerie sound returned. This time it was very close. Friend darted to the doorway and pawed aggressively at the floor. Snarling, he took a stance. With his haunches raised and tail ruffled, he paced back and forth in front of the doors, not allowing anyone close enough to exit the building.

At dawn, opening a shutter, Bearfox looked outside and shook his head. It had snowed again. Needing to replenish their wood stock, William and a worker hitched up the sleigh. They found a nice landing where a lot of seasoned, dried deadfall could be easily accessed. Tethering the horse, they entered the woods. They made the distance to some of the closest deadfall and bucked them into lengths. It was while they were loading the firewood into the converted sleigh when they heard again the haunting sound from the night before.

Stopping, they stood silently and peered deep into the forest. It was eerie enough to send chills down their spines.

Then once again, there was silence. "Reckon, we pick up our pace a bit, Lester. Whatever it is that makes that God-awful sound don't sound pleased that we're here."

Lester nodded, "No kidding. What do you figure it might be?" he asked.

"You've lived around here longer than I have. I reckon you'd be the one to know what it might be." William made a point to say, hoping Lester had the answer.

"Nope. Never heard that sound until the other night," Lester said as he tossed the last piece of wood into the sleigh. "Well, that's the last piece. Let's head back," he said as he untied the horse from its tether.

As evening approached, they made sure that there was enough wood stacked inside the saloon to last a couple of days in case something unexpected transpired. They secured both entrances and locked the windows. The potbelly stove in the lobby, as well as the one on the second floor, was stoked. With the children safely tucked into their beds, William blew out the lantern. Then he and the others talked softly in the darkness, listening intently to every sound that emitted from outside. Friend lay on the floor in front of them, and he too waited and listened for any unusual sound. That night, though, no haunting shrill echoed. The town of Hinterville stood silent.

The next morning, the children played outside in the fresh snow and were warned not to venture far. The sun that day was unusually warm, and they removed their heavy parkas. Playing with Friend and throwing snowballs, the children were startled suddenly, and they froze in fear. Friend curled up his top lip and, snarling, he stood motionless. It was not like anything they had ever seen before. Friend became aware of the children's fear, and he darted forward. This gave the children the opportunity to break their gaze. Turning, they ran towards the saloon screaming.

Shileen embraced the children as they darted forward, trembling with fright. They could only point towards a knoll.

With their rifles in hand, the men ran the distance. Over a little crest, Friend was rolling vigorously on the ground, attempting to familiarize himself with any scent that the animal or whatever it was may have left behind, but he scented nothing.

Walking a short distance into the woods, the men found no tracks, broken branches, or pieces of fur. Their only hope was that the children could tell them what it was that they had seen. Maybe then, they could ascertain what it was that was living with them in the mountains surrounding Hinterville. Turning, they made their way back to the saloon and the tale that awaited them.

The children described what had startled them. It was a man who looked to be a hundred years old. His hair was long and greying. Draped over his shoulders were animal skins. What frightened them the most, they said, was how he appeared so suddenly and floated, his feet not touching the ground. They described how his eyes looked cold and dark. It was hard to believe such a story. Yet, the children seemed sincere. *Could they have made up such a tale?*

Bearfox believed part of the story. He recalled an incident when he and Terae were children. They were returning from a visit with Oowatchy, making their way home along the twisted path that led from Oowatchy's tepee to the Wakashan village. They were talking amongst themselves when, in front of them, suddenly appeared an old man who also floated. Draped across his shoulders was the flesh of many dead men. His face was contorted with an evil smile, and he pointed at them both, then vanished. They ran back to Oowatchy, frightened and speechless.

Oowatchy told them that they had seen the Wakashan Devil. He said that if throughout one's life the Devil was spotted twice, the seer would be faced with certain death. *Did the children see the Wakashan Devil?* Bearfox hoped that was not the case. As the day progressed, the wind picked up and began to whistle relentlessly. By early evening, frozen rain pelted the outer walls of the saloon with a constant battering. The saloon was cold even with both fires burning. It was obvious something had to be done about the constant draft that billowed in from the windows. Lester recalled seeing a large piece of canvas buried in the rubble of one of the old shanties, and he went to retrieve it. Exiting the saloon, the harsh wind blew his hat off. Chasing it as it slid across the frozen earth, he slipped, knocking himself unconscious.

When the others realized exactly how long he had been gone, they went to look for him. Searching, they called out his name to no avail. They assumed that because of the wind, he was unable to hear them. Curious, they walked the short distance to the barn, thinking perhaps he was there. Again, their search was futile. They put some hay out for their livestock and broke the ice that had formed in the trough. Exiting the barn, the wind that blew peppered their skin with frozen rain and snow. Dashing the distance back to the comforts of the saloon, they hoped Lester had returned. He hadn't.

Dressing more warmly, the men left again to search for Lester. There were four of them this time, and they split up. They searched for an hour, then finally met again in the middle of town. The men, cold and discouraged, returned to the saloon. Tomorrow, in the daylight, they would have to do a more thorough search if Lester hadn't shown up by then. Adding wood to the fires, William looked outside into the darkness. The snow blanketed the little town with drifts. In places, whirlwinds were dancing and twirling. It was a pretty enough sight, yet it was also a bitter reminder that it was freezing outside.

Turning, he descended the stairwell from the second floor. Entering the lobby, he was overcome with exhaustion; he needed sleep. He bid good night to those who remained awake. Drifting off, he soon dreamt. In his dream, he found himself lying on a bed where beautiful bare-breasted women surrounded him. They were running their fingers all over his body. Yet, it wasn't pleasure he felt. They were the fingers of *Hell,* and the fingers burned his skin. Waking abruptly, he shook his head and rubbed his eyes. The sun was still a few hours away, but he was unable to sleep. He checked the fires and made sure they were stoked.

Warming up some coffee from the night before, he ate some bread. Looking outside, he sighed. The snow was deep. He knew he would have to give it his best effort in trying to find Lester. He tried to picture what might have taken place. His first thought was that Lester had been a victim of some animal or worse yet, that thing that the children presumably saw. Sitting at the table, he contemplated all possibilities.

As the sun rose, it dawned on him. *What if Lester had tripped and fallen?* The snow would have partially buried him by the time they realized he was gone, making it hard for him to be seen. Silently and with determination, he exited the saloon. He turned and walked a short distance. Coming across a snowdrift, he noted its peculiar position compared to all the others. Kneeling down, he began to dig with his hands. Removing the frozen layer, he dusted away the powder that lay beneath it. In the snow, he found the frozen body. That day, they mourned the death of Lester McNeil.

Lester's family consisted of only his mother, brother, and sister. His father had been shot and killed in Medallion while upholding the law. One day, a man strode into town and stirred up trouble. He picked a gunfight with one of the drunken locals. Hearing the commotion outside, Big Ed McNeil confronted the man. Ed wasn't even armed with a gun. Still, the newcomer drew his weapon and fired, ending Ed's life. The McNeils were left fatherless and had to fend for themselves. Lester grew up fast, becoming the man of the house. He worked hard, always making sure his ma and siblings never went without, and now, after all that, he too was dead.

Brandt knew the McNeil's well and had spent time with them; it was decided that he, Bearfox, and Adam would take

Lester home to Medallion. It would take them a week and a half to make the round trip to Medallion and back again to Hinterville. They would leave the following morning. For the remainder of the day, the men worked on securing the saloon and repairing the drafty windows. They gathered wood for both the saloon and the travellers.

A few bundles of hay were loaded into the wagon for the horses, but also to help keep Lester's corpse secure. Clea made a batch of biscuits for the men to pack while Adam made sure they took with them a couple of the rifles and ammo. Shileen looked through all their blankets and found a few woollen ones that she gave to the men.

Bearfox double-checked everything, making sure they were packing only the things they would need. "So far, the white man's world has disappointed me. Too many innocent people have been dying since I've been introduced to your world."

Shileen consoled him and told him some words of wisdom that she had heard somewhere along the way, and she recited them to him. "Remember this, Bearfox, 'Life is what you make it, not how it sometimes seems; so live your life to its fullest and your life will meet your dreams.' Those are words of wisdom, brother."

"Those are good words. Perhaps I am being a little hasty," he replied. Early dawn the next day, Bearfox exited the saloon. He walked the short distance to the barn, rounded up the horses, and led them to the waiting wagon. After hitching them up, the three men exited Hinterville and soon disappeared on the northern horizon.

Mac Henry was crossing the Wakashan Mountains and decided to stop off at the little village. He had some news for the Wakashan, although perhaps not good news. Entering the village, he was swarmed by them. They were always excited to see Old Mac. Dismounting, he strolled over to the comforts of the Soaring Eagles tepee.

Soaring Eagle greeted him and smiled, "Hello, my friend. Come and sit by my fire; you look weary."

"Thank you, chief," Mac began. "I have travelled some distance to bring news to you. Perhaps not the best either."

Soaring Eagle looked at him with concern. "What is this news you bring, Mac?"

"I recently heard a tale that the small township of Hinterville has been attacked by marauders. Our friends the Vanfells and Bearfox would have been in that particular area near the same time this all took place. It concerns me somewhat."

"How can you be sure they would have been there?" Soaring Eagle questioned with trepidation.

"I ain't sure, only thought it was somethin' you and your people might need to know. I was goin' travel there myself and check, 'cept I was closer to here than there."

One thing about the mountains, thought Soaring Eagle. *News always spreads slowly.* This alone worried him. "Come with me, Mac. We must inform the others. I will send Lightfoot and Big Weasel to see what comes of this news you tell." Exiting the teepee, Soaring Eagle called upon the others and told the story that Mac had told him. "Lightfoot and Big Weasel, you will travel to Hinterville at first light. We must make sure our chief and friends are safe."

"Come, Big Weasel, we must make preparations," Lightfoot said as he looked over to him.

"Yes, let us prepare," Big Weasel replied. "Tomorrow we go to Hinterville."

Settling in for the evening, Shileen and Clea made certain that both potbelly stoves in the saloon were filled. It was 7:00 p.m. Bearfox, Adam, and Brandt had been travelling for ten hours. Those at the saloon hoped that the companions were able to travel at least twenty miles. That would put them five miles closer to White Pass. With any luck, the travellers would make the pass by early noon the next day and be out of it by the following evening. Tucking the young children in, Shileen kissed them good night. What tomorrow would bring was anyone's guess, but, morning would come, it always did.

By early morning that following day, Big Weasel and Lightfoot had already begun the trek to Hinterville. Their route was shorter than the Vanfells and they were expected to make it to Hinterville in two days. They would cross the Wakashan Mountain range and bypass Elk Ridge. They would be approaching Hinterville from the west. The worst part of the trip would be when they crossed the frozen muskeg of Beaver Lake. As long as they were careful, they could manage it unscathed.

Bearfox and his two companions reached the pass by early morning as well. Brandt was quite surprised to see that the weather was not as bad as he had imagined. The wind, however, was not pleasant and made for slow travel. They stopped at the halfway mark and built a fire to thaw out. They drank hot black coffee and huddled as close to the fire as the flames would let them. They rested only long enough to make the transition from freezing to comfortably cold. Taking up their seats in the wagon after the short rest, they once more continued on their way.

Back in Hinterville, William took notice of the changing weather. As the day progressed, it went from mild to arctic. Stepping outside to retrieve wood for the evening, he noticed that the moon was barely visible through the falling snow. Tomorrow, he would have to head into the bush and gather more wood. Their supply was dwindling fast because of the tricky weather. He would not go as far as he did in the past. Instead, he would only go the distance to the west forest, less than a mile away. There was a good stand of birch deadfall that he knew of. Setting down the armful of wood, William removed his heavy parka. He could smell the aroma of baking. Walking into the lobby, he got a whiff of pipe tobacco. Standing, he inhaled deeply. It struck him as uncanny, but it was definitely pipe tobacco that he smelled. It smelled like the same kind that his pa smoked on occasion. William sighed as he reminisced.

Shileen was seated at the table with the others, and they were eating freshly baked muffins. He took his usual spot at the table and helped himself. Shileen asked if Friend had come in with him. William shook his head. He had forgotten all about Friend going out with him. Opening the saloon door, he called; he waited a few short seconds and called again. Finally, Friend showed and entered. Curling up on the horsehair rug beside the potbelly stove, he quickly dozed off.

Returning to his seat at the table, William helped the others finish off their snack and the pot of coffee. They told a few stories to the children, then put them to sleep. Up before dawn the next day and riding bareback, he headed west of town. In the distance, he watched as the hill of birch came closer. Finally approaching, he dismounted the horse and tethered it loosely to a poplar tree. Looking at the stand of birch, he chose two of the bigger and began bucking them into manageable lengths.

A short distance away, Big Weasel and Lightfoot were sneaking up on their old friend. They had spotted him from up on a ridge and were relieved to see he was alive, *but what was he doing there?* They waited silently and watched as he went about his work. At the right moment, Big Weasel came darting out of the undergrowth, screaming, "Bear! Bear! Bear!"

William didn't even look back and instead began running. When he heard the rumbling laughter, he knew that it was Big Weasel. Stopping, he turned, and sure enough, there he stood along with Lightfoot.

"How have you been, my friend?" Big Weasel asked.

"We're all fine. By the way, welcome to Hinterville." It took a few minutes for William to explain to the two braves what exactly had taken place in Hinterville: the attack, the dead, and their inheritance of the town. He refrained from mentioning anything about the ghostly figure the children claimed to have seen. At the moment, it seemed irrelevant.

It was quite the reunion when they finally made their way to the saloon. The look on Shileen's face when William and the two Wakashan braves entered was that of both shock and surprise. Big Weasel picked her up and hugged her gently. "Waiting two years to hug a pretty thing like you is too long a wait, and that is why we are here," he said as he set her back down. Next, he looked at Clea and smiled. Honey and Sinclair, somewhat shy, looked on from the second-floor balcony, not sure if they should run and meet him. He noticed them peeking, and he waved them on. They ran to him, laughing and giggling, excited to see the big Wakashan brave.

Chapter 17

Bearfox and his companions made it out of the pass by early evening. They were grateful that they wouldn't have to spend the night there. Finding a place to camp north of White Pass, the travellers built a fire and a break against the wind. It was only the third day, and they had already travelled half the distance. Medallion was now only a few days' ride away, provided the weather continued to cooperate. The problem was that Lester's body began to stink. The two horses were slowly eating the hay that Bearfox had surrounded the dead man with, and each time they fed them, the smell worsened. Only at night, as the temperature dropped, did the odour become less obtrusive.

Back in Hinterville, unable to sleep, Shileen sat at the table with the oil lamp glowing dimly. She was reading from an old newspaper that they had found tucked away. A story about the founding of Hinterville caught her eye. Roy Vanfell founded it in 1801. The story went on describing how Roy had dressed the day he so graciously cut the ribbons to the town's entrance.

This is what it read: *'Dressed in his usual attire of buckskin and furs, Mr. Vanfell today opened Hinterville to the public. The rancher, trapper, and prospector again kept his promise to help build a strong economy for Medallion and the cattle industry.*

It struck her as odd that Roy wore buckskins and animal furs, and a chill ran down her spine. She wondered if William had known that. The story also went on about how much Roy contributed to the expanding town of Medallion. The Double-U, it stated, employed more than five of the town's families. Roy also gave a gold claim away to one of the town's less fortunate families so that they could feed themselves. It was then that Shileen began to understand why so many people in the Hinterville and Medallion areas held Roy in such high regard. He was practically a saint. Shileen folded the paper and sat in wonderment. She wished that the same blood ran through her veins. She appreciated the way the Vanfells treated her with kindness and respect. Closing her eyes, she slowly drifted off and fell asleep at the table.

By noon the next day, Bearfox and his crew had travelled another ten miles closer to Medallion. The sun was hot, and Lester's body was beginning to ripen. The stench, overwhelming and rancid, forced them to stop frequently. Pulling the wagon to a halt, they disembarked. Sitting at a distance, the travellers wondered whether they could handle the stink for the rest of the trip.

In Hinterville, William, Shileen, Clea and their two guests sat at the table drinking tea. They had spent much of the morning exploring the town. As they sat, William took his turn looking over the newspaper that Shileen had mentioned to him that morning. He was enchanted by what he read about his uncle. He wondered if he would be able to uphold the Vanfell name. It seemed so prominent, so upstanding. He knew he would have to do his best in preserving the values his uncle believed in. To him, this meant that as soon as both Hinterville and the Double-U were up and running, he would hire back the same people if he could. The rest, William hoped, would fall into place.

By early evening, despite earlier concerns of not being able to travel with the rotting corpse, the others had actually done well. The McNeil farm was now less than a day's ride. Preparing for the oncoming evening, Bearfox fed the horses some of the hay. He noticed there was no stench. All he could smell was hay. Looking to make sure the body remained in the wagon, he was shocked at what he discovered. Lester's body had fallen out. Somewhere back the way they came laid the body of Lester McNeil. It was too late to search now; they would have to wait until daylight.

Rising with the sun, they turned the wagon around in search of Lester's corpse. Five miles later, they came upon the torn blanket that had wrapped the body. Lester, though, was gone. They decided that wolves or some other animal must have taken the body. It seemed odd because not a track was visible. *There could be no other explanation.* Turning back in the direction of Medallion, they continued onward. It was going to be hard explaining to the McNeil's about their son's death and now his missing corpse.

It was nightfall when they knocked on the door of the McNeil home. Brandt introduced Bearfox and Adam to the widowed McNeil, and she shook their hands. She seemed frail yet full of life. As they sat, Brandt inhaled deeply and explained their visit. Brandt decided to stay back in Medallion and help widow McNeil out for the winter. Bearfox and Adam bid farewell and gave their condolences once more. Then they left to return to Hinterville.

Stopping briefly in Medallion, they picked up a few provisions for the return trip. While Adam was at the mercantile, he overheard two people talking about six renegades that were seen south of Medallion. Apparently, the renegades had killed a trapper. They took what he had in furs and burned his cabin to the ground.

As Adam exited the store, he spotted Bearfox buying grain and hay for the horses. He, too, had been informed of the renegades by the stable hand. As Adam approached, Bearfox met him and helped him with the supplies. "My friend, there is bad news. We must take a different route back to Hinterville. Some trouble has taken place. Six men have killed and robbed a man and are now being tracked by a posse. The stable hand has suggested we take the Old Crow route to avoid a confrontation." Bearfox said as the two continued on to the wagon their arms full of supplies that Adam had purchased.

"I heard. What a shame, huh? Killing a trapper for his furs seems petty to me. I know the Old Crow route. It might take us longer, but I'd rather be safe than face six renegades," said Adam with a half-smile. They travelled for five hours before making their first stop. "I say we should carry on for a bit. There is a plateau about three, maybe four miles from here. I know of an old cabin we can stay in. It'll be better than sleeping under the stars. Looks to me like we are going to be in some nasty weather either way. What do you say, Bearfox?"

"I say you are crazy, but lead the way, my friend." Bearfox smiled and nodded as they carried on.

Back in Hinterville, a lot had transpired. With Big Weasel's brawn and Lightfoot's help, they managed to stock up on enough wood to last the winter. They made the necessary repairs to the rickety barn and made further repairs to the saloon to prepare it for winter. With things looking up for their friends, Big Weasel and Lightfoot decided to return to their tribe the following day, bringing the news to those waiting to hear. That evening, they played a few Wakashan games. Big Weasel told them that he was going to return and stay the winter with them. He said they needed someone like him around.

"I'd never deny that, Big Weasel. We could always use a fella like you around." William admitted with a smile full of hope.

"It is settled then," said Big Weasel as he nodded his head.

William reached across the table and shook the ten-pound ham-like hand of Big Weasel. "It is settled."

Lightfoot, too, said he would return and bring his niece Sky with him.

"By all means, Lightfoot. You and your niece Sky are welcome," Shileen interjected with a smile. "It will be nice to have another woman around here."

Finally, Bearfox and Adam exited the forest onto a plateau. The cabin was silhouetted against the evening sky on the far side. It was a small cabin. Inside, there were two beds, a log table and a potbelly wood stove. It would definitely do for the evening. As the fire warmed the inside of the cabin, Bearfox exited and fed the horses. He looked in the direction of Hinterville and wondered if the renegades had been there.

That night, the six men did visit Hinterville. They were surprised by what they found: Big Weasel. He had been asleep for only a short time when something made him wake up. Listening, he heard horses galloping closer and closer. Then he heard voices in the distance. Standing, he silently exited the saloon. He crept around the corner and stood vigilantly on guard. As the horsemen approached, he armed himself. Standing in the shadows, he waited and watched.

There were six of them, and his instincts told him they were not friendly. Dismounting, they surrounded the saloon; they were about to kick in the door, that is, until they saw the shadow of Big Weasel, who quickly beat them into submission, and managed to get the six men into the barn where he tied them to the rails of Black Thunder's stall. He knew if they tried anything, Black Thunder would put an end to it.

Exiting the barn, he saw three more horsemen approaching. Standing in the shadows, he watched as they came into view. The moonlight glinting off the badge worn by the one horseman confirmed that it was the law. Big Weasel called out. "If you are looking for the men who ride those horses, they are over here."

The three riders trotted over, and Big Weasel introduced himself. He led them into the barn and to Black Thunder's stall. Looking at the six men, now semi-conscious and confused, the sheriff laughed. "How the Hell did you manage that alone?"

Big Weasel shrugged his shoulders. "They were not as smart as they thought they were. They are small in both heart and size," he smiled.

William, woken by the voices, joined them and introduced himself. He invited the sheriff and his deputies to spend what was left of the night in the saloon. The sheriff appointed one deputy to watch over the outlaws. However, Big Weasel intervened, saying his horse would make sure they remained. William nodded that it was true and added the security of Friend. There would be no way that the six men would attempt an escape.

Returning to the warmth of the saloon, William introduced the lawmen to the others. They seemed friendly enough. However, one of the lawmen was Hubert's brother, with a mouth as foul. The sheriff told the deputy on more than one occasion to button his lip. It was not long after they were seated that Big Weasel decided to do something about the young deputy's attitude. Reaching across the table, he grabbed the deputy by the top of his head and punched him square in the mouth. The deputy fell backward and was knocked out cold. Blood spewed from his mouth as one of his teeth skidded across the wooden floor. He lay there unconscious. The sheriff didn't raise a brow. His deputy got exactly what he deserved, and he nodded his approval to the big Wakashan.

In the distance, Bearfox and Adam were beginning to rise. The fire in the cabin went out in the early morning, and the two companions were feeling the chill. Looking outside, there was a heavy fog making visibility less than safe to travel. They would have to wait until it settled before they could continue back to Hinterville. In the mountains as high up as they were, it would be a death sentence to travel in fog so thick.

Adam re-lit the fire while Bearfox checked on and fed the two horses. The morning air was arctic, and the horses were covered in a gentle frost. They neighed slightly as Bearfox retrieved a bucket of grain for them. He knew the horses could withstand temperatures well below freezing. Still, Bearfox felt compassion for them. Scattering hay in front of the horses, he patted them and returned to the warmth of the cabin. The kettle on the stove was beginning to boil, and

Adam added coffee. They would drink a cup or two. Perhaps by then they could continue. If the fog didn't dissipate, they would be better off remaining at the cabin. The problem was that every day they were held back meant winter was one day closer.

That morning, once the sheriff, his men, and the prisoners were on their way to Medallion, Big Weasel and Lightfoot began their journey back to the Wakashan village. They would return in ten days. William watched as the two Wakashan entered the western wood and disappeared out of sight. Already it was lonely.

Finally, five hours after Bearfox and Adam rose, the fog had dissipated. They wasted no time hitching the horses up and heading for Hinterville. They travelled all day. Resting on a crest, they looked down at the valley they would be crossing. The valley was called Lost Cause because it was covered in shale. Not even grass seemed to grow. Now it was snow-covered, and going across it would be treacherous. They would have to take their time if they were to cross without injury. "It will be dark soon. We must set up for the evening," Bearfox pointed out as they looked out across the valley.

"Yeah. I suppose," Adam agreed as he too looked on. Settling for the evening, Adam let Bearfox in on a secret. "There's a creek on the other side called Mary Jane Creek. My father staked a claim along it somewhere. He said that there was enough gold in it to make all the others that he worked look pitiful.

"He told me that one time he pulled out a nugget the size of a silver dollar. If I could find the claim number and stake, I could work it myself. What do you think, Bearfox? Would you and William consider helping me find it in the spring?"

"I cannot speak for William. Myself, though, I might consider it," Bearfox responded as he added a piece of wood to their fire. Adam smiled and nodded his head as they continued to converse well into the evening.

It had been a lonely day in Hinterville, and an even lonelier night. The children had gone to bed early. They were exhausted from all the playing they did over the past week with Big Weasel. They were sure going to miss him. Adding wood to the two stoves, William once more thought he could smell pipe tobacco. Peering through an upstairs window, he looked to the sky. Thoughts of his family palpitated in his mind.

At the edge of Lost Cause Valley, Bearfox and Adam were feeling the bitter cold. Their fire blazed, yet it did not warm them. They spent a few hours building a windbreak, and now the wind whistled from the other direction. The only thing left for them to do was an old Wakashan trick. Gathering their horses, Bearfox made them lie down. He curled up with his bedroll next to the horse's underbelly, gesturing to Adam to do the same. "It will keep you warm, my friend. It is what the Wakashan do in weather like this, with no shelter. As long as the horses remain down, there will be no chance of freezing to death."

Finally, dawn approached. They were grateful to be alive as the night had been bitterly cold. If not for the horses' warmth, they would have perished. They absorbed the heat from the early morning sun. The valley floor was bright and blinding because of the gleaming snow. Bearfox removed two large pieces of birch bark from a nearby tree. Cutting slits in the two pieces for eyeholes, he handed one to Adam and tied it around his head to prevent snow blindness. The two slits worked to deflect the ever-dangerous reflection of the bright snow. They travelled the distance to the other side without as much as a scrape. There was one more pass to cross before the terrain would ease up.

Finding the Old Crow trail again, they continued onward. The trail, although barely visible, was passable. In certain areas where the big cedar trees grew, it was as black as night.

The snow was hard and icy, and it cracked beneath the horse's feet. The sound echoed in the eerie silence. They travelled for three hours until they were again smothered in the sun's glowing warmth. They stopped and rested. Bearfox checked one of the horses, which had picked up a terrible limp from the icy trail. Sure enough, the ice had gouged the horse's foot. The only thing they could do was to remove him from the harness. They would have to lead him the rest of the way. Tying the horse to the rear of the wagon, they started off once more.

They travelled until dusk and came upon an old wooden sign reading 'Mary Jane Creek'. The creek itself was covered in snow and ice. Adam broke through and retrieved a kettle of water. It tasted heavenly compared to the snow they melted. Leading the horses to the creek, they let the animals drink their fill. Bearfox built a makeshift Wakashan wigwam out of poles and cedar boughs. There was no way he wanted to sleep under the stars that night. It was only dusk, and already ice particles were blowing this way and that. Tonight, they would stay warm. Adam gathered wood for the fire and gladly made a dinner of beans.

In the distance, while they ate and stayed warm by the flickering flames, they heard the howling of wolves. With each minute that passed, the orchestrating howls seemed to grow closer. "Perhaps we should retreat to the cover of the wigwam. We will be safer inside than out." Bearfox suggested. With Adam in agreement and rifles in hand, they retreated to the wigwam. Bearfox lit the fire in the middle of the floor. At first, the wigwam filled with smoke, causing the two companions to choke and cough. Finally, the smoke found the exit and began to billow out through the roof.

They awoke the following morning to the hot glow of the sun. Today, they would make the distance to Hinterville. By nightfall, if all went as planned, they would be riding up to the saloon and the comforts it held. Off they set, unhindered by the weather. By early evening, they could smell smoke from the saloon fires. It would be only a short while before they would be entering the little town. Tonight they would have a hot meal and sleep in comfort. Approaching, they noticed that the barn and corral were mended, the saloon windows repaired. Even one little shanty was almost rebuilt. There was enough wood piled near the saloon entrance to keep it warm and cozy throughout the winter.

The two riders looked at each other and shrugged. Odd as it seemed that so much was done, they were glad to be back. Dismounting, they were greeted by none other than Friend. He sauntered over to each of them and licked at their hands. Entering the quiet saloon, Bearfox hollered their return.

William was the first to greet them. "Welcome back. How did it all go? Where's Brandt?" he questioned.

"It is a long story," Bearfox started. "Brandt is with the McNeil's; his help was needed there. As we travelled, Lester's body fell out. We turned back to look for it, but found only the blanket that wrapped him up. We never found him."

"What?" Shileen asked in disbelief. "Where could a frozen, dead body go?"

"We think that wolves or something else may have carted it off. Perhaps in the spring we will find his bones," Bearfox responded.

"Spooky, I reckon," William said as a chill ran down his spine. "I guess we ain't going to know more until spring. Hope you got the place memorized."

Bearfox tapped his temple with a finger. "I remember the place," he assured.

"All right. Well, there ain't nothing we can do now. Let's get these supplies put away," William gestured as they began to unload. There were a couple of sacks of grain, some coffee and sugar, canned goods, ammo and gunpowder, as well as hardware items and prospecting tools. Adam had even picked up some nice material that could be used for clothing, curtains, and bed linen.

Clea seemed happy that Adam had returned unscathed. She had a deep crush on him. Adam felt the same towards Clea. The golden band he picked up in Medallion proved that. He would not offer it to her yet, though. Instead, he would wait until he felt certain that she, too, wanted him. Engaging in conversation, William mentioned the visit from Big Weasel and Lightfoot. "We had a visit from Big Weasel and Lightfoot while you were gone. The others back at your village are fine. I guess they were sent to check up on us," William paused for a moment as he reminisced. "Mac mentioned to them that Hinterville had been ransacked, and he guessed we were near it. Soaring Eagle sent them."

"Ahh, so that is why so much work has been done." Bearfox smiled.

"Yep, you'd be right; we couldn't have done all that alone. They're coming back, they claim, to spend the winter here. Lightfoot is bringing his niece, Sky. Should be interesting this winter, I reckon. Whilst they were here, Big Weasel took down six renegades that killed a man, a trapper, I think he was."

"Yes, we heard that news in Medallion. Adam and I travelled back along the Old Crow route to avoid any confrontations. It is good that Big Weasel was here. I'm even more pleased that he, Lightfoot, and Sky are returning. Big Weasel works hard and is afraid of no one. Lightfoot is good at everything. They will be of great help as we continue to rebuild your town."

"I reckon as much," William agreed.

The next morning, while they were sitting at the table, they heard the saloon door open. Startled and curious, the men stood to meet and greet whoever had entered. Standing near the entrance was a big, burly guy who stood at least six feet five. He was dressed in buckskin. He reached out his hand to introduce himself. "My name is Kyle, Kyle Henry. Mac is my brother. I understand you have all met him."

By now, Shileen was standing next to William and answered the question before he could. "Yes, we have. Has something happened to Mac?" She asked with concern.

"Hard to say. I was sent a wire by the mercantile merchant back in Sushwa. It said all of Mac's supplies were ready for him, but he hadn't shown up yet."

"That does not sound like Mac Henry," Bearfox commented.

"No, sir. I heard from a friend of mine that Mac was contemplating coming here to Hinterville. On my way, I checked out one of his trap lines. I can tell ya he hasn't been there in a while. My guess would be a couple of weeks. Seems he dropped off the face of the earth. It is not like Mac not to pick up his winter supplies. I thought if he was coming here, I might run into him," said Kyle.

"If he's coming here, Kyle, you're quite welcome to wait. There's a lot of room. So far, though, Mac ain't shown up here yet."

"Thank you." Kyle said with appreciation. As they contemplated the possibilities, they sat in discontent. They knew Mac. He was probably one of the best woodsmen known in those parts. It was unlikely that he got lost. It was unlikely that others killed him. Mac had no enemies other than the Toukia, and they were no longer a threatening menace. *What then could have happened to old Mac?* By the day's end, Kyle and the others agreed to wait a week in Hinterville to see if he showed up. If he did not show within the week, Bearfox would summon help from his people and begin a search.

Chapter 18

In a little gold town to the north called Hell's Bottom, in a big, deep bed laid Mac. He'd been celebrating his good fortune of a rather large gold deposit he had finally found. He had discovered one of the richest gold deposits in the history of Hell's Bottom. In his hand, he clutched a gold nugget. To his right were four empty bottles of the saloon's best whiskey. His head pounded destructively as he edged himself up to a sitting position. Looking about the room, he reached for the fifth bottle. Pulling the cork out with his teeth, he took a long swallow. The whiskey cleared his head enough for him to stand and get dressed. He knew it was time to leave Hell's Bottom.

He had heard during his visit that the Vanfell family had survived and were now rebuilding Hinterville. It wasn't until he heard that name again that he realized exactly what it all meant, and he kicked himself for not clueing in sooner. The Vanfells he had met were obviously one and the same. Not even when he spoke with Soaring Eagle in regard to the tale heard about Hinterville being ransacked and the fact that Bearfox and the others may have been close to the town when it all took place, did he realize what he realized now. *Stupid,* he thought to himself as he exited the room.

At the stable, he retrieved his horse, paid the boarding fee, and then tipped the young stable hand. The boy thanked him and, with a grin, ran off. Mac waved and started for Hinterville and the long and lonely trail that lay ahead. That evening, as he bedded down, he realized that he had forgotten to turn in two satchels to the Gold Commissioner of that region. There was no sense in turning around, although he knew that carrying that much in gold was asking for trouble. There was nothing he could do about it now. Lighting a fire, Mac wrapped himself up in his bedroll and soon gave way to his tiring eyes. He woke with the morning frost and, dusting himself off, retrieved the two satchels. It was too dark to travel, but within the hour, the sun would begin to rise. Mac took advantage of this and prepared a pot of coffee. The hot brew was welcoming. It was something to help get his day started rather than whiskey.

He looked around for a place to ditch the gold. Unable to find a suitable place, he decided to carry it with him. There was a location closer to Hinterville that he knew of. Loading up his gear and keeping one hand near his pistol, he continued onward. One more night and he would be in Hinterville. By noon, he had travelled the distance to where he was going to hide the gold. It was in a shrubbery of wild roses that grew tall and thick every spring.

That was not Mac's reason for putting them there. Rather, it was because near that place, he was once mauled by a grizzly. He was years younger then; still, it made him shudder. Mac remembered the bear's breath, how rancid it smelled, and the ear-piercing growl the bear made. He recalled how he reached for his knife and, with adrenaline pumping, slashed off the grizzly's ear. Then, from out of nowhere came the big Wakashan named Big Weasel, hatchet in one hand and knife in the other. The big grizzly, startled by the Wakashan brave, tucked its tail and headed for higher ground. Old one ear was never seen again. Mac smiled at the memory.

Pushing aside the thorny branches, he set the two satchels inside. He knew the gold would be safe. Backing away, he smiled as the branches formed a thorny shroud around the satchels. Turning, Mac mounted his old buckskin. He rode for another five miles before he needed to rest. Sitting, he realized he was feeling his age. In his late forties, he had outlived most of his family except for Kyle. He never married legally. He preferred the no-strings-attached type of relationship. He was not sure if he ever regretted not settling down. On the other hand, perhaps it was better that he hadn't. Rested, he returned to his saddle.

Near dusk, he began to feel nauseated. He hadn't eaten much in the last while other than liquid rye and malt. He blamed the way he was feeling on that reason. Tonight, he needed a warm meal. Stopping, he made up his camp and cooked a meal out of his dwindling staples. The combination of grits and beans was quite filling. Now he stretched out, his head resting on the rolled-up bedroll. Gazing into his fire, he thought he heard a voice that sounded as if it were in both a native tongue and broken English. Odd as it was, Mac extinguished his fire. He led his horse to a clutch of trees and tethered him there. Walking over the crest, he crouched and looked around. Nothing stirred, moved, or sounded. The evening once again grew silent.

Returning to his fire, he added wood to the embers until finally flames snapped to life. Lying out his bedroll as near as he could to the warm orange glow, he fell exhaustedly asleep. The following morning, fresh snow covered the ground. The air, though chilly, was also exhilarating to the old trapper, and he inhaled deeply. Loading up his gear, he headed towards Hinterville. Having travelled for a few hours, he took a short rest. Looking down the valley from a ridge, he noticed a pack of wolves in the distance as they crossed the valley below. He made sure his rifle was loaded and kept his hand close to it.

Rolling a cigarette, he noted that the sky was beginning to turn grey. Putting on another thick jacket, he descended the rocky ridge. Only another two or three hours, and he would be within shouting distance of Hinterville. As he crossed the valley, he heard a God-awful sound. It was like nothing he had ever heard. Stopping, he looked in the direction from which the sound came. Again, the sound echoed, so loud and close that his steed reared up and knocked him to the ground. Standing, he looked quizzically around but saw nothing and once again silence fell.

Finally able to gather his horse, he once more set off. Riding along the brush line so as not to bring notice to himself or, for that matter, run into whatever it was he had heard, he stayed vigilant as he coursed his way hidden in the shadows of the thick forest of evergreens. A few minutes passed, and the forest remained silent. He was starting to relax and feeling a lot less vulnerable when, once again, the haunting scream echoed. This time, he scrambled into the undergrowth with his rifle in his hand. He scared off his ride, knowing that his horse would only go a short distance.

Crouching behind a fallen log, he looked in all directions. He saw no signs of a man, but he stayed well alert. He crawled from tree to tree. Whatever it was that was out there, Mac knew he had best keep moving. After about a mile, he settled for a rest. An eerie sensation came over him. Looking around, he heard the sounds of running feet crashing toward him, then the loud laughter of his old friend, Big Weasel. "Goddamn it, Buck. You're the one who's been makin' that God-awful sound, ain't't'cha?" retorted Mac, pissed off and relieved all at the same time.

Big Weasel only laughed. "Nice to see you, old friend," he said. The two embraced, and Big Weasel patted his old friend on the back. "Come," he said, "Lightfoot and his niece are over that knoll. We are on our way back to Hinterville. Will you join us?"

"Of course, I will as soon as ya help me round up my steed," Mac replied with a grin from ear to ear. Rounding up Mac's horse, the companions set off. It was good to be in the company of the three Wakashan. *How odd,* Mac thought, that only the other day he had thought of Big Weasel. They were now only minutes out of Hinterville, and they could smell the cooking smoke that wafted towards them. The scent tantalized the companion's senses, and they sped up their horses. As they rode over the last hill before entering Hinterville, Big Weasel began to holler "Bear! Bear! Bear!" loud enough to wake the dead.

Instantly, the saloon doors flew open, and the occupants ran out screaming with joy as the four riders strode in.

Dismounting, they handed out hugs and handshakes. Mac was surprised and pleased that Kyle was there, and he smiled at his brother. "How'd ya know I would be headin' this way?"

"Simple deduction on where else ya might be headin'. I reckoned this to be the closest place to where you might be." Kyle shrugged, glad at least that his brother was alive and well.

It had been quite some time since old Mac had seen William, Shileen and the two children. Tonight, they would celebrate their reunion. Rubbing his stomach, he looked at Shileen and smiled. "Been a while since I last ate a meal made by a woman as good-looking as you."

Laughing, Shileen took Mac by his arm and led him into the dining room. Sky was pleased to be with normal people again. Travelling with Big Weasel and her uncle had been quite difficult at times, especially with all Big Weasel's antics and practical jokes. Sometimes a girl got bored with belches and indignities. Yes, she was glad to be in the presence of women again. Kyle and Mac stuck around for almost a week, and then the two brothers headed back to Sushwa.

Chapter 19

Throughout the winter, William, Shileen, and their four guests, along with Clea and Adam, restored the town. On April 12, 1827, William, Bearfox and Adam loaded up a wagon and began a month-long journey to the Double-U. The others remained behind. In mid-May, the three travellers arrived at the Double-U. William dismounted and looked around at what they had pursued since September 1825. To him, it seemed like an eternity. During that time, he had gone to battle with the Wakashan and lived amongst them. He'd lost his family and gained another. Now, as he looked over the Double-U, he realized how much it all meant.

Undoubtedly, he had been transformed from a youth to a weathered young man. William smiled. The Double-U was exactly how he had pictured it. The house was showing its age and the lack of maintenance. The yard was completely overgrown, where at one time flowers and vegetables certainly grew. There was a lot of work ahead of them: fences to be mended, corrals to be rebuilt, and even the bunkhouse was in dire need of repairs.

Walking over to the well, Bearfox pumped it a few times until the cool water began to flow. Taking a drink, he looked up and smiled. This was it. This was the Double-U. A dark forest surrounded the grasslands, which extended further than the eye could see. Except for the disarray of the buildings and fences, it was a beautiful place. Granted, it needed work, but it was nothing they couldn't handle. After all, they had rebuilt an entire town. Repairs to the Double-U would take only a week.

Entering the house, they were overwhelmed by its size. The bottom floor was scantily furnished with velvet Victorian chairs, wooden tables, and high-back couches. The dining room was quite spacious, and off it, there was a large cooking area. A ranch-style veranda skirted the dwelling. The second floor housed six larger-than-life bedrooms furnished with sitting chairs, nightstands, desks, closets, dressers and big double beds in each room.

In the backyard was a fire pit large enough to roast a side of beef or, for that matter, an entire cow. From there, one could watch the sunset. Walking over to the bunkhouse and entering, they startled a family of raccoons. The bunk bed mattresses were completely disembowelled, the stuffing strewn here and there. There was a powerful stench of urine, feces and rotting food. The coons darted this way and that. There were at least eight of them.

Stepping back, the threesome nodded in agreement that they would have to build another bunkhouse. The coon's could keep that one. If nothing else, they would keep the mouse population down. If they turned out to be a nuisance, then they would rip down the building and shoo them off. Until then, they would leave the vermin alone.

Finally, after their tour they unhitched the wagon, and each mounted a horse. They decided to take a quick look around at the fences that might need repair and check the grazing pastures. A mile from the house, they came across a creek. On the other side, in a serene meadow, were four wooden crosses. Here was where Roy and his family finally rested in peace. They continued for another hour and returned to the Double-U before sundown. The fences out on the range were intact. They would have to string up only a few wires. The fences nearest the house, the barn, and the corral were in need of both minor and major repairs.

The house itself needed only a few quick repairs and a couple of windows. The three agreed that within a week, the Double-U would be up and running and in the market for some good cattle. As the day's progressed, they worked fourteen-hour days right through until the first week of June. In that time, they built a new bunkhouse; the barn, corral, and fences were mended and ready for livestock. The garden was dug up and fertilized with old horse and cattle manure. They planted only potatoes and corn, deciding to leave the rest of the gardening for the women when they arrived. They knew it was quite late to plant, and the produce they would yield would be insignificant. Next year, they would have a better start. All in all, the Double-U was in tip-top shape and ready for business.

First, they would need fifty or so head of cattle, a few good wrangling horses, pigs and some fowl. The place to find these was at the cattle auction in Hudu. It was a four-day ride from the Double-U and the place where Roy always did business. Naturally, it would be where William would do his. An auction took place in June and ran through the end of the month, and then again in October. William wanted to get there at the beginning of the auction, when some of the stronger, healthier livestock were being sold.

Bearfox wanted to stay behind and hold down the fort. There was work to be done, and he wanted to do it. On June 10, William and Adam headed for Hudu. They would be back at the Double-U toting cattle around July 3, if not sooner. They took into consideration the difficulty they might face in returning with the cattle. Fifty head was no small herd to be driving, especially for greenhorns.

The day they left, Bearfox made repairs to the plough and the farm wagon. He located the old branding pit out behind the barn and found the irons close by, corroded with rust. One could barely make out the *UU* brand. They needed cleaning. Walking back to the barn, he swung the irons over his shoulder, *his project for tomorrow.* Watching the sun descend from the back porch that evening, he decided that instead of retreating to the big empty house, he would gather his gear and head for the bunkhouse.

Setting the coal oil lantern down on the rustic table, he chose his bed, the one furthest from the door. Tossing his gear on the top bunk, he pulled up a chair and put his feet on the table. This was home. In the corner of the bunkhouse nearest his bunk was the potbelly stove that they managed to take away from the raccoons. He chuckled as he remembered the difficulty they had in doing so. Staying awake for a couple of hours, he stepped outside to check his horse and to listen to the sounds of the night. Finally blowing out the lantern, he curled up on his bunk and slept.

Twenty miles to the east, William and Adam set up an evening camp in the valley that ran its course right through until Hudu. It was cool in the valley, and they had a small fire burning to ward off the chilly air. They too were bedding down for the evening. Tomorrow would be another long day. Adding one last piece of wood to the glowing flames, they set out their bedrolls. They set out on their journey the following morning before sunrise.

Bearfox, rising quite early the next day as well, retrieved the scythe to mow down the long grass that had taken over the yard. It wouldn't take him that long, he decided. He had been at it for only an hour when he came upon an overgrown root cellar. When he opened the door, the hinges pulled out. Setting the rotting door on the ground, he entered the dark, musty cellar. It was large enough to hold bushels of produce. There was even enough room to hang a few sides of beef. *It is good to have such a place,* he thought as he looked around, then exited. Working until dusk that evening, he managed to cut all the grass and rebuild the door for the cellar. Satisfied that his day wasn't wasted, he sat outside the bunkhouse and watched as the evening stars began to flicker, mesmerized by the sounds of the night.

Back in Hinterville, nine new residents moved in. There was a young doctor and his family, a bartender that Shileen hired, a store clerk and his wife. She rented two of the shanties to the doctor and the blacksmith. She charged each of them ten dollars a month. The blacksmith's wife worked as the saloon's cook. She was paid twenty-five dollars a month, and from that amount, Shileen deducted the rent. The doctor paid up front for two years. Things were going quite well in

Hinterville. Shileen hadn't put any posters out advertising rentals or employment. Instead, word was spread through Kyle, Mac and the Wakashan. She was surprised at how many people rode through. Some stayed, some didn't. She hoped that more homesteaders, storeowners and even a few land developers would consider moving to Hinterville. For now, however, it would remain as it was. *No use overbuilding the town if no one else moved in.*

On June 15, the town mourned the loss of Friend. He had been missing for about a week. What happened to him no one knew. They only wished he would return. By June 20, they had given up all hope. He was lost to them forever. Around this same time in Hudu, William and Adam picked up the livestock that they had come for. William paid five dollars a head, totalling two hundred and fifty dollars. He was given the name of a farmer who sold pigs and chickens. He would seek him out after they returned to the Double-U. They began their trip back on the 23 of June 1827, arriving on July 2. A lot had transpired since they left. Bearfox had definitely been busy.

The following morning on July 3, they started the task of branding the cattle and setting them loose to roam the range. The work was hard and exhausting. It took them two days to brand all fifty head. Obviously, they were in need of a second and third set of branding irons. One just wasn't enough, as it took too long to heat. With multiple sets, they would always have one hot. Letting the last steer out into the range, they yelled in triumph. Finally, the work was done. Now the vigilant task of watching over them would begin.

William had left behind in Hudu an advertisement in a store window that the Double-U would be looking for wranglers, ranch-hands, and housemaids to start in August or September. Previous employees of the Double-U were encouraged to answer. He figured that for the first year, they would only be able to hire four or five employees. He hoped that he could hire back the employees who had worked there before. However, he wasn't going to favour anyone. He'd hire those who came first and who were qualified. He knew that fairness in this type of business would be a virtue. As the days progressed, it became quite evident that Bearfox made the bunkhouse *his* living quarters. The extra bunks turned into shelves that held his carvings, gear, and personal belongings. There was no choice, really, except to build another bunkhouse.

The day came when William decided it was time to head back to Hinterville and bring back the others. It would take about a month to get there and a month back. He would leave the Double-U in the capable hands of Bearfox and Adam. He gave them permission to hire five workers and left them with enough cash to purchase six pigs and a few dozen chickens from the Cranston farm that lay in the next valley. On July12, he began his journey.

Two weeks later, Adam headed towards the Cranston farm, only half a day's ride. As he approached, old man Cranston met him at the gate. Adam introduced himself and said that he was sent by the Double-U to purchase pigs and chicks. Mr. Cranston took him out to the barn, and Adam selected and paid for the livestock. Loading the last of the animals into crates and into the wagon, Adam himself swung up and took hold of the reins. "I hope we can do business again," he said.

"Oh, you can count on it, Adam; you can count on it," Mr. Cranston assured.

"Good. Well, I should be heading back," Adam replied as he bid the Cranstons farewell and headed back to the Double-U.

William meanwhile had made exceptional time and was five days' ride from Hinterville. Travelling had been good with the added bonus of no snow and sound weather. As he set out his bedroll, he sensed eyes watching him. Stoking the fire, he gazed into the darkness. He could faintly make out the yellow glowing eyes of a wolf. Loading his rifle, he sat motionless. If there was one, there were probably two; and if there were two, there was probably a pack. *Dumb luck,* he thought to himself. *I've travelled this far only to be torn up by wolves.* He kept his fire well stoked that evening, prepared for what the night might hold. Back on his horse early the next morning, he travelled for only a few hours when he came upon a carcass of a dead wolf. He could not tell for sure because of the decay, but the choker that lay beside it told him that it was *Friend.*

Chapter 20

Two days later, William was sitting on his horse on the outskirts of Hinterville. From that distance, he could see how the town changed. When he rode into town, Big Weasel spotted him and met him at the stable. The big Wakashan welcomed him back, and together they walked to the saloon. It was August 11 1827. Entering the saloon, the others came running to his side, and they embraced. All the work and despair that they had endured was finally paying off. The Double-U was back in business, and Hinterville was growing and generating an income. Things could only be better if Friend were still alive.

Days later, William, Shileen, Lightfoot, Clea and Sky, as well as Honey and Sinclair, said their goodbyes to Big Weasel, who had decided to remain in Hinterville for now at least. He would keep things on the up and up, he said, as they left for the Double-U. On September 23, the procession approached their new home, the legendary Double-U ranch. Shileen was completely overwhelmed. The place was magnificent. The children, too, were quite enchanted.

Bearfox welcomed them, curious about where Big Weasel and Friend were. William told him what had happened to the wolf and that Big Weasel was keeping his eye on Hinterville for the time being, but had mentioned he would follow them to the Double-U in time. He was saddened at Friend's demise and said a quick Wakashan prayer. He couldn't believe Big Weasel's decision to stay behind; nonetheless, he was glad that he had. "He will protect what is yours as though it were his. He will do well," said Bearfox.

Not much had taken place at the Double-U other than the addition of squealing piglets and tweeting chicks. With the addition of Lightfoot and the two Indian girls, there would be no need to hire hands that year. Now they could manage. After all, there wasn't much work to be done. The Double-U had only been up and running for a few months. There wasn't any harvesting to do. They had planted too late for that. The livestock they were raising could easily be looked after with the current help.

Within two weeks of being back, everyone settled. The children took care of the chicks while Clea and Sky maintained the large ranch house. Shileen was partial to doing everything else, including feeding the pigs; she thought that they were cute. William and the others rode the range and kept the cattle happy. They were constantly building new corrals and putting up new fences. They gathered wood, chopped it, milled it, and cleared brush for new grazing pastures. As the weeks progressed, the days became cooler and shorter.

It was around this time that they began seeing a pair of rogue wolves living close by. The pair hadn't caused a ruckus, so William let them be. At the end of November, as the bitter winds swept the fields and it came time to round up the cattle, something remarkable happened. When a few of the cattle broke from the herd and drifted toward the open range, one of the rogue wolves unexpectedly intervened. With swift, deliberate movements, the wolf turned the cattle around and gently chased them back into the safety of the herd. Then, almost as if fading into a dream, the wolf slipped back into the forest's shadow. Watching from across the frosted grass, William felt a jolt of awe and gratitude. *What kind of wolf would do that?* His heart whispered, *Friend.*

William would never know, of course. He called out Friend's name, his voice echoing with desperation, but never got a response. If it were Friend, he was now in his element—distant, unreachable, and swallowed by the silence. "See, I told you, you'd never be a coat," he said softly as he turned his horse and followed in behind the fifty head of cattle meandering homeward. After the cattle were sorted and put into the corral near the house, they were counted to ensure they were all there. They were. Perplexed still at the rogue wolf, he looked into the distance and smiled. How he hoped that the wolf was Friend.

Soon, winter was in full force. Big Weasel had come to stay until the end of next season, and those at the Double-U were glad to have him. As January arrived, some of the cattle became ill, leaving no recourse other than to kill them. The cattle, suffering from some ill-fated disease, were examined by the cattleman from across the valley, who called it *Flesh Craves*. "Your Uncle Roy had the same thing happen to him, son. Not much else you can do. Keep your eye on the others. As for these six, you have to shoot them and burn their carcasses. Even animals shouldn't feed on the meat."

"Do you know how they got it?" asked William.

"Not a clue, son; not a clue," replied the cattleman. "I can tell you this much for sure. It was only shortly after Roy had this happen that all Hell broke loose. First, old lady Vanfell died, and then the children. Well, you probably know the rest, son. I can tell you it wasn't a pretty sight. Hell, one day the boy nearly ate his own arm off. Roy tried his hardest to restrain the boy, but the boy turned on Roy and took a bite at him. We finally got the boy tied down, and two days later, he died. I'm not sure what else I can tell you, sorry."

"That's all right. You told me a lot more than I knew. I had no idea that is how their deaths came about."

"That is indeed how their deaths happened, son; that is how indeed," said the cattleman as he bid farewell and vanished into the distance.

William looked at the six steers they managed to separate, his heart pounding with dread. As he loaded the rifle, panic surged when one of the bigger steers rushed at him, pinning him with brute force to the rail fence. The animal's head smashed into his stomach again, pain exploding through his body as four ribs cracked. His vision blurred from agony, and the rifle slipped from his trembling hands, clattering to the dirt. As the steer stepped back to charge once more, fear and desperation clawed at William. In a flash, Big Weasel vaulted over the railing, hurling himself at the animal. He wrestled the steer to the ground, rage and concern twisted across his face, then drove his knife deep into its neck. The dying steer bit him savagely. Big Weasel rose, shoulder bloodied, jaw clenched in pain, and pulled William gently to his feet. "Are you all right, my friend?"

"I think so. How about yourself?"

"I am okay; a little scratch is all."

"Little my behind," William said as he pointed at Big Weasel's right shoulder.

"It is nothing, my friend. Come, we must get you back to the house. You have some broken ribs, I can tell. I will tend to myself later." Helping William get settled in his room upstairs, Bearfox and Big Weasel returned to the corral armed with rifles.

"Look at them. Look at how they wish for a quick death."

"A quick death they shall have. They are minions of evil. They are no longer beef. They crave blood, cousin. We have seen this before," said Big Weasel.

"Yes, I remember. We must tell the others; we must prepare for the worst."

"We cannot tell them, Bearfox. The Wakashan no longer possess the power to contain its evil."

"If it becomes so and we have not warned them, what then will they think of us?" asked Bearfox.

"It would not matter. It would be too late. All we can do, cousin, is wait. If this evil continues to wake, then all will be lost. We mustn't acknowledge it. That is what it wants, acknowledgement, and giving it will only make it so."

"Yes, you are probably right," Bearfox responded, as they both took aim at the six crazed steers. Their rifles erupted in gunfire, and finally, the last steer fell upon the ground. They would have to keep a close watch on the rest of the livestock. Only the spirits knew how this evil worked, and only the spirits knew when and where it would strike next. Dousing the carcasses in coal oil, they set them ablaze.

Shileen was still wrapping William's ribs when both Big Weasel and Bearfox returned.

"How many are broken?" asked Bearfox.

"Four, I reckon," replied William. "Did you finish off the steers?"

"Yes. We are burning their carcasses now," said Big Weasel.

"Good, I hope none of the other animals end up like that."

"We will keep our eyes on them. For now, you must rest. It's going to be some time before you'll be up and about."

"You got that right. A few weeks at the least," said Shileen, "but I'm sure we can handle it, Mr. Willy," she chortled.

"As for you, Big Weasel, come here. You need to have that bite looked at. I didn't know bovines could do that."

"They usually don't, not can't," chuckled Big Weasel.

"Nothing to worry about. It's only a scratch," Shileen responded, as she looked it over.

"Good," said Big Weasel. He knew, deep down, a cold dread twisting in his gut, that, regardless of the severity of the wound, he could still become infected with the *demonic plague* that the Wakashan had defied long ago. "It's getting late, my friends. I bid you goodnight," Big Weasel said as he stood.

"I agree, cousin. I too shall bid goodnight. It is late and my fire barely burns in *my* bunkhouse and it needs tending," said Bearfox.

Chapter 21

In February 1828, weeks after the cattle incident, William was able to venture outside. The weather was finally turning nice again. January had been exceptionally cold, but now the sun shone, radiating its heat. It was a gorgeous day. He walked up to the men working on removing snow and ice from the flat roof of the pigpen. "Nice day out, isn't it? Looks like we'll be in for a great spring," he said.

"I sure hope so," Adam responded. "A man can get sick of shit weather as we've had as of late." He leaned on the shovel and looked down at William from the roof. "How's the ribs feelin', Will?"

"Well enough that they're allowing me to walk some. They hurt every now and again, but I reckon that is to be expected."

"Leastwise you're healin'; that is always a good sign," Adam replied as he went back to work.

Nodding, William smiled and turned away. He walked over to the rear corral and leaned against it. Here, the snow was still knee deep. Squinting, he looked into the distance. Soon, spring flowers would begin to bloom, and they would be able to let the cattle back into the open range. That is when the real work would begin.

This year, they were going to plant vegetable crops and a grain field. He hoped that by then his ribs would be completely healed. It had already been close to a month since they were broken. Sometimes the pain was excruciating. Even the short distance he walked made his ribs ache. He rested a while longer, looking around the Double-U. What a transformation the ranch had undergone since June. Here it was only eight months later, and the Double-U could never have looked better.

Returning to the house, he stopped off at the horse barn and looked in on the horses. They appeared to be in good spirits, but he could tell they were already getting spring fever. "No worries, fellas; spring will be here soon enough, I reckon." Hearing his name being called, he exited the barn and looked towards Bearfox's bunkhouse.

Bearfox was waving him over. "Come here, my friend. We must talk."

"Sure, what is it, Bearfox?" William asked as he approached.

"I have something I must speak to you about. When the cattleman was here, he said these cattle have flesh craves, did he not?"

"Yep. Why do more of the livestock have it?" William asked with deep concern.

"No, but I am afraid Big Weasel has contracted something. He has not been himself lately. Yesterday I saw him behaving strangely."

William looked at Bearfox somewhat confused. "How's that?"

"He sat and stared blankly. He asked me to take his life. Said he was afraid of what he was becoming." Bearfox answered, he knew what Big Weasel was referring too, yet he did not want to mention it to William, not yet at least.

"I reckon he has been curious lately, but it ain't nothing except probably cabin fever. There isn't much for him to do here." William responded. Knowing full well Bearfox was alluding to something more sinister.

"No, my friend, it is deeper than that, I assure you," said Bearfox. "You see," he began, "this flesh craves, as the cattleman called it is a curse that once destroyed many Wakashan, it is a demonic plague. It has been dormant for many years. I was only a child when it first crossed me. It only gave me a meek taste for human blood, and only once did I taste it.

"The Wakashan first encountered this curse a hundred years ago. It made many ill. It caused great fear. My ancestors did battle with this evil. Only five Wakashan survived." He paused there for a moment as his mind raced back to his childhood, when he himself became violently ill. "Then, as a child, the evil infested me, and I became very ill. I desired warm blood. Big Weasel bears the scars that I left. It was then that the Wakashan again were cursed. Oowatchy was the only one who had the power to defeat it. Since then, it has happened one other time.

"That was here at the Double-U. Four years ago. I am certain of this, from what I have seen and from what that cattleman spoke of."

"You mean to tell me that this thing can affect both man and beast? And that the symptoms include thirst for blood? Come on, Bearfox; that's a lot of horse crap, I reckon." William said hoping not to have insulted his Indian friend.

"No. It is not horse crap. It is true, and yes, the symptoms include thirst for blood," Bearfox said with purpose and conviction.

"Still sounds like horse hooey to me, Bearfox. There is nothing that can make a man crave blood. Likely some kind of ailment cured with medicine, is all."

Bearfox shook his head with frustration. "It is an evil too great for any white man's medicine. The Wakashan are also powerless. Oowatchy is gone."

"If this is what you claim it is, what are we supposed to do with Big Weasel? I'd hate to see him in such a state if one exists."

"Only Big Weasel can help Big Weasel. He knows the symptoms as he has seen them. He also knows that the Wakashan are powerless against it. If he gets this evil inside, I may have to do what he has asked of me, which is to take his life," said Bearfox reluctantly.

"I reckon you're talking crazier by the minute. Maybe it's you who has cabin fever," William commented as he tried to break the tension. He wasn't sure he believed what he was hearing. Bearfox, though, seemed sincere.

"I plead with you, William, please listen. It is an ancient evil brought on by a demon."

"See, Bearfox, now you're talking demons. You've flipped your lid, I reckon."

Bearfox continued regardless of the comment. "The evil one is named the Wakashan Devil. His only weakness is Wakashan medicine. He can only be stopped if he can be fooled into thinking that he has been stopped. We must never show this evil weakness."

"I tell you, Bearfox, I appreciate legends and all, but I tend not to believe them."

"It is not a legend." Bearfox was more aggravated now, and the voice he used emphasized that.

"Why are you only telling me this now? Why didn't you mention this before?"

"There is only one reason, my friend. I did not want to concern you or the others. The Wakashan believed that if we were to speak about it outside of the Wakashan, then this curse would return. I know now that is not the truth. We've not spoken of it, and it has returned. Yet, I wish not to tell the others. As a friend, swear to me you will not repeat what I have said."

"I swear, Bearfox. I think that if I did, everyone would think I was crazy. I mean no disrespect either."

"I understand. I thank you for listening." Bearfox turned and entered his bunkhouse closing the door behind him, as a gesture that he no longer wanted to speak.

Shrugging, William, walked back to the house, and was met at the door by Shileen. "What were you and Bearfox talking about so discreetly?" she asked.

"It was nothing really; besides, he made me swear not to repeat it." William said as he brushed by her.

"Nothing? Then why did he make you swear not to repeat it?" Shileen questioned at the secrecy.

"He is your brother. Why not go ask him?" William replied keeping his word not to repeat what he and Bearfox had spoke of.

"I will, then." Shileen walked the short distance to Bearfox's bunkhouse. Knocking on the door, she called his name. "Bearfox, are you there?"

"Yes, yes, come in, my sister. What brings you?"

"I watched as you and Willy talked. When I asked him what you were talking about so discreetly, he told me to ask you yourself, so here I am."

"Very well, come sit. I will tell you." Bearfox commenced by telling Shileen what he had told William. By the end of the discussion, Shileen wasn't convinced. Bearfox sat silent for a while. *How could he explain the difference between what Shileen and William both called cabin fever and what the Wakashan knew as a demonic plague? How could he explain to her that it was not a simple ailment, but rather a possession of the soul? Had she not understood?*

"It is not what you and William say it is. The cattleman who was here all those weeks ago called it flesh craves, but it is truly a demonic plague. It is an evil possession of the soul, and can spread from man to beast. If Big Weasel gets this sickness, he will kill to tame his thirst for blood," he pointed out.

"It isn't an evil, Bearfox. There cannot be such a disease that causes a man to thirst for blood. It is something willed, not forced by sickness."

"Then why did I crave blood when it found its way into my soul? Why does Big Weasel wear the teeth marks I left in his shoulder all those years ago?"

"Because you were led to believe that what you had was Flesh Craves. You were taught these things from when you were a child. It is a Wakashan legend," replied Shileen.

Bearfox shook his head. "It is more than legend. It is true. However, for the sake of arguing, I will put our fate in your hands for now. I hope that you are right. Otherwise, I will have no choice other than to kill my cousin."

"Please, Bearfox, don't talk like that. Big Weasel is perfectly fine, and he will remain that way. There is nothing wrong with him. If he seems distant, it could be that he is coming down with an ailment such as the flu. It's nothing, a bit of rest and food won't cure," said Shileen as she stood to exit. "Goodnight, Bearfox."

"Goodnight, sister. May the Gods watch over us all."

Walking back to the house, Shileen could not get the pictures out of her head that Bearfox had painted in her mind, pictures of a man craving human flesh, pictures of a disease that caused cannibalism. She thought back to her dream where Honey held a human beating heart in her hands, her teeth crimson. It sent shivers down her spine. *Something so awful could never really happen,* she convinced herself.

It took only a few weeks to see the results that Bearfox had described. This time, though, they were different inasmuch as who they affected. It was Honey who contracted the deadly symptoms. Shileen followed her medical experience and administered the medicine that was supposed to rid her daughter of the painful convulsions and overwhelming thirst. She was convinced that the medicine would work. However, as the days went on, Honey's condition only worsened.

One night in late March, when Shileen administered the elixir, Honey, frothing from the mouth, reached up and grabbed her in a violent rage. Her face contorted as she tried desperately to sink her teeth into Shileen's flesh. Shileen was able to subdue her young daughter only when Honey's body finally rested from what Shileen believed to be muscle spasms. She burst out of her daughter's room, frightened at what Honey was becoming. She was so young, so innocent. Shileen's fears were that her daughter would die. The medicine, the prayer, none of it was working.

Seeing that Shileen was in distress, Bearfox approached her side. "The little one. She is not healing, is she?"

"No. Her body screams to be healed. Something is not letting it. I haven't got the medicine or even the knowledge to fight it off," Shileen said as she began to sob.

"We must get her back to the Wakashan village. It is all that will help her now. Perhaps Wakashan ceremonial prayers and incantations can help her heal."

"You are asking me to allow you to take my daughter back to the Wakashan village where you believe the Wakashan Gods can heal her," Shileen exclaimed coldly.

"Sister, please, calm yourself. Listen to me. Your medicine has not helped. The young one will not get better. If you do not wish her to die, believe in me. The Wakashan can help, but in our own way. You must believe this. Are you afraid that we will harm your daughter, my niece?"

For a moment, Shileen looked into her brother's eyes and found in them the reassurance she was looking for. Her eyes welled up, and she put her arms around Bearfox's shoulders and sobbed. "Bearfox, I am so sorry. I didn't mean to sound so horrible. I believe in you and your people as much as I believe that your people can heal my daughter. Please accept my apology."

"Those were feelings, my sister. You do not need to apologize to me. Your feelings speak for themselves. You have been put into a position where one you love so dearly is faced with a terrible illness. It is only a reaction to a dire situation," Bearfox replied. "I would expect the same from any mother."

"How long, Bearfox? How long will it take to see my daughter again?"

"The Wakashan village is miles away. We will travel swiftly, and perhaps in thirty dawns we will arrive. The spiritual ceremonies will commence immediately. Still, it could take weeks to heal her, but we will not stop until it is so. I will send one of our people if it takes longer than two months," he said. "One other thing, sister. How many winters old is the little one? I ask this because it attacked me when I was twelve winters old."

"Honey will turn eleven this year in July. Please, Bearfox, do not let anything happen to her."

"Not to worry. I will protect my kin with my life and will give it up to protect her. She will be safe in my hands."

The following morning, they bid farewell to the Wakashan braves and the ailing Honey. That was March 16 1828. Five days later, as the travellers rested, Honey began having convulsions. Bearfox darted to the wagon where the ailing Honey lay. As he peered in, Honey looked at him, her eyes cold. She was frothing at the mouth like a wild animal. Then, without a word, she buried the cold steel blade of a knife deep into his abdomen and, in one motion, removed his innards. Bearfox didn't stand a chance, and his limp body fell to the ground. Honey rose and stepped out of the wagon. She crouched near the back and waited patiently for her next victim.

It was Lightfoot who approached next, curious to know what was taking his friend, the Wakashan Chief, so long. As he approached, Honey sprang at him without so much as a murmur and slashed the blade across his throat. Lightfoot made a low gurgle sound and then fell silent as the steamy, dark blood from his severed jugular vein spewed out on the grass-covered ground. Honey was enthralled. Her eyes were big with desire for blood. She looked towards the fire. Slowly, she crept into the tall grass towards Big Weasel, who sat near the flames watching them dance. His big body would be hard to take. However, Honey's desire for blood was greater than any man's will to live.

She crawled silently towards her next kill, making low, sinister growls as she approached. Then, she pounced onto his back and sank the knife's blade deep into his cranium. His blood spurted up like a fountain, and Honey lapped at the warm plasma as it squirted her chin and face. Engorging herself, she bit at the Wakashan's cheeks and face until her teeth meshed with his. She ripped and tore at the dead Wakashan's flesh like a hungry wolf. Fed and full, she set the wagon ablaze and dragged the bodies of her victims to the undergrowth. Their flesh would feed her for the coming weeks until she could move on and find a more distant killing ground.

It was not until late June of that year that Soaring Eagle visited the Double-U that the disappearance came to light. William spotted the rider coming and mounted his horse to meet the oncoming rider. Shocked that it was Soaring Eagle, he thought Soaring Eagle was sent by Bearfox to report on Honey's condition. However, he was there because of a vision. "Soaring Eagle. How have you been? Are things going well with Honey's recovery?"

Soaring Eagle looked at his friend quizzically. "I do not understand, Vanfell, what you have questioned."

"Honey became deathly ill, and Bearfox believed the Wakashan could help her recover. He and the others, along with Honey, headed to the Wakashan village in late March." William was confused now, and his heart beat a mile a minute. "Don't tell me, Soaring Eagle, that they never made it. Please don't tell me that."

"I am sorry, my friend, they have not," replied Soaring Eagle.

William bowed his head and shook it. "What do you suppose could have happened? Could you have missed them along the way?" he asked.

"That question I cannot answer. It is a possibility. I left in late April, which means they should have been quite close to the Wakashan village by then, depending on what route they may have taken. I know if Bearfox was returning, he would have followed the same route that I took, and that would have been through Beaver Lake. I did not see any sign of past travellers. I am sorry, my friend."

Chapter 22

During the weeks that followed, William and Soaring Eagle both travelled back to the Wakashan village, but there was no sign of the four travellers. William returned to the Double-U in early August, breaking the news to the others as gently as he could. Shileen was horror-struck as a mother would be, and for months she did not speak a word.

In July 1829, a year after Honey's disappearance, it was decided that Shileen would return to Hinterville. The heart-wrenching pain of living in the last place where she saw her daughter alive was more than she could bear. She remained in Hinterville until her death in the early 1840's.

William continued operating the Double-U until 1848. He then handed the Double-U over to his cousin Sinclair. Taking up residence in Hinterville, he lived out the remainder of his life as Mayor. He died tragically at the hands of a young woman in 1856 at the age of fifty. His body was found partially consumed. It was believed that his killer was the wolf child that hunted the woods in and around Hinterville.

It was a legend started years after the disappearance of Honey and the three Wakashan braves. It was a legend told to those who travelled in and out of Hinterville about a young woman who stalked passersby and fed on them as a wolf feeds on its prey. People had been disappearing for years before the story started, and after it became a legend. The legend, however unlikely, was more fact than fiction.

The first disappearances took place during the winter of 1828. Of the six people who went missing, the remains of only four were found. As the years progressed, the death toll and disappearances increased. Search parties were sent out on occasion, only to return with the dead, sometimes with nothing at all. Hence, a legend of a clan was born. It was much like the Toukia clan from years gone by, but ruled by a woman. It was said that the clan would stop passersby and ask for directions to one spot or another, or they would call out for help until someone stopped, then attack. They would entice young men into the bramble and embark on killing them. Some of the younger children were, on occasion, spared and taught the way of the clan. They kept their breeding population up by kidnapping young men and women.

When men and women from outside the clan fathered or gave birth to three children, they were either spared or made to work as slaves to the Queen. Some were murdered and feasted upon. The men were usually castrated and left in shackles until they died, their bodies being burned in pits until only bone remained. The skeletal remains were then pounded with heavy mallets until the bones were reduced to mere dust for use in spiritual ceremonies.

In 1849, Honey gave birth to Shala. Honey bore three children, two of whom died from eating diseased, rancid human flesh. Shala was now Honey's pride and joy, and she loved her daughter, as mothers should. Shala was strong and bore a resemblance to Honey. As she grew, her killing techniques became unsurpassable. She led the clan's best hunting party for over five years. Her first kill was at the age of thirteen. She tempted a young man who was a few years older than she was with her voluptuous body and breasts. When the lad followed her into the forest, she pounced on him and drove a knife deep into his cranium.

As her first victim's blood spewed from the deadly wound, spraying her in the face, she lavishly licked the plasma off her chin, much the same way her mother had done many years before. As Shala grew, so did her desire for human flesh. She was nineteen now. Her kill count was more than that of all the girls who were in the clan and of the same age.

Chapter 23

In the spring of 1868, three girls loped through the misty morning, enticing the traveller deep into the woods. Satisfied that they had led the young man far enough off the beaten path, they hid, salivating, in the undergrowth, waiting to attack. His corpse would feed their clan tonight. When the stranger passed within striking distance, they pounced from their ambush, knives and spears glinting in an assault of metal claws.

The blond youth spun toward the raucous cries. Too late, he saw the flashing blades. The bloodlust in the feral eyes of his assailants, dressed in buckskins, told the story; *they were from Hell.* The tallest, a white girl, hurled her spear at close range, a snarl twisting her cherry mouth as it pierced his shoulder. With a cry of shock and pain, he tore it from his bleeding flesh and whirled around, wielding the spear at the trio, warding them off. His attacker drew a knife from her moccasin and brandished the long blade.

He lunged toward her. Dizzying pain from his wound threw him off balance; losing the grip he had of the spear, it fell to the ground, useless now. All three girls charged him, slashing at his chest and torso, slicing into the palms of his hands as he tried to protect his face and eyes. Overwhelmed at last by agony and exhaustion, he slumped to the ground.

Shala, the eldest of the three girls, decided that the young man's life would be spared. Instead of food, he would become a breeder. The clan needed good, strong breeders, and this young man had proven his strength. "We must keep him alive. He will make strong children," Shala announced.

One of the girls asked, "Strong children for whom, Shala. Isn't your hunger for this man's flesh more appealing than the desire to have him as your own?"

Shala studied the prisoner's broad back and silken blond hair. "More food will walk up this path," she said, "but not every day do we come across such a man as this."

That night, as the clan members gathered around their fires, she asked to speak. "I am nineteen winters old," she stated. "I believe my time to add to this clan's lineage is now. I have led the best hunting party for five winters. I have earned my position as next to be bred, so that I may bear three children. I desire the responsibility of raising a family of hunters. Please, my Queen, grant me this," she said as she bowed to the Queen.

None of the things Shala asked for could be denied her. She had come of age. "Shala, for nineteen winters I've watched you grow. You have proven your qualities to become a clan breeder. Your offspring would be a great addition to this clan. I cannot deny you this. If it is what you have decided, I will grant this to you. Is this truly what you want?" asked the chieftain queen.

"Yes, it is what I desire," replied Shala.

The queen rose. "Tonight, Shala will become a woman," she stated. A hush fell over the clansmen as each young man willed that she would choose him for her breeding purposes. The men dreamt of her and lusted after her long, slender legs and wild auburn hair. Her aqua green eyes gleamed with penetrating moxie. Out of all the female clan members, Shala was the most desired.

She decided, however, that her lover would be the young man her hunting party let live that very day. First, he would have to be brought back to health. His wounds would have to heal, and he would have to prove himself to the queen. He would be put through endurance tests to condition his mind and body. If he failed at any of the tasks, he would be put to death by Shala herself. If he upheld, he would be kept alive until Shala birthed three children.

The fires of the evening crackled and popped as the young man awoke from his slumber. In his feverish mind, the Double-U rises out of the plains like a mirage in the desert. The sound of trickling water draws him onward. He searches for the source, aching to taste the cool, sweet water of home.

So near, within his grasp even, the ranch house recedes, further and further. He follows, his arms outstretched. Then suddenly, he walks into a green field where men are branding a herd of white-faced cattle with the UU brand of the Vanfell ranch. It is a familiar, arresting sight, and he stands transfixed. The branding iron sizzles against the hides, releasing an acrid stench of burning flesh and hair. He feels eyes upon him. Yellow eyes, terrible and surreal, watching from the forest. The baying chant of demons resounds in the forest surrounding his home. The scent of fresh blood wafts toward him on the chilling breeze.

The cold roused him, and he lay sore and stiff on the hard dirt floor, his tongue thick and dry. He could barely swallow, far less call and beg for water. He struggled to his feet and stumbled toward the door. The shackles biting into his ankles proved too short, and he fell back. Outside around the burning fires, the clan was saluting Shala and her new role as clan breeder. The clan originated from a family named Vanfell. The queen was an adopted descendant of the Vanfell family. Her childhood name had been Honey. Now, she was old and frail. She had started the clan. She reigned over it for forty years. Now she knew it would be only a matter of time before her daughter, Shala, took the throne.

She inhaled deeply the aroma of tobacco mixed with the dried leaves of a sacred plant. She admired the gem-studded calumet in her hand. Loose folds of skin blanketed her eyes from the flames as she puffed on the Pipe of Unity, once passed from hand to hand around circles of Wakashan braves. Her name belonged to another world, another time, not this nomadic existence she had chosen. She shook her head in thought. *No, there had been no choice. From the time she had been captured by the bloodthirsty Toukia, she had craved human flesh.*

For three weeks, the young man Shala, spared that day, lay in shackles on the dirt floor of the shanty, seeing his captors

185

only once a day. They brought him food and water, and occasionally one of the young women would cleanse his wounds, a veil draped over her face so she would remain faceless in his mind. As he regained his strength, the visits became more frequent. The food he had been fed was replaced with undercooked meat, but he ate it ravenously nonetheless. He could only speculate who his captors were or what his role might be. By fall that year, he had completely recovered. He was released from his shackles, but he remained imprisoned.

He had learned by now not to speak to his captors unless they spoke to him. Each time he tried in the past, he had been threatened with a knife to his throat or a javelin to his chest and forced to remain silent. One night in early fall, two women approached his stone prison. He watched them through the small window, noting that each was armed. He slowly returned to his straw bed and sat down. The wooden door slowly opened, and a woman approached him. Her face was concealed in the darkness. She slipped a hood over the young man's head and tied it snugly around his neck.

"You must lie on your back. Do not try to remove this hood or your life will end," said the first woman as she stepped aside. The young man followed the woman's instructions, and for a few minutes, the hut became completely silent. Then he heard another person approach his bedside.

The woman began massaging him and pouring a warm, oily substance over his body. Then she mounted him. For three months, this was a nightly occurrence. Then, just as the visits began, they halted. Who the woman or women were remained unknown. Nevertheless, his purpose was now clear.

The young man's name was Leif Vanfell. His legacy was the Double-U and Hinterville. Leif grew up most of his life in Hinterville with his mother. During the harvesting season, he resided at the Double-U, learning the cattle ranching trade from his father, Sinclair Vanfell. His father was getting on in years and decided he wanted to spend his remaining days on the Double-U's back porch. In fact, Leif was returning to Hinterville on that fateful day that he was taken captive. Although it had been months since his capture, he remained optimistic that he would eventually be rescued. He now knew that his captors were the 'clan' described in legends and stories that he had heard while growing up.

He lived with the clan. He ate the meat brought to him, knowing all the while it was human. Slowly, he gained their trust. In the spring of 1869, he and four other clan-abducted men were released from their prisons. They were shown boundaries and told that if they crossed them, they would be executed. Names were never discussed. Among the clan, several young women were pregnant. The clan men were dressed in loincloths and buckskins and were apart from the women. Most were in their early forties; some were decrepit and sat crossed-legged, constantly chanting.

An old lady sat shaded from the hot sunlight beneath a canopy made up of cedar boughs and animal skins. On each side of her sat two women in a semi-circle as if in a trance. Neither spoke to the other. Fires burned in stone hearths, cooking and drying the latest kill. The pungent stink of human flesh as it cooked was thick in the stale air. Black flies buzzed constantly. It was a scene none of the abducted would soon forget. They had spent the last seven months encased in their stone prisons surrounded by four lonely walls. All that kept them warm throughout the past winter was a small fire in one corner of their stone cellars that was kept alight by one of the clansmen and out of reach of the prisoner.

Many times those fires burned out, and the prisoners were left shivering. The flimsy blankets covered in fleas and lice were insufficient without a fire burning. On those occasions, the prisoners resorted to covering themselves not only with blankets but also with the matted-down straw used for their beds. They lived like caged animals. Now, outside in the open air with the sun shining, nothing mattered.

The thought of escape was too much for one of the men, and as he tried to dart into the forest, he was instantly brought down with whistling arrows. The clansmen ran forward and disembowelled the dead man. His guts they tossed into one of the fires, and as the innards sizzled and popped, the clansmen began methodically skinning and butchering. Children gathered and watched the spectacle with glee. One child began gnawing on the dead man's ear, which had been tossed onto a pile of snacks, however, not before being scolded for trying to take a finger.

Leif turned his head in revolt. The old lady sitting beneath the canopy noticed the look of distaste on his face and abruptly sent one of the women sitting beside her to seize him and bring him forth. "Bring me that man. The one who looks away," she exclaimed as she pointed at Leif. The young woman stood and swiftly approached him.

"You, blonde one," the woman said.

Leif looked at her and then pointed at himself. "Me?" he asked.

"Yes, you, blonde one. The Queen has ordered your presence."

Taking this opportunity to speak as much as possible, Leif replied. "Ordering my presence?" he questioned. "Why does she order my presence?" He knew exactly why. The woman saw him turn in disgust and almost throw up. He wondered if it would be the cause of his death. Thinking quickly, he asked, "Before I go to her, may I have some of that meat?" he said, pointing at the pile of tidbits. Looking from the corner of his eyes, he noticed that the woman must have heard him. She rose and gestured to the young woman, allowing him to take a piece.

The young woman looked at Leif. "The Queen says that yes, you may," the young woman said as she encouraged him over to the pile of small body parts. Leif stepped forward. Looking at one of the clansmen, he reached over to the pile and picked up the first piece his fingers touched. The entire clan grew silent as he put the piece to his mouth and slowly began to chew. Turning, he walked the short distance to where the woman sat.

The woman looked at him quizzically. He reminded her of someone she knew as a child. "What is your name?" she asked.

"Does it matter? I no longer exist in my world. I live in yours now. My name was forgotten months ago," Leif retorted.

"Do you wish to live? I can have you killed and thrown on a spit. However, I think you deserve more than that. Now tell me, what is your name?"

Leif stared silently at the woman in front of him. Afraid that if he opened his mouth, he would be sick. The aftertaste from the raw flesh was threatening to make him vomit. He took a deep breath, then spoke. "My name is Leif. Leif Vanfell."

The woman sat silent, her mind racing with thoughts of her childhood. She knew now who this young man was. "Vanfell?" she repeated.

Leif looked at her and nodded. "That's right. My father is Sinclair Vanfell."

Without skipping a beat, the woman gestured for her guards to seize him. "Put him back in his cell. Bathe him, feed him and then bring him back to me," the woman said as she stood and entered one of the mud huts.

The guards grabbed Leif by the back of his arms and pushed him back into his stone prison. As soon as they were out of earshot, he darted over to the hole used for defecating and urinating. Kneeling, he spewed what was in his stomach until nothing remained, and his guts began to ache. Falling to the floor, he lay in wretched pain.

A short time later, he was brought a platter of food. The meat this time was at least cooked, and swallowing it was not nearly as bad as when it was raw. A few potatoes came with the meal. They were covered in charcoal, obviously roasted in an open flame. Leif consumed everything that was on his platter. He was then whisked away to the bathing area, stripped, and made to stand still as gallons of sun-warmed water poured over his naked body. Two of the women approached carrying rags. They scrubbed him down, shaved the small amount of hair that was growing on his face, then made him walk through the little village butt naked to one of the mud and straw huts.

Inside the hut were the old woman and what Leif could only guess was her daughter. They sat on a goose-down-filled mattress. To the right was a table. There was a stone fireplace, and embedded into the clay were two human skulls. Leif walked a few steps forward. The old lady stood and raised her hand. "Vanfell child. You will reside here. You will be dressed in clean clothing, bathed every second day, fed three meals a day and allowed outside thrice a week. Believe me, child, you are not our friend. These things are given to you because we must keep you healthy.

"These things are given because my daughter has chosen you to be the father of her offspring. That is why you still live. When she has borne three children, you will be released from this house. Your fate will be decided then. Do not try to escape because it will be futile." The old woman looked at him sternly and with conviction. Leif could tell she meant business. "The guards outside have been ordered to kill if you should try. The rules of talking that you have learned will also apply here. You will not speak unless spoken to," she said coldly as she signalled to her daughter. Together, they exited the hut.

Leif looked around the domicile. Compared to where he had lived that past winter, this place was a palace. He could do without the skulls. They seemed to stare at him as if in great agony. Leif walked over to the table and sat down. The hut door swung open, and one of the clansmen walked in. "These are the clothes that the Queen has asked me to bring," he said.

"Thank you," Leif replied. He stood and retrieved the handful of clothes. The clansman nodded and exited the hut. As the days turned into weeks, Leif had two encounters with the old lady's daughter, whom he got to know as Shala. One was during her ovulation of some month, whatever month it was.

Another encounter was when he was forced to have carnal knowledge with the old woman. Because of her age and Leif's inexperience, he was not able to perform. Shala pranced over to his side and, while her mother looked on, held a blade of cold steel against his throat. "You must perform for my Queen, or I will decapitate you this instant. Do you understand?" Shala exclaimed. For Leif, it seemed to go on forever. Finally, the queen expressed fulfillment, rose, and left. "You have done well, my pet Leif. The old woman cannot bear children. She still has desires. Now rise and follow me," said Shala.

Leif stood and followed Shala into the cooling evening. She brought him to the bathing area, disrobed him, then cleansed his body. "You will have to perform for our Queen like that whenever it is requested of you. If you do not, you will die. In time, my pet, I will be queen, and that filthy bitch will no longer have a say. Until that time, you must obey. Do you understand?" asked Shala, gesturing to Leif that he could now speak.

"It sounds like you do not approve. I will do what I can to please your Queen, but it is you I desire," replied Leif.

"Enough. Do not speak to me like that. How can you desire one who eats its own kind?" she asked.

For a moment, Leif said nothing. "I have watched you for several months. I know how you detest who you are. The way that old bitch runs all of your lives is pathetic. What makes you so sure that you are any different from me?

"You only eat human flesh because it is what was taught to you. If you hadn't, you would have starved by now. I know this because I have eaten it for the same reason, not because I desired it, but because I wanted to live. I will escape from here one day, Shala. Won't you come with me?" Leif questioned.

Shala was looking up to the darkening sky. "You are stupid. What you have said is reason enough for me to kill you right now. Plead for your life, pet!" Shala exclaimed as she brought the knife to his throat for the second time that evening.

"I will not plead for my life. If I have to live like this, I have nothing to live for," retorted Leif.

Shala grabbed him by the back of his hair and forced him back to the hut. "You, my pet, are lucky that I do not slit your throat and drink your blood. Now get into your cage. Go now," she exclaimed as she tossed him into the hut. Leif was thinking back on that now. Since then, he had not seen Shala or the nasty old bitch, whom he came to know her as.

Again, weeks passed, and finally, once again, he was visited by Shala. She was dressed in prismatic colours, and in her eyes was a gleam of lust. "My pet, Leif, rise before me. Disrobe and lie down. I am not ovulating tonight, and the Queen does not know I am here. I have come on my own because of desire. Breed with me and then tell me about your home."

"Hold on. It is not 'breed with me', it is 'make love to me'," Leif resounded.

Shala looked at him with confusion. Whatever it was, she cared little. She wanted to feel his manhood deep inside. "What is make love? I desire your manhood, that is all."

"Fine then, let's breed," Leif said as he removed his loincloth. Someday she would understand. For now, he desired her too. The two fell into each other's embrace. It was early twilight when Leif rolled off Shala for the third time that night, spent and exhausted. For a few minutes, neither one spoke as they caught their breath. Leif turned and looked at Shala. "What do you wish to know about my home?" he asked.

"Everything. The freedom, the things you can do, the food, the places you can go and see, everything, my pet. I want to know everything," she replied. They talked until early dawn. Leif told her about all the splendours that his world held. In the end, Shala exited, Leif hoped, with reasons to revert. He watched as she pranced across the courtyard, her silhouette made visible by the rising sun. *Will I ever be free of this place...* he silently wondered.

Leif thought back to when he was first captured, the horrors he had seen and heard, the screaming women, children, and men as they were brutally killed and ripped apart to feed the cravings of the clan. He knew their lust for human blood and flesh was forced on some while bred into others. In Shala's case, it had been bred into her like the bloodlines of a wolf. Leif knew that he must break the chain. If he could convert Shala, then together they could escape and expose the clan.

Chapter 24

One evening in June, he again performed for the Queen. Again, Shala stood vigilantly at her mother's side as Leif gave her pleasure. Glancing over, he could see the hatred that burned in Shala's eyes for her mother, *the dirty old bitch.* Soon the deed was done, and the old lady stood and put on her clothing. "Filthy bitch," Shala muttered as her mother walked out into the evening air. "Stand, my pet, the cleansing water awaits," Shala gestured as she looked at Leif who was sitting on the edge of the bed.

Leif stood and followed Shala. "Shala, why do you let her get away with this? It revolts me every time I must submit. Why don't you put the cold blade of steel against that bitch's throat? You and many others would have a chance for freedom in my world. The young children could live normal lives. Remember what we talked about? My world would welcome you. That nasty bitch and her puppets must be dealt with. Believe me when I say you do not need human flesh any more than I do," Leif began.

"You know nothing, pet. My people have been around for forty years. The majority of us have never tasted anything but human flesh. I am one of those people. I have never tasted beef that you spoke of so desperately, nor any of the other meats your kind eats. I have lived on human flesh my entire life. Two of my sisters died from eating rancid flesh from a sick man. Did it stop my people then? No, it did not. I'm afraid, my pet, that this is my world and one I cannot leave," Shala was convinced.

"That is not true, Shala, and you know it. The truth is that you have been treated like an animal your entire life. Think about it. The way your people force innocent people into breeding with your men and women is not what free people do." Leif shook his head, "In my world, all men and women are free to choose their own destiny. It is not forced as it is here in your so-called world. People are not forced to stay cooped up in small buildings or allowed outdoors only when granted. Please, Shala, pay heed to what I say. This is not the way you have to live," replied Leif.

"Quickly finish washing yourself. I will visit you again this evening. Perhaps we will breed, for I desire you. I have never felt this way before. I believe in what you say. I wish I could live in your world, but I cannot. I would be crucified for what I am. Instead, my pet, you will for now reside in mine." Shala guided Leif back to the hut, then locked the door as she turned away and skirted over to where the clan lived, apart from the breeders and food.

Leif walked over to the bed and slumped into it. *How could he get through to Shala?* He had tried talking and reasoning, but she continued denying what he claimed. Standing now he walked over to the door. Peering through the gaps, he could see that the four guards were beginning their shift change. He had been studying their shift changes since he was first put into the house of shame and despair, and for months, he watched the changing of the guards. He wanted nothing more than to escape, and by studying this perhaps he would get the upper hand and freedom would once more be his. That evening he waited for Shala until the stars in heaven began to shine, but she didn't return. In the end, he curled up on the bed, closed his eyes, and waited for sleep.

The next morning, he rose from bed at the crack of dawn. Today, according to the mental calendar in his head, was one of his days out. He waited anxiously for the door to open. He looked forward to these days when he was allowed out and able to mingle with the others. Although the perimeter in which he was expected to stay was small, and at times the stench of death was enough to make one sick, he appreciated the space. To his despair, the doors that day did not open. Instead, just before noon, he heard a commotion outside in the courtyard. Peering out of the small window he watched as the clan slaughtered more food. They gathered a number of men, and as they cried out and pleaded for their lives, the clan disembowelled them where they stood. Blood-curdling screams of terror, horror and pain echoed as each man fell to his death. Leif counted five in all.

He felt sick as the clan's young children gathered around with glee as the butchering took place. Leif watched in disgust as the last body was skinned and deboned. His hatred towards the clan grew with potency that day as he thought of those the clan had killed. Until the fires burned out that night, in his mind, he killed each of the elder clan members over and over again.

In the morning, the door to his hut swung open, and Shala approached his bed. "Pet Leif, rise. Today you will hunt with my party. Our scouts have spotted a caravan approaching from the east. They report that the food looks healthy. Today you will prove yourself to me," Shala said as Leif rose from his slumber.

"What's that you say? You expect me to hunt with your party?" he asked, dumbfounded.

"That is right, pet. Today you will hunt with my party."

Leif's mind raced with how he could escape. This could be the perfect opportunity. "Will I be armed?"

"No. You will play the role of decoy. Shall you fail? We will slaughter you as we do them. Is that understood?" Shala demanded. There was a look in her eye that told him that she was expecting him to try an escape. Her eyes also told him that if he tried, the consequences would be dire.

"I understand," Leif replied.

With that, Shala led him out into the early dawn. The sun, as it began to rise in the east, cast shadows on the horizon along the eastern mountains. Shala's hunting party met the two as they entered the courtyard. The remains of what the clan had killed the day before lay in a waste pile covered in flies as the liquids and solids seeped from the bloody mess. The stink of defecation and undigested food was a cross between vomit and rotting meat. Leif's eyes watered from the stench. Gritting his teeth, he waited for the party to begin moving. They huddled a short distance away, obviously discussing the day's strategic attack against the unsuspecting people in the caravan that waited for them in the distance. Finally, Shala waved him over. "You will go with these three," she said as she pointed at the three women he was to accompany. "They will tell you what to do. Listen to them with care and conviction. There is no room for error."

Shala and the two others darted off into the bush. They ran through the forest like a pack of hungry wolves thirsty for a kill. Their destination was an outcrop of rocks that overlooked where the killing would take place. Leif followed the other three young women along a well-trodden path that led to a stand of willow that emptied into a rushing creek. He realized as he stepped through the stand how well it obscured the path they had taken.

Looking around as they proceeded, Leif tried to find a landmark, something that he could use to find the path again. It was all so mesmerizing that he almost felt dizzy. He had not seen such beauty in almost a year. He clumsily followed behind the three women, awestruck at the sheer beauty of the open air. After a few miles downstream, the women climbed an embankment that led them to another well-used trail. It snaked along the creek in both directions.

They stopped for a few brief minutes to catch their breath. Before continuing, they slipped a dark hood over Leif's head. Then they led him for a short distance in a direction he could only guess. Stopping again, they removed his cover. They had travelled to a heavily wooded area overgrown with fir and birch. The sun was behind them now, which meant they were now travelling southwest.

They carried onward over a few ridges and then stopped. From there, they could look down onto a valley floor. One of the young women pointed downward. "The caravan will be passing this way before the sun sets. Leif Vanfell, you must take a position down near the road. Any passersby, you must stop. Pretend you are hurt, dead, or lost. Anything to get their attention. Leave the rest to us. Shala is nearby, so do not attempt an escape. This, Vanfell, is a test and one that you must pass. Shala will explain the reason when it is over. Dare to escape, and you will surely die. Go now, Vanfell. Stop the passersby."

The three young women watched as Leif descended the rocky face. He stumbled a couple of times, causing a few lacerations to his shins and knees. If nothing else, the wounds would be convincing when he pleaded for help from passersby. Finally, at the bottom, he walked over to the opposite side. There, he had a better view of the oncoming caravan and anyone else who approached from either direction. Hours went by without so much as a deer crossing. It was completely quiet. Yet he sat still and alert, waiting.

As the sun began to go behind the western horizon, Shala and the other young women approached. "You have passed my test, pet. I believe in your faith. This morning, when we left, we were leaving behind that evil place and its people. The six of us intend to accompany you to your land and home.

"We must travel well into the night. The clan will miss us before sunrise. They will send out search parties. When we are not found, they will suspect us to be dead or traitors. They will kill us without mercy if they ever see us alive again. Let's make haste." Shala demanded as she gestured for them to get moving.

"What about the young ones, the small children. What will become of them?" questioned Leif.

"Once we have returned you to your place, we will travel back. We will smuggle the young ones out and head for greener pastures. We will head deep into Beaver Mountain. A place I have heard about lies on the other side. We will make that place our home," replied Shala.

"Why do that? I have offered you and the others sanctuary at the Double-U, the farmlands I told you about. Shala, there is plenty of room. My father's land stretches further than the eye can see in all directions. We raise beef, vegetable and grain crops. It is a magnificent place. Those of the clan who are not old and set in their ways would be welcome in both Hinterville and at the Double-U," explained Leif.

"You do not understand, my pet. As I walk here beside you right now, I crave to taste your flesh and blood. I do not wish to have this urge, but it is one I cannot fight. That is why my people cannot live amongst your kind. We are different."

Leif looked into Shala's eyes. "Shala, when we arrive at my home, please, you and them," Leif began as he gestured to the others, "stay at my place as my guests. You will find that my people are no different than yours. We eat beef and pork; that is the only difference. Eat my food, Shala, as I ate yours. None of you would be locked up as I was or restricted from anything that is human nature. I think you would come to like my place, and together we could prosper."

Shala looked at the others, contemplating. "Your place is a place each of us has dreamt about and knew existed, somewhere. If they agree, so will I."

A big smile broke out across Leif's face as he turned and asked the defecting clan members if they wished to accept his offer. Not surprisingly to him, it was unanimous. "There is your answer, Shala. I assure you that none of you will come to harm or be foiled. Now, can someone explain where we are?" Leif replied.

"We are only a few miles from where we captured you last year. I hope, pet, that once we get you there, you will recall where to go from there. No one from the clan, except a few elders, has passed through there," replied Shala.

"Get me there, and I will take you to my home," assured Leif. The assemblage hiked relentlessly until the first light of dawn. By now, Leif was recalling some of the places they passed. He remembered vaguely seeing them when he came to on those one or two occasions after being beaten into submission and taken captive. Now he was recalling some of those familiar places again. They were quickly approaching the region he knew. He knew that from where he had been taken captive was a five-day hike to the Double-U, the land he grew to miss.

The travellers finally reached their destination early that evening. They rested a short while, nibbling on nuts and berries. It was all they had to nourish themselves until someone was able to kill an animal or find some eggs. By now, they knew that a search party from the clan had been summoned and sent to look for them. They couldn't stop now, and so they continued on, hungry and afraid, but not defeated.

That night, as the travellers carried onward, the clansmen who had been sent to search for them returned to the clan empty-handed, clueless about where Shala and the others had gone. "I'm sorry to report we do not know where they have gone or what has become of them. Shala knows this area too well to have left behind any sign. She has out-skilled us if indeed she has taken sides with the breeder," said the search party's leader.

"If she has defected to the other side, we will find her and her hunting party. We will torch their bodies and burn them at the stake. In two days, if they have not returned or their bodies have not been found, we will banish her, and there will be a bounty put out on her and her followers. We will send scouts to all the towns from here to the Dakotas. We will find each of them, and they will pay with their lives," retorted the Chieftain Queen.

Chapter 25

As the moon rose in the darkening sky, the travellers stopped and laid out cedar boughs, conversing as they did so. "There never was a caravan, was there?" Leif asked already knowing the answer, it was all a diversion.

"No, my pet, there wasn't," answered Shala.

"Why was I hooded back at that creek we left in the distance?" he questioned next.

"It was for our protection. I believed you were going to try to escape. If you had managed such a feat, we would have been in jeopardy. It was good that you were hooded because if we cannot live amongst your people, the party and I can return to that place, and your people would not be able to find us so easily. That is enough questions for tonight. We will talk more as we travel. Close your eyes, Leif Vanfell," Shala said as she lay down.

"Shala, before you fall asleep. Can you tell me what month this is?" Leif asked solemnly.

"It is June, pet."

"Thank you, Shala. I have been without months for so long." Leif had guessed it to be June and was relieved when Shala confirmed it. Looking to the stars, he counted how many months it had been, then sighed heavily. For thirteen months, he had been locked up like an animal, and for thirteen months, he had been bred like one, too. He wondered back to the first two women who approached him that first time. The one who stood beside him, he knew, was the bitch Queen. He could tell by her voice.

As for the one who mounted him, he had no idea. He doubted it to have been Shala. He would have remembered her firmness and scent. The one to have mounted him in the presence of the Queen could have been any of the pregnant young women he saw in the clan. Slowly, Leif gave in to exhaustion and curled up on the soft cedar boughs. Closing his eyes, he slept, relieved at last to be free.

The blinding rays from the rising sun woke the travellers. Soon they were again travelling in the direction of the Double-U. By mid-afternoon, they stopped at the sight of a blue grouse. Taking the opportunity to fill their stomachs with the fresh fowl, Shala loaded an arrow, and in an instant, the grouse was dead. Leif was only able to put down a few morsels of the raw bird, while the others indulged wholeheartedly until all that remained were feathers and bones. They rested a short while and spoke sporadically.

"If we had horses, we'd already be at the Double-U," Leif said, contemplating. "Why does the clan not have horses?" Now that he thought about it, it seemed odd.

"That is simple, Vanfell. Horses are easily discovered. They need special rearing. The clan has at times used the white fang to help move from one place to the next and also at times to hunt," one of the young women replied.

"White Fang?" Leif asked, not knowing what Shala meant by that. Not until she explained it, did he understand.

"That is right," Shala began. "My mother had a kinship with a wolf as she grew up. Over the years, the white fang became tame to us, perhaps because we shared with them the land and protected them from slaughter.

"I remember as a child, I too grew close to the white fang. As the years and seasons changed, the wolves we had grown up with or at least some of us had grown up with, became distant. Many of the wolves were killed for sport and their fur. The few that remained loyal to us died of old age and the loss of freedom to be wild. Now we no longer have that connection," she stated.

"But for everything lost, isn't something found?" William questioned as much as pointed out as they sauntered on.

Shala looked at him confusingly, "Explain this question; I know not how to answer."

Leif sighed and half-chuckled. "In other words, Shala, is it a bad thing that the wolves left and returned to the wild? Think about how odd that must have been for them. Then, think of your own life. I guess what I am trying to say is follow their example. If the wolf can return to its wildness, then shouldn't you and those who wish to leave the clan be able to be civilized?" He felt bad saying it that way, but there really wasn't another way to explain the question. The clan, after all, was not *civilized*. "It is determination and a willingness or instinct to change, isn't it?" Leif added philosophically.

"I understand your question. It is a good one, Vanfell. I will think of this as I remain a guest at this place you call the Double-U," replied Shala. "For a man, you are quite wise, Vanfell."

"And you, for a woman." Leif smiled.

By June 9, the travellers began the final leg of their journey. What lay ahead was one more pass and a short ascent to Crow Trail. From there, it was only twenty miles to the Double-U. They spent another evening down low in a clearing, and by the next, after travelling all day, they were standing on top of the world, or so it seemed to the women.

The blackness of the evening made one feel as though they were flying in perpetual space. As the wind picked up, it blew the evening clouds toward the yellow moon. They seemed to be close to them at that altitude, and they believed they could reach out and touch them. It was a spectacular sight. "This is beautiful, Leif Vanfell. I have never felt so free in my entire life," said one of the young women.

"It is striking, isn't it? This is called Crow Mountain, the tallest mountain in this range. By tomorrow evening, we will begin to descend," he grew silent as he inhaled deeply. "We need to seek shelter for now. This mountain can get cold without warning. There is a remnant of an old log cabin not far from here. Follow me, ladies," he said as he turned and commenced walking. The cloud cover broke, and again the moon lit their way. The four walls of the cabin stayed erected over the years. The roof, though, had caved in. It always seemed curious how half of it had fallen against one of the walls, inadvertently creating a lean-to. It had remained like that for as long as Leif had been alive. Many passersby used it to protect themselves against the harsh elements of Crow Mountain.

That evening, they huddled closely together, keeping each other warm with body heat. The wind blasted from the north, bringing in its wake a downpour of cold rain. The odd crack of lightning snapped like a bull's whip, causing the group to jump and chilling them to the bone. Finally, the storm retreated, and silence fell over the mountain. The cloud cover dissipated, and the moon again lit up the sky. A warm, early summer wind followed and gently caressed the soaked earth.

Chapter 26

On the third day after Leif and the women escaped the clutches of the clan and barren mountains where the clan lived, the Queen gathered the clansmen and women. "Shala and her hunting party have not been found, nor the man she chose to be her breeder. She and her party have alienated us, 'their people'. Today, I will pick some of you to venture onward to the outside.

"Those whom I pick will travel to where I believe Shala and the others have gone. If they are found at either of these places, you may kill them at your discretion or bring them back to receive their penalty. If you kill them, I will want to see proof. Bring back their heads." She called out the names, and the four women and two men stepped forward. "The rest of you return to your duties. The six of you follow me."

The six clan members followed their Queen into her domicile. "I have chosen you six because I have trust in you. Listen to what I tell you and then head to the outlands. Shala and the other girls have headed towards the place I left many years ago. The young man with her is a Vanfell. The town of Hinterville belongs to them as does a cattle ranch called the Double-U."

There was a short pause as she reminisced about those places that she had left so long ago. "These places," she began once more, "lie outside our hunting grounds. It is northwest of here on this side of the Beaver Mountains. The Double-U is closer than Hinterville by many miles. The six of you can decide on who will travel where. Do not bring attention to yourselves. When you are hungry, do not kill what you cannot consume. Now gather your things and set forth. Track those who have betrayed us and bring them back or kill them however you see fit," demanded the Queen.

The six chosen clan members bowed. "We will find them, and we will slaughter them where they stand and bring back with us their rotting heads," said one of them as they left her and began their journey.

Leif and his companions were reaching the summit of Crow Mountain. It had been an excellent day to travel. They stopped one last time before descending into Vanfell territory. Leif pointed down at the valley. "Down there is the land owned by the Double-U. We have to follow that valley for a day, perhaps two. Then we will be able to see the open range of the ranch. From there, it'll take us a few hours to reach the Double-U," Leif announced with gratification and relief.

"Vanfell, how are you going to explain us?" asked Shala.

"I've been thinking about that, Shala. It is going to seem odd when I approach with six young women. I assure you, the ranch hands will not ask too many questions. They will be too busy looking," Leif replied as he chuckled.

"Vanfell, this is not a joking matter. How will you explain us?" Shala demanded an answer.

"Well, the truth always works. I will not tell anyone that any of you were ever involved with those bloodthirsty demons of Hell. I will tell those who need to know that you are the ones who rescued me from their clutches. I will protect all of you with the Vanfell name, I assure you of that.

"As I have said, Shala, there is plenty of room in both Hinterville and the Double-U for all the young ones. The land that is owned by the Vanfell name is large and plentiful. Come on; now, we must carry on."

By early evening, they descended Crow Mountain. As the seven companions stopped and rested, they drank from a nearby stream. "So this is Vanfell territory? It has sweet water. I like it here already," said one of the young women.

"Yes, this is Vanfell territory. I welcome you as my guests."

"Soon it will be dark, Vanfell. Let us stay here tonight," said Shala.

Leif nodded. "Sure, I don't mind. It is beautiful way out here, isn't it?"

"Yes. I like the sound of that stream. I feel at peace here, Vanfell. So far, you have not lied about anything you spoke of. You are a great and trustworthy companion. I have strange feelings for you, Vanfell. When you speak and are close to me, my insides flutter. I have never felt this way. Have you put a spell on me, Vanfell?" Shala asked half-jokingly.

"No, I haven't. I feel the same way for you. I have tried explaining it to you many times, Shala. You'll figure it out," said Leif teasingly.

Shala shook his arm, "Tell me now, Vanfell. What is this I feel?"

"Yes, Vanfell, tell us what Shala feels," requested the young women.

"Very well," started Leif. "I believe, Shala, that what you and I both share for one another is known in my world as love. It means that I would spend the rest of my life with you. Not just now, but even back at the clan," Leif smiled and nodded. "If I knew I had a future back there and that I would not eventually be slain and savoured by your people, I would have stayed and lived at your side until my dying day. In other words, Shala, I would have learned to adapt to your way of life if only to be at your side," he tried to explain.

Shala and the others looked at him, obviously still confused. "I see. I need to dwell on that for a while, Vanfell. I think I understand, but for now, it escapes me. I will let you know," Shala said as she looked at him.

Leif nodded. "Okay, Shala, you do that," he said as he chuckled coyly. *Everything is always half-backwards with Shala,* he thought. That evening, they feasted on raw fish that they caught in the little creek. It was easier for Leif to eat than the grouse. As the warm evening darkened, the young women removed their clothing near the shore of the creek and bathed. Leif joined them but remained in his breeches. It felt good to wash away the four days of dirt and sweat that were beginning to leave a lingering stink in the air. Cleansed from sweat and dirt, the companions retired for the evening. They lay on the valley floor in a patch of clover and slept.

At dawn, they rose and continued their last day of travel. By midday, they crossed over the valley and up a ridge. From there, they could see the open range of the Double-U, plush with grass and clover. There was a meadow to one side of the big open field, which Leif explained was from a fresh water spring. In the distance beyond another forest stood the Double-U. "Once we get there, we'll be home in only a few hours. As a kid, I used to hunt this area. We are not far from the Double-U. Are you ready to continue?" asked Leif of the others.

"Yes, lead us, Vanfell, to your home," replied Shala.

They continued onward and were coming upon the meadow when they spotted a couple of horses and their riders in the distance. As the horses approached, Leif knew that the men were a couple of the Double-U's hired hands. He hollered and waved his arms in the air. The riders approached quickly and were awestruck at who it was that waved.

"For the love of God, if it ain't Leif!" exclaimed one of the riders as he swung off his horse. "How have you been, son? We all thought you had been killed. It has been over a year. Your old man is going to be comforted when he sees you. His ticker has been giving him problems ever since you never made it home all those months ago when your horse came trotting back. Welcome back, son."

"Who ya got with ya there, Leif?" the second rider asked with a drawl.

"It's a long story. I'll tell you this: if it weren't for them, I wouldn't be standing here now." Leif pointed out with conviction.

"What are their names? I ain't ever seen these pretty women before. They from around here?"

"It doesn't matter where they're from. Just know that they are my guests. I'll introduce everybody when we get to the Double-U. Why don't you two ride ahead, hitch up a wagon, then come back and get us? We'll keep walking," replied Leif.

"You bet, Leif. You want me to bring your old man?" the first rider asked.

"Nah. Don't even tell him. I want to surprise him. I'll explain everything tonight," Leif said.

The rider mounted his horse, and together the two riders headed back towards the Double-U.

"Who were they?" asked Shala as they continued.

"They work for the Double-U. The man who got off his horse has worked for us since I was a child. His name is Jessie. The other guy goes by the name of Neilson. He's worked for us for going on nine years. He's a good wrangler, but lacks manners."

"How many others work for your family?" asked one of the young women.

"When I left, there were five full-time wranglers, including Neilson, a blacksmith, and his son, who came to live with us. There are two lead hands; one of them is Jessie. They are the ones who put everybody to work. We have an Indian cook and her three children, now. That's not including the men we hire seasonally. At any given time, there are usually between fifteen and sixteen workers, but only twelve people, including my old man and me, are permanent. Don't know if it's changed since then."

Three hours later, the men returned with the wagon. "Brought ya all some jerky and water. There are also some apples in the bag from last year," Jessie said as he pointed out the bag.

"Thanks, Jess. We appreciate it." Leif handed the women some jerky, knowing it was meat they craved. They took the few pieces reluctantly and began to gnaw. The wagon turned and headed towards the Double-U. At dusk, the big ranch house came into view. The women sighed in awe. It was the largest dwelling they had ever seen. As Jessie pulled the horses to a stop, Leif stepped down and helped the women off the wagon. "This is the Double-U. Welcome," he said as he turned and saw his father standing behind him.

"Son, is that you?" questioned the old man standing on the veranda.

"Pa!" Leif jumped forward and hugged his father.

"Thank God you are alive. Where have you been, son? I lost hope that I would ever see you again. Jessie, immediately send someone to Hinterville. We must let the old woman know that her son is alive!" exclaimed Leif's father. "Who are these angels with you?"

Leif explained who the women were, leaving out the fact that they once belonged to the clan. "They are my friends. Without their help, I would not be here now. They wish to stay with us, and I have granted them this."

"Yes, yes, by all means. There is plenty of room for all. Come now, you all must be hungry. I will have Char fix some sandwiches."

Leif followed behind his father, leading the women into a big room that held a long table. He gestured for the women to sit. His dad slipped into the other room and was gone for a short while. When he returned, he brought with him a platter of bread and meat. "Please, help yourselves. It is beef and chicken. I'm sorry if the beef seems a bit rare. It was from last night's meal, and the men around here like their meat kind of on the bloody side," he said as he set the platter down.

The newcomers didn't even raise an eyebrow. Before long, they had consumed the entire roast and half a chicken. "It's sure good to see healthy appetites," replied Mr. Vanfell, his face gleaming with pride that at last his son had returned.

Two weeks later, he passed away in final compliance with old age and a lingering heart condition that not even he was aware that he had. Leif stood over his father's grave as tears rolled down his cheeks. Kneeling, he put a hand on the mound of dirt. "Until we meet again, Pa; until we meet again."

That was June 22,1869.

Chapter 27

One evening in early July, the Double-U took a blow that changed the course of Leif's life and the Vanfell Legacy. Unexpectedly, they were attacked with a barrage of flaming arrows gliding in from all directions, hot and fast. In only seconds, the ranch house and barn were engulfed. Shouts of surprise and cries of pain echoed as Leif and his men fought back in an array of gunfire. Hot lead whistled through the evening air as those attacking fell one by one.

Regrettably, when it was over, a number of ranch hands scattered the ground, pincushions for the many arrows that were buried deep into their corpses. A look of surprise and pain was preserved on their faces for eternity. The attackers, all of whom were identified by Shala as clan members, lay amongst the bodies in puddles of blood.

On that fateful night, the Double-U suffered a loss of all but four men. Most of the buildings that the Vanfells owned were destroyed in the fire. The flames, hot and intense, shot to the sky, whipping through the house and filling the air with thick acrid smoke. Nothing could be done. The survivors stood back and watched as it crumbled into history.

With dawn's approach, they began the painstaking burial of all those who perished. Fifteen graves in total were dug, and fifteen bodies filled them. The four clan members who savagely attacked were planted in the ground at a different site, their graves marked as *'Unknown'*.

"What are you going to do now, Vanfell? Everything is lost?" questioned Shala with sincerity and concern.

"I'm going to pay off the families of these dead men with two years' wages. I'm not going to try to rebuild here yet. It's too tragic for me. A lot of my family have laboured here and died here. The cattle that remain, I'll send to market or auction. What's left of the house I'll have torn down, and the land it sat on will be turned into pasture. Then, if I ever rebuild, it will be at the base of Crow Mountain, the place you found so beautiful."

"I think I love you, Leif Vanfell," Shala replied.

"I love you back, Shala," said Leif with a smile.

"There is something else, Vanfell."

"Yes, Shala, what is it?"

"Because my people have sent these assassins, they will continue sending them until they are certain that I am dead. The filthy bitch that is my mother has probably ordered my head on a platter. I am afraid that we would never know when they might attack next. That is why I think it is best that I and the others of my party leave this place. That is why I say I love you. I don't think we will ever meet again."

"Shala, your people will never stand a chance alone, not now, not with those hunting you. Tomorrow we say goodbye to Vanfell territory. You must lead me back to that place so that I can avenge the deaths of those we buried."

"I will not do that, Vanfell. Even with your rifles, you alone cannot fight the entire clan. I will only lead you there if my party and I can help you in the attack. The children and captives can be saved. If you allow us to fight by your side and promise me, Vanfell, that you will, only then will I submit to what you ask."

Leif nodded in agreement. "That's fair, but I have conditions, too."

"What would be your conditions, Vanfell?"

"That you and your party remove all the children and those who are held captive. That you do not fight in the battle. When they are safe, I, and I alone will attack and kill all those who remain. The more children and prisoners that you and your party can help to safety, the better," Leif made clear.

"It would have to be an evening strike, Vanfell. The children are all housed in one building. There is usually one night master who watches over them. I think my party could slip in. I agree with your terms, Vanfell," said Shala.

"Good," Leif replied. The two of them walked back the short distance to where the others gathered near the smouldering remains of the big house. Every now and again, they would spot something that hadn't been destroyed. They managed to retrieve an assortment of this and that. "Well, men, that's about all we're going to get from this mess," said Leif as he tossed a few things onto the pile of clutter they had retrieved.

As evening approached, he wrote out bank notes to each of the survivors and entrusted Jessie with a handful of signed bank notes to be used however he saw fit. "All I want, Jess, is to have what remains of this old house torn down, same as with the barn. Then, fallow up the earth the old girl stood on. The bunkhouse is still standing. You might as well use that for now.

"I figure you got about a year's worth of work if you want it. I will leave it up to you who you might want to keep on. I am going to head to Hinterville after I return with Shala to her people. I want to make sure she gets there. We have decided to leave at first light. If you want the job, Jessie, it is yours for the taking. You can give me your answer in the morning."

"No need for that, Leif. I can give you my answer now, but first, what are your true intentions, son?" Jessie questioned.

"Sorry, I don't follow, Jess. What do you mean? I told you what I was doing."

"Leif, I ain't blind nor do I have a bad memory. Doesn't it seem odd to you that those who attacked were dressed in the same manner as your guests when they first arrived? I know who and what they are, Leif."

"Thanks for your concern, but this is my affair. I'm not looking for assistance." Leif committed.

"I ain't offering you assistance, Leif. I know you better than that. You're like your old man. You're gonna do things your way, no matter what. I am asking you to use your head.

Think about it. Can you guess how many of these people
there are? Is there three, four, more than five?" Jessie looked
deep into Leif's eyes. "You're an awful good shot; I know
that. Hell, I taught you. Still, you aren't going to be able to
pop off the number of rounds it's going to take to slow them
down. They would be on you in no time. I say you're doing a
foolish thing, Leif."

"You're probably right, but what would you suggest I do. I
am not willing to risk the identity of Shala or the others who
helped me escape. I do this thing on my own, Jess. Then no
one except me is held accountable for what might transpire."
Leif looked down, then back up at Jessie. "Besides, it's going
to be open season on the sons-of-bitches. The only ones my
bullets aren't going to hit will be children. Anything that
walks on two legs once Shala and the others have cleared out
will start dropping like flies," Leif tried to convince himself
as much as convince Jessie.

The truth was, he wasn't so sure that he could pull it off by
himself. "If it gets too out of hand, I'll head to higher ground,
but those who may remain standing will fall as easily. If it
takes me 'til my dying day when I'm done, they will be too,"
Leif concluded.

"I don't doubt that. Ya still aren't getting the picture, Leif.
If you and I both go at this, then your chances as well as
Shala's and the others are now times two. It might sound like
I'm offering you my assistance. In fact, I'm telling you how it
is gonna be." Jessie wanted to make clear.

"I would never let your old man down like that. You try
and leave without me, I'll shoot you in the leg myself." He
was looking directly at Leif, and the look on his face told Leif
that he wasn't going to let up.

"Now, we're gonna work on this together," Jessie
continued, "whether you want to or not. As for the work that
needs doing here, I suggest you keep the others on. Not one
of them has a place to go. I'll tell them what needs to be done
and that you and I are gonna take care of the monetary needs

of Neilson and the rest who laid their lives down. I'll let them know to expect us back in early fall. What do you say, Leif? Either we're in it together, or you're gonna be limping for some time to come," replied Jessie half-jokingly.

"Since you put it that way. I guess I don't have much choice. The only thing is, I don't think I'll be returning with you in the fall. I figure once all this is said and done, I'm gonna spend the winter in Hinterville.

"The old lady doesn't yet know what kind of travesty has taken place here. Besides, I'd like to see the old town again. Maybe in the spring I'll head back this way," Leif explained. They sat in silence for a few short minutes.

"Well then, I'll tell them to expect me back in the early fall," stated Jessie. The remainder of the evening went quickly, and the ten survivors all bedded down in the bunkhouse. Jessie slept next to the door with one eye open, figuring Leif was going to get the jump on him, leaving him behind and that he wouldn't get a shot off.

At dawn, Leif, Jessie, Shala, and the five women headed towards the place of Shala's birth. They would be judge, jury, and executioner. Their mission simple, to annihilate *the clan*. They travelled by horse for three days until the forest became too dense. From there, they walked on foot, packing the munitions and their meagre supplies. They were equipped with eight rifles, a dozen pistols and enough ammunition to take out the entire clan. They hoped that if any prisoners were able to fight, they could arm them and that they, too, could fight alongside. That had been Leif's initial plan the entire time.

On the fourth night, they quietly talked amongst themselves before bedding down. In the distance, they could hear the creek that would lead them to the entrance of the clan's guild. Leif thought back to the time he had been forced to live there, *the daily occurrence of mayhem and the blood-soaked ground, the screams at night as someone else was tortured mercilessly.* He could even hear the sound of those first spring days when he was allowed outside, of men and women smashing human bone. *The pulverizing sound echoed in his head.* He remembered watching as the innocent children of the clan partook in the cannibalistic feasting. They knew nothing else. Most of them were exposed to it the first day out of the womb. Leif wondered how it would affect the rest of the children's lives, or whether it would at all. He fell asleep as the thoughts palpitated in his mind.

They hiked for one more day until they were within only a few hundred yards of the clan's compound. They crept close, like lions on the prowl, until the huts were in full view. Silently, they sat tight, keeping their eyes and ears focused on the sights and sounds surrounding them. It would be only hours now. They went over their plan one more time.

"Remember, we have to get the children and prisoners out of there without alarming anybody. Once they are safe, the straw huts need to be set ablaze so we can see those we are shooting at. That's also the time when we will know that anyone worth saving is safe and out of harm's way. Then, we'll open fire on anything that moves. Lighting the huts on fire is the key. Are we all clear? Any questions?" asked Jessie. The travellers remained silent, only nodding. "Good. And God help us," he added.

The last few hours dragged on for eternity. They waited until the last coal lantern was blown out and the compound was dark and silent. Then Shala and her party made their move. The two men watched intently, waiting for the huts to be ablaze. Only three prisoners joined them and were able to fight. The others were too ill or young to be of help. Minutes later, the first hut went up in flames. It illuminated the compound, and the clan members ran this way and that, screaming in agony and pain as the men opened fire, their bullets ripping through the flesh and bone of the clansmen and women. The sound was that of a hundred galloping horses and cracking whips. The smell of gunpowder was inhaled with every breath they took. The remaining huts lit up in succession as the roaring flames that seemed to be from Hell engulfed the compound. They quit firing when the rifle barrels glowed orange like a branding iron and the last clansmen fell silent. It was a complete massacre, ending an era of repugnance and anarchy. The clan had been nullified. The victors sat in silence, watching as the compound slowly crumbled to the ground.

As the sun rose, they gathered in the courtyard. Bodies littered the ground, burned beyond recognition, while others were riddled with bullets. The attackers dug one hole big enough to take all the dead. They filled it half full with wood, then stacked the dead. Covering the bodies with the remaining wood and debris from the huts, they doused it with coal oil. Shala threw the flame that ignited the pyre. They left that place with five children, three more women and four more men strong. Like a platoon, they trudged back the way they had come.

When the civilized land came into view, two of the men continued on alone to destinations unknown. The other two found employment with the Double-U and returned with Jessie. Leif, Shala, and the children, along with the rescued women, set out for Hinterville. However, only the rescued women and orphaned children ever arrived. Their travelling companions led them to the outskirts, then wished them well and headed to parts unknown.

Resting on a ridge that overlooked Hinterville, Leif looked down on the Vanfell town. He would return one day. For now, his only thoughts were of Shala, the woman who had saved him, and the children he had helped save. They would be settling soon in a different place, a different forest. Perhaps once he was sure that Shala would be safe, he would return. Leif looked one last time at Hinterville, then turned his steed. "It is a great day to travel, isn't it, Shala?"

"Yes, Vanfell, it is." Shala said as they trotted off.

Macbeth

What are these,
So withered, and so wild in their attire,
That look not like th' inhabitants o' the earth,

Bloodlines